Praise for

PHILIP R. CRAIG's

incomparable

MARTHA'S VINEYARD MYSTERIES

"Reading [Craig's] books is like a pleasant holiday, visiting old friends (his recurring characters) and enjoying a popular resort area, all without leaving the comfort of your favorite chair."

Los Angeles Daily News

"Diabolically clever . . . Craig vividly portrays the island mystique."

St. Louis Post-Dispatch

"Refreshing . . . entertaining . . . nicely crafted mystery that is worth spending some time on."

Knoxville News Sentinel

"Excellent . . . engrossing entertainment."

DeLand Sun News (Fl.)

"Reading Philip R. Craig is armchair traveling at its finest."

Alfred Hitchcock's Mystery Magazine

"It wouldn't be summer without a new Martha's Vineyard mystery."

Boston Herald

Other Martha's Vineyard Mysteries
by Philip R. Craig

VINEYARD ENIGMA
VINEYARD SHADOWS
VINEYARD BLUES
A FATAL VINEYARD SEASON
A SHOOT ON MARTHA'S VINEYARD
A DEADLY VINEYARD HOLIDAY
DEATH ON A VINEYARD BEACH
A CASE OF VINEYARD POISON
OFF SEASON
CLIFF HANGER
(*to be published as* VINEYARD FEAR)
DEATH IN VINEYARD WATERS
A BEAUTIFUL PLACE TO DIE

VINEYARD DECEIT

A MARTHA'S VINEYARD MYSTERY

(Originally published as *The Double Minded Men*)

PHILIP R. CRAIG

AVON BOOKS
An Imprint of Harper Collins*Publishers*

This is a work of fiction. Names, characters, places, and incidents are products of the author's imagination or are used fictitiously and are not to be construed as real. Any resemblance to actual events, locales, organizations, or persons, living or dead, is entirely coincidental.

AVON BOOKS
An Imprint of HarperCollins*Publishers*
10 East 53rd Street
New York, New York 10022-5299

Published by arrangement with Charles Scribner's Sons

Map illustration by Aher/Donnell Studios
ISBN: 0-06-054290-X
www.avonmystery.com

First Avon Books paperback printing: December 1993

Printed in the U.S.A.

10 9 8 7 6 5 4 3 2 1

To Gen Prada and Joyce Goldfield,
and in memory of Al Prada,
who, long ago, welcomed me to their island
and into their Vineyard Family.

Particular thanks to Dr. Thomas W. Adams—physician, poet, potter, gardener extraordinaire, and specialist on poison plants.

"A double minded man is unstable in all his ways."

—JAMES 1:8

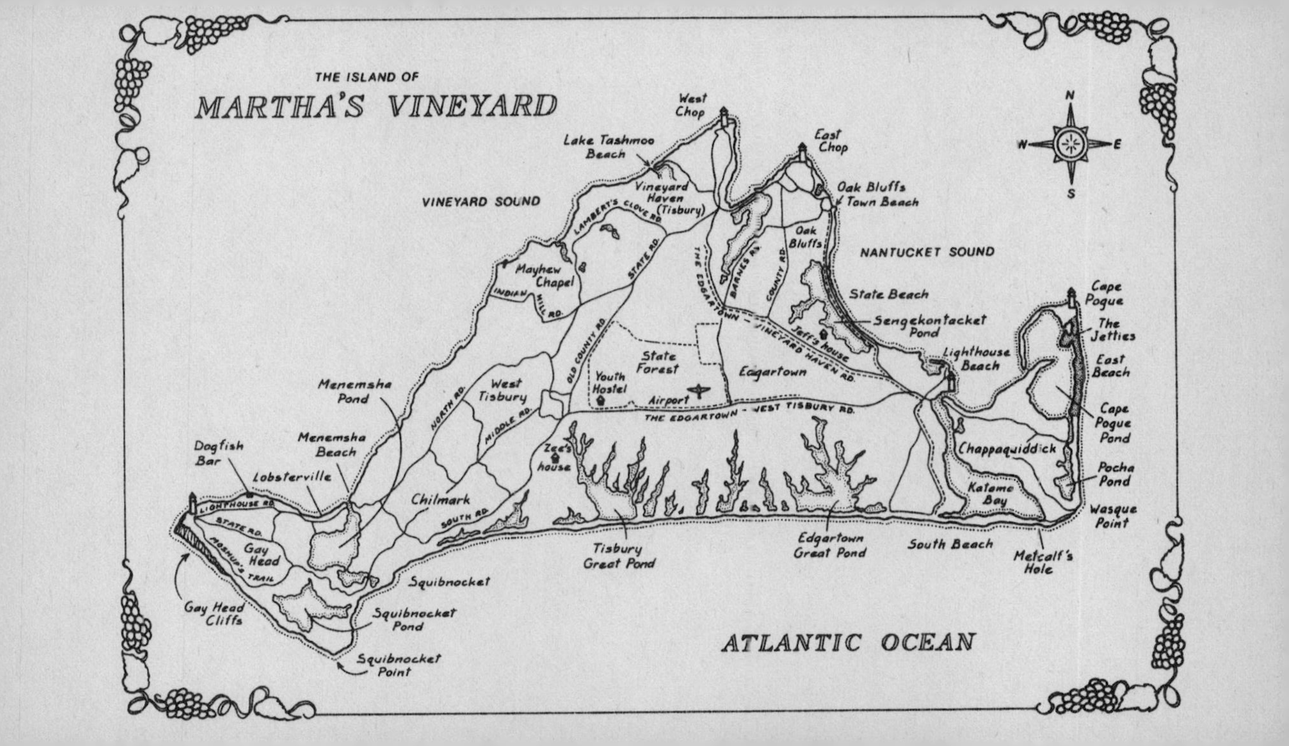
THE ISLAND OF
MARTHA'S VINEYARD
N
E
S
W
VINEYARD SOUND
NANTUCKET SOUND
ATLANTIC OCEAN
West Chop
East Chop
Lake Tashmoo Beach
Vineyard Haven (Tisbury)
Oak Bluffs Town Beach
Oak Bluffs
LAMBERT'S COVE RD.
STATE RD.
BARNES RD.
COUNTY RD.
THE EDGARTOWN - VINEYARD HAVEN RD.
Jeff's house
State Beach
Sengekontacket Pond
Lighthouse Beach
Cape Pogue
The Jetties
East Beach
Cape Pogue Pond
Chappaquiddick
Pocha Pond
Katama Bay
Wasque Point
Metcalf's Hole
South Beach
Edgartown
Edgartown Great Pond
State Forest
Youth Hostel
Airport
THE EDGARTOWN - WEST TISBURY RD.
OLD COUNTY RD.
Mayhew Chapel
INDIAN HILL RD.
West Tisbury
NORTH RD.
MIDDLE RD.
Zee's house
Tisbury Great Pond
Chilmark
SOUTH RD.
Menemsha Pond
Menemsha Beach
Dogfish Bar
Lobsterville
LIGHTHOUSE RD.
STATE RD.
Gay Head
MOSHUP'S TRAIL
Gay Head Cliffs
Squibnocket
Squibnocket Pond
Squibnocket Point

VINEYARD DECEIT

■ 1 ■

The first time I saw the Padishah of Sarofim was the morning when he nearly killed Zee and me with his cigarette boat.

It was just after the change of the tide in the Cape Pogue Gut when Zee hooked a fish. We were drifting in my dinghy and had the gut all to ourselves.

"Hey," said Zee, "there's life in the sea, after all." She hauled back her rod and reeled down and hauled back again. "This is a good-sized fish or else a fighting little fool."

It was the only hit we'd had since we'd putted over from Edgartown to seek the wily blues, so I reeled in and watched her work the fish.

It wasn't hard to watch Zee. She was wearing her short shorts and a shirt with its tails tied around her waist and the blue bandanna she liked to wear around her hair when she fished. She was sleek as an otter.

"Maybe it's a bass," I said.

"No, it's not a bass," said Zee. "It's a bluefish. I know a bass when I have one on."

"Do you want me to help you land it? Fishing is man's work, after all."

"Pardon my repressed laughter. Where's *your* fish?"

"I'm deliberately not catching any so you'll have an improved self-image. Bad self-images are no-no's these days."

"My self-image is just fine, thank you. Gosh, this guy really is giving me a tussle."

True. The dinghy was being towed across the slow tidal current. I got interested.

From the other side of John Oliver Point rose the rolling thunder sound of a powerful engine as a fast boat came up from the south end of Cape Pogue Pond. I hate and fear overpowered boats being driven too fast. They're a danger to their riders and to everyone else in sight.

Around the far end of the point came a shining cigarette boat, throwing a spray of white water behind and riding a roar of sound. The boat curled along the inside of the Cape Pogue Elbow and came full speed into the gut, straight at us.

Jesus Christ! I grabbed the starter rope of my little Seagull outboard and gave a yank. The trusty motor kicked right over, but it was far too late. Before I could swing the dinghy away, the cigarette boat was on us. Zee's mouth moved, but her voice was lost in the roar of the boat's engines.

At the last moment the helmsman altered course a trifle. The boat missed us by a yard, severing Zee's line. A second later the wake capsized the dinghy and dumped Zee and me into the water. When I came up I looked for Zee. She was treading water, still hanging on to her rod. The dinghy bobbed upside down beyond her. We were all drifting slowly out into Nantucket Sound on the falling tide.

"Are you all right?"

"Yes. You?"

"Yes."

Beyond the gut, the cigarette boat slowed and swung around and came back. There were three men aboard. They eased up near us.

"Are you all right?" This from the dark-eyed helmsman. There was a British intonation overlying an accent I didn't recognize.

"You missed us by at least a foot, you stupid man!" Zee was furious.

The helmsman darkened even more, and his mouth tightened. An olive-skinned man with a hatchet face frowned. A blond young man dropped a ladder over the side. "Come aboard," he said, leaning down and putting out a hand.

"I don't want to ride with a maniac," said Zee, coughing. "Get away from us before that fool at the wheel really does kill us both!"

"Please," said the blond man.

Zee waved her fishing rod at the helmsman. "I had a good fish on, you dunderhead! You cut him off! People like you shouldn't be allowed to drive! My God!"

The helmsman glared, and the man with the hatchet face spoke to him in a language I didn't know.

The water was warm, but we were still slowly being carried out to sea. I swam to the cigarette boat and climbed aboard. "Awfully sorry," said the blond man, giving my hand a fast shake. "Please, miss, come aboard."

I reached down a long arm. "Come on, Zee."

Spitting water, she swam over and handed up her rod, then climbed the ladder and glared at the helmsman, dripping.

"Just to make sure I've got the right man," she snapped, moving toward him, "it *was* you who nearly cut us in two, wasn't it?"

The helmsman lifted his chin and looked first at each man on the boat and finally at her. "It was indeed, madam. And what were you doing there, anyway?"

"You incredible jerk! I was fishing there, but this is what I'm doing here!" And before he or anyone else could move she hit him in the nose with her fist.

He gasped and raised his hands to his face.

"There, you wretched man!" cried Zee.

He staggered back. His legs hit the side of the cockpit and he went overboard backwards. Zee looked slightly abashed. The man with the hatchet face looked suddenly deadly. His hand dipped under his light summer shirt and came out with a flat semiautomatic pistol. He was very quick. He swung the pistol toward Zee, and I barely had time to step between them.

"No, Colonel!" The blond man's voice was loud, but he did not step in front of the pistol.

The Colonel did not shoot, but neither did he lower the pistol. It was lined up on my solar plexus. Long before, I had been shot just a bit south of that spot and I still had the bullet nestled up against my spine.

From the water came a strangled shout in that unknown language. The helmsman was thrashing in the water. The Colonel hesitated, then glanced down at the helmsman and back at Zee and me.

Zee leaned over the side. "Now you know what it feels like! Swim over here, if you know how. Or are you as bad at swimming as you are at driving a boat?" It was clear that she had not seen the Colonel's pistol. "Come on," said Zee, reaching down. "That's it. You needed a little cooling off, hotshot."

The helmsman came up the ladder, Zee's hand clenching his shirt. I looked back at the Colonel, and the pistol was gone. He and the helmsman held a short intense conversation while the blond man scurried away and returned with towels.

The helmsman glared at Zee, and there was a seepage of blood from his hawklike nose. The Colonel's eyes were hooded like those of a snake. The blond man was conciliatory to all. "Okay, folks, let's all just relax. You, sir," this to me, "will you take that boat hook and see if you can snag your dinghy's painter when I come up alongside of her? That's it."

I hauled the dinghy close, tipped it right-side up, and pulled it up the side of the cigarette boat so some of the water would empty out. When I eased it back in the water, it floated. Gone was my good graphite rod, a Penn 704 reel, and a tackle box full of gear. I pointed this out to the blond man and added that my outboard would now have to be rinsed and possibly repaired down at Pirate's Cove, the local boatyard in Edgartown.

"Don't worry, sir," said Blondie. "We'll take care of everything. We're just delighted that you're both all right. These things happen, in spite of our best efforts to prevent them. Allow me to introduce myself. Standish Caplan, State Department. My fault, this, I'm afraid. Allowed his . . . er . . . Mr. Rashad to take the wheel at the wrong time. A thousand pardons. You must allow us to take you into Edgartown. May I know your name, sir?"

"J.W. Jackson," I said, angry about the pistol now that it was no longer pointed at me. "Who's your gunman? We don't see many like him down here."

The gunman and I stared at each other. He identified himself. "Colonel Ahmed Nagy." His voice was dark and had a cut to it.

Standish Caplan stepped smoothly between us, now that there was no pistol. "Mr. Jackson, Mr. Rashad. Mr. Rashad, Mr. Jackson. Gentlemen, please shake hands. No damage done, ha, ha, save a few wet clothes. Tempers cooling, I hope. Miss . . . er . . ."

"Zeolinda Madieras," said Zee. "Mrs. Zeolinda Madieras." She was still glaring at Rashad, but her lips were beginning to twitch. I knew a laugh was coming, and it did. She shrugged her shoulders. "Let's call it even, then. Take us home. I need a shower."

Rashad touched his nose. "In my country women do not strike men."

"That must be some sort of country! Maybe you should go back to it, where you'll be safe," flared Zee.

Rashad's eyes grew bright. He lifted a hand.

"Don't even think it," I said, but I was really watching Colonel Nagy.

"Madam, gentlemen, please." Standish Caplan was somehow between Rashad and the Colonel on one side and Zee and me on the other. "Please, let us put all this behind us. Let me take the wheel and see if we can get Mrs. Madieras and Mr. Jackson and their boat safely home. Awfully sorry about the fish, Mrs. Madieras. We will be glad to replace everything else, but we can't replace your fish, ha, ha."

"Ha, ha," said Zee. But she seated herself on one side of the cockpit and waved a languid arm. "Home, Standish."

We parted at Pirate's Cove Marina.

"Your names are in the book, yes? Well then, I will be in touch," said Standish Caplan, handing us each his card. "Now I must take the . . . er . . . Mr. Rashad home and get him some dry clothes. Awfully sorry about this whole thing. Terribly glad you're both all right."

The Colonel leaned toward me. "We will remember you," he said in a voice like a knife. He looked at Zee. "And the woman will not be forgotten either."

He stood back and put a hand on the edge of the cockpit. He watched us with his hooded eyes as the cigarette boat rumbled away down harbor. Rashad turned once and looked back. His eyes seemed to burn with dark fire.

Beside me, Zee shivered in the warm August air. "Take me home," she said. "I want that shower."

We walked along North Water Street past the great captains' houses, crossed Main at the Four Corners, and went up South Water Street past the huge pagoda tree that some captain or other had brought over from Asia in a flowerpot a century and a half earlier. We turned down toward The Reading Room, got my ancient, rusty Toyota LandCruiser from where I'd left it, in spite of the NO PARKING signs, on Collins Beach, and I took Zee home.

At the time I had no idea that we'd crossed swords with the Padishah of Sarofim or what that would lead to.

2

Behind every great fortune lies a great crime, as someone (Balzac?) observed. Certainly that is true of the Emerald Necklace of Sarofim. The theft of the emeralds had provided the beginning of a great family fortune two centuries earlier, and crime followed them to Martha's Vineyard. Kidnapping and killings were only two of the evils that arrived with the necklace, and Zee was to be only the first island victim. Even now, chicanery and violence seem inexorably linked to the emeralds. They glitter from the dark shadows of their own history. Where did they really come from? What gem cutter cut them, what goldsmith set them? How many times have they been wrested from someone who had stolen them from someone else? How much blood has been shed for them? How much is still to be shed?

When I first heard of the Sarofim necklace, I had been enjoying clams, beer, and country music in my yard. It was about a week after the incident in Cape Pogue Gut. Standish Caplan had been as good as his word. He had sent me a generous check, and my outboard motor was again purring smoothly. Emeralds were not on my list of things to think about. I was dreaming about Jeremy Fisher's eighteen-foot catboat.

I had been clamming the day before in Eel Pond, where I'd been having some luck lately. Good clamming spots get discovered and clammed out pretty fast on Martha's Vineyard, so when we find one, we keep it to ourselves. My secret still seemed secure, and I'd got my bucketful in short order, brought them home, soaked them all night in salt water so they would spit out their sand, and now had them ready for frying. My mouth watered as the oil heated and I whipped up some tartar saucc.

You can dip your clams in a batter or in flour or in both before frying them. I use a batter. To get it to stick to your clams, you make sure the clams are dry and then chill them in the fridge until just before you dip them in the batter.

To the sound of Hank Williams, Jr., singing of the joys and sorrows of honky-tonk life, I cooked and ate, washing the clams down with Yuengling lager, an excellent beer (from America's oldest brewery). Yum. What could be finer than beer and clams and C-and-W music on a fine August day on the beautiful island of Martha's Vineyard? I took my portable radio and more clams and beer out into my yard, stripped down, and sat gingerly in Archie Bunker's chair, the wonderful, comfortable but fragile old wooden lawn chair I was going to fix up right someday. Two of the Bad Bunny Bunch, who had evil designs on my garden, hopped reluctantly back into the oak brush and trees as I lay in the warm sun beneath a blue sky. Tan renewal time. I could eat, drink, and do that too.

Beyond my garden and the trees and across Anthier's Pond, the August people could be seen, distantly, sopping up the summer sun on the beach or on their sailboards. Beyond them, out toward Cape Cod, where a line of lazy clouds hung against the sky, the sail and motorboats moved across the Sound. The wind was gentle from the southwest and sighed through the trees around my house.

I was finishing up the last of the clams and thinking about the eighteen-foot fiberglass catboat that Jeremy Fisher, who had decided at eighty-something that he was no longer up to singlehanding around Vineyard Sound, was willing to part with for a very decent price, which I could not afford, when I heard a car coming down my driveway.

My driveway is long and sandy and I don't get a lot of cars coming down it, although I don't mind when one does. I also don't get dressed if I'm perfecting my tan. After all, I'm in my own yard and whoever is coming wasn't invited and must take what he or she finds at the end of the road. On the other hand, one never knows, do one? What if it were the President of the United States? What if it were the Pope?

Just because they've never come down yet doesn't mean they won't.

I placed the empty clam plate in a diplomatic position and took a pull on my beer.

The car belonged to the town of Edgartown, had blue lights on top, and was being driven by the chief of police. He stopped the car, and we eyed one another across the lawn. He shook his head, opened the door, and got out.

"You're too late," I said. "I spent all of the Brinks money on clams and I just ate the last of them."

"Decadence," said the Chief. "Aren't you embarrassed to be lying out in the open like that, in view of low-flying planes?"

"I realize that it's envy of my manly endowment that makes you talk like that," I said. The Chief had never come to my house before, so something was going on. I got up and pulled on my shorts. "There, now you don't have to feel embarrassed. I didn't mean to show you up, but you've nobody to blame but yourself. You should have called and told me you were coming."

"You off-islanders don't even know what well hung means," said the Chief, digging his pipe out of his pocket. "The chamber of commerce sent me to talk to you about this habit of yours of lying around naked. We have a lot of rich female tourists flying in here, you know, and when they look down and see you, they fly right home again, thinking that all the men down here are underdeveloped. It's wrecking the summer economy."

I finished my beer and picked up the clam plate. "Come up on the porch," I said. "I'm going to have another beer. You care for one?"

"Nope. On duty." He stoked up his pipe and followed me up the steps into the screen porch. The sweet smell of his tobacco filled my nostrils, and once again, as always when I smell a pipe, I gave serious thought to smoking my own again. I still had my rack of briars and corncobs even though I hadn't smoked in years. I'd once smoked cigarettes too, but I missed only my pipe. I sometimes suspected that the Chief deliberately lit up to give me grief. Now he puffed and looked out across my garden to the Sound. "Nice view," he said. "How much land do you own here?"

"About fifteen acres. Just enough to keep people from getting too close to me. My father bought it a long time ago, when land was cheap. I couldn't afford to buy it now."

"Baird's old hunting camp," said the Chief. "My old man used to come out here with Baird and some of their pals. They'd bring their guns and a few bottles and a box of grub and spend weekends pretending to hunt while mostly they drank whiskey and played cards and told lies. My old man brought me up once or twice when he thought I was old enough to shoot." He gestured toward the pond. "There used to be good duck hunting out there, not that we ever actually got around to shooting very many."

"My father told me once that if you had all the whiskey that had been drunk in this place and if you poured it out, you'd have a river running all the way to the pond," I said.

The Chief allowed himself a fast smile. "That's about right." Then the smile passed, and he stopped looking at the Sound and looked at me. "One of my special officers just retired to Florida. I want to replace him and wondered if you, being an ex-big-city cop and all, would take the job. I need all the extra officers I can get for a special detail that's coming up. You might even like it. One night. Good money. Fancy clothes; a tux, probably."

"I don't own a tux."

"The customer will pay for it. You interested?"

"If the money's good, every off-duty cop on the island is probably interested. Aren't there enough of them?" Cops everywhere love off-duty special details. They make excellent money and can always use it; usually, too, the special details require very little work; whenever you see a cop standing beside an open manhole or beside a telephone company truck or outside a farmers' market, directing traffic, it's a special detail.

"You must have won the lottery," said the Chief. "You don't seem too interested in making some money. I've already got every loose cop on this job, but I could use one more inside the house, and much as I may regret saying this, you're my first choice."

"It's been a while since I carried a badge."

"It's a part-time job at best. You interested or not?"

I thought about it. "Enough to talk about it some more. This must be a big deal, if you've used up all of the island's off-duty fuzz. What's it all about?"

"It's not just island law," said the Chief sourly. "We'll have state cops and some feds too."

"My breath is bated."

"You know the Stonehouse sisters . . ."

"No."

"Yes you do. Amelia Muleto. Old Ray Muleto's widow. She's one of them. Her twin sister is Emily. She married Edward C. Damon. Owns that big place over on Chappaquiddick. You know, down harbor the other side of the narrows. White boat house big enough for the *QE2*. Keeps the *Dog Star* tied there. Sixty-foot yawl. Big cigarette boat, too."

I did know Amelia Muleto. She is Zee's aunt by marriage, but I'd known her long before I'd met Zee. And I had once met her sister, but I hadn't known they were the Stonehouse sisters and explained that to the Chief.

He puffed on his pipe, undismayed by my ignorance. "In that case, you probably don't know about the emeralds, either."

"No."

"Or about Edward C. Damon being appointed ambassador to Sarofim."

"As a matter of fact, I did hear that. He's one of the fat cats who bankrolled the campaign of the new President of the U.S. of A. and he's getting Sarofim as a reward even though he doesn't speak the language or know anything about the Middle East in general or Sarofim in particular."

"You're a snide bastard. How much do *you* know about Sarofim?"

"I know it's got more oil than it can pump in a thousand years and a king or sheik or whatever who likes movies and women."

"I see you read *Newsweek*. Gosh!"

I gave him a wise smile. "Tell me about the emeralds. They sound more interesting."

"The way I get the story, a couple of hundred years ago one of the Stonehouse ancestors hired himself out as a mercenary to someone who wanted to replace the king or whatever of Sarofim. In the war that followed, Stonehouse got into the palace and away with enough of the royal treasury to establish a family fortune. He sold most of the jewels for cash, made some smart investments in land and the East India trade, and ended up with a peerage that he gave up to come to America and make even more money. But he never sold this emerald necklace. It's been passed down through the generations until now. And now the king of Sarofim wants it back. National treasure."

"And is he going to get it?"

"He is. The Stonehouse girls—girls! They're in their sixties, at least—are going to hand it over to the king himself. You get the idea: cementing the historical friendship between the two sovereign nations, ending an ancient grievance between the royal family and the Stonehouse family . . ."

"Guaranteeing Edward C. Damon a good start as potential ambassador to Sarofim . . ."

"You got it. The show is scheduled to take place in Damon's house. His Royal Whatsis was on the island a week ago and he'll be back again in a couple of days. In Disneyland right now, I think. Anyway, it will be a very, very grand affair, with Important People from Sarofim, Washington, Boston, you name it, here for the event."

I thought of Amelia Muleto. I had never heard her say anything particularly flattering about Damon. If I were Amelia, the widow of a poor man, I wouldn't hand over my emerald necklace for the sake of my brother-in-law's career, especially if I didn't care too much for him. I suggested as much to the Chief.

The Chief sucked on his pipe. "Not sure the girls have much to say about it, actually. Trustees' decision, or some such thing. Anyway, word has it, quite unofficially, that Sarofim is paying big bucks for the necklace. Under the table, of course. That way, all parties are satisfied. The Stonehouse sisters get megabucks, which Amelia at least certainly can use, the king of Sarofim gets to return triumphant to his homeland bearing the necklace that no previous king could get back, Edward C. Damon gets his ambassadorship, the President smiles, and so forth. You interested in the helping me out or not? The security precautions are sapping me dry."

"I get to wear a tux? And hang around the rich and famous?"

He nodded. "This time, at least."

I was thinking about Jeremy Fisher's catboat. The second deadly sin shares me with the other six, and I try to enjoy them all.

"Why not?" I said.

"I can give you one reason, maybe. The king or whatever they call him of Sarofim is not necessarily the kind of guy you want for a pal. Some people think he's a dictatorial shit. His old man kidnapped women for his harem—a *harem,* for God's sake! I didn't know they still had them—and gave them to his secret police if they didn't go along with it. The police screwed them and then cut pieces off of them and tossed the bodies back in the streets as a lesson to the uncooperative. They did the same thing to men the king didn't like. Cut off their peckers and put out their eyes and then killed them. That sort of thing. Amnesty International didn't like the old man and they don't like this guy any better. Of course that's just what I've heard through the grapevine. Maybe it's all just bad-mouthing by somebody who doesn't like the family."

"Where'd you hear it?"

"Spitz. FBI guy who's on the island arranging security from the federal end. He didn't know if it was true or not, but he passed it along. One of those guys who distrusts our foreign policies. In J. Edgar's day he'd have been on the hit list instead of carrying a federal badge. Times change. Spitz may be unhappy about the king, but he likes having a few days on this blessed isle of ours. You still want the job?"

"Sounds too good to miss."

"I'll give your name to the selectmen. They have to approve your appointment. The big party is next Saturday night. There'll be a briefing that morning out at the Damons' house. Nine o'clock. Security will walk the grounds, learn the ways in and out. That sort of thing. Thornberry Security is running the show."

Thornberry Security was a big outfit. When I'd left the Boston Police, Thornberry had offered me a job. I'd declined.

"I'll be there," I said.

"Islands may be the aristocrats of the earth's surfaces, but there are just as many crooks and wacko people here as anywhere else," said the Chief. "I don't want anything going wrong while those rocks are in this town, so I expect everybody to keep his eyes open. They can steal them someplace else, but not here. You still have a pistol?"

A pistol? I tried to look unsurprised. "Yeah. The .38 I carried in Boston."

"Well, carry it that night too. Or I can give you something from our armory, such as it is."

"You're taking this pretty seriously."

He pointed his pipe at me. "I hear that there are people around who'd love to mess this deal up and I don't want anything going wrong, even if the king is as bad as some say. Thornberry will tell you all you need to know at the briefing." Then he had an afterthought. "You won't shoot yourself in the foot or anything like that, will you? You do still remember which end the bullet comes out?"

"As I recall, you stand behind your gun when you shoot. That right?"

"Just like pissing," said the Chief. "I knew you had what it takes for this job."

■ 3 ■

In August the bluefish seek cooler waters up north of Cape Cod, giving joy to Boston and Maine Coast fishermen. They drift south again in September, just in time for the Vineyard Striped Bass and Bluefish Derby, but for a month or so, they're hard to find from the Vineyard shore. Nevertheless, Zee and I were hunting them along East Beach on the far side of Chappaquiddick. We were in my Toyota LandCruiser, stopping at each point—Wasque, Leland's, Bernie's, the Jetties, Cape Pogue, and all the nameless little outthrusts of sand in between—and casting without any real hope of getting anything. There was a northeast wind that had cleared away the humidity for a couple of days and brought a hint of fall to the island. Across the Sound, Cape Cod was looming, and off to the southeast we could see Muskeget hanging on the edge of the horizon. Sailboats were moving over the waters, and there were fishermen working the shoals out in the Sound. Over us there was a clear blue sky. The sun was warm.

Zee was again wearing shorts and a shirt with the sleeves rolled up and the tails tied around her waist. Her wonderful long black hair was tucked up under her bandanna. Her skin was brown and smooth. When she made her casts, the motion was like a movement of dance, something you might see in a ballet.

As she was reeling in, she turned and looked at me. "Well, are you going to fish or not? You don't catch them unless you put your plug in the water, you know."

"I'm waiting for you to get one first, because even though I'm a very macho guy I'm also very polite."

"Sure you are," said Zee. "And you want me to have an improved self-image, too."

Zee made another cast. She was breaking in my brand-new eleven-and-a-half-foot one-piece graphite rod and was throwing a diamond jig a long way out. All to no avail. I watched her reel in again while I leaned against the Toyota and listened to the radio inside. I was tuned to the classical music station on the Cape, which was presenting Beethoven's Ninth, the world's heavyweight musical champion. When I die, I want my ashes poured out (downwind, of course) over the Wasque rip while somebody plays a tape of the fourth movement of the Ninth.

Zee came up to the LandCruiser and changed lures. She smiled at me. We had been changing lures all the way up the beach. We'd started with Roberts and then tried Missiles, poppers, swimmers, and then metal in various shapes—Kastmasters, Hopkins and diamond jigs. And we had caught nothing. Now Zee was putting on a little broken-backed Rebel, blue with a yellow streak on its belly. I looked at it skeptically.

"Well, why not?" asked Zee. "It can't do worse than what we've tried so far."

"True enough. You've inspired me to try again myself." I peered into my tackle box and extracted a pink Nantucket Bullet, got her rod, and snapped the lure onto her leader.

"That's the stuff," said Zee. "Never say die. Just because you've never caught a fish in your life using that thing doesn't mean you're not going to catch one today."

"Absolutely."

"If you do catch something, of course it'll belong to me because you're using my rod."

"Use your own rod, then, and give me back mine."

"This rod is too good for you. You should really give it to me."

"Fat chance."

We walked down to the water and made our casts. Fifteen minutes later we still had no fish. No swirls, no hits, no anything.

"The dead sea," said Zee.

We went back up to the car and got out the coffee. It was a beautiful morning, and we were the only people on the beach. I pointed this out to Zee.

"Possibly because everybody else is smarter than us," she said. "They don't go fishing when there are no fish."

"Dumbness has its own rewards," I said, leering. "I have you all alone on a beautiful beach on beautiful Martha's Vineyard and I am plying you with strong drink."

"I don't think this is the kind of drink the world's Romeos use," she said, sipping her coffee and looking at me with her dark eyes. "Besides, as I recall, you don't even like beach parties. Sand in the food, sand in the drinks. That sort of thing. I'd have thought that sand in the crotch would be equally undesirable."

"It's not that I'd enjoy it," I said. "It's just that it's part of the 'Romance on the Vineyard' scenario, and, being the kind of guy I am, I have obligations. I mean, here we are. Beautiful, passionate woman, handsome, virile stud, bright sun, blue water, empty white sands, hormones bubbling, you unable to resist your erotic impulses. I have to satisfy you whether I really want to or not. I just want you to know that I'm prepared to do my duty as a manly Vineyard man."

"You're a person driven by moral imperatives," said Zee. "The way I see it is this: we lay out the bedspread I notice you just happen to have in the back of the Toyota, we dig out the towels, we put away these worthless rods, we strip and go for a skinny-dip, and then we see what happens."

The Trustees of Reservations, who own East Beach, do not approve of nude bathing or nude anything else taking place on their property, but they were not around at the moment.

"You have good ideas, Cornelius," I said. "When I am king, you may have my hat."

An hour later a pickup came up from the south and we got back into our clothes. The driver was Iowa, a retired guy from the Midwest who now lived on the Vineyard year-round and fished all of the time. Iowa stopped in front of us and glanced at the rods on the roof rack.

"Anything?" he asked.

"Not since daybreak," said Zee, fastening a button on her shirt.

"You been up to the lighthouse?"

"Up there and back this far. Not a fish."

"You try the gut?"

"No, and we didn't try in the pond. Maybe you'll find some there."

"I doubt it," he said gloomily.

"If you don't go, you don't know," said Zee, quoting a trusty fisherman's maxim.

Iowa looked at the bedspread and at the sand in our hair and smiled. "It's a nice day anyway, fish or no fish. I'll toss a couple of lines at the Jetties and then try the gut. Maybe there's a stray out there somewhere."

He drove on, and we stripped again and went back into the water to rinse off. Then we dressed and drove back to my house for showers and clothes without sand in them. Afterwards we sat on my balcony and drank sun tea and looked out over the pond. Beyond the pond was a strip of land bearing the road between Edgartown and Oak Bluffs. In two places bridges crossed over channels connecting the pond to the Sound beyond. On the far side of the road were miles of gentle beach greatly favored by island visitors with small children. Already the beach road was lined with cars as the August people poured onto the sands.

"Tell me about your Aunt Amelia's emeralds," I said.

Zee looked at me with surprise. "How do you know about Aunt Amelia's emeralds?"

I told her about the Chief's visit.

She smiled. "So you'll be there Saturday night for the big event. I'm glad. I'll be there too. Aunt Amelia says that Aunt Emily insisted upon it. Apparently Aunt Emily wants me to start mingling with proper society again."

Zee was not-long divorced from the doctor she'd helped put through medical school who had then replaced Zee with a younger lovely who, unlike Zee, adored him as much as he believed he deserved. Dr. Paul Madieras, known to me as Dr.

Jerk, and his new bride now lived somewhere on the mainland, while Zee glued her life back together working as a nurse in the Martha's Vineyard hospital. Zee had come to the Vineyard from Cambridge after the divorce because Ray and Amelia Muleto, her father's brother and his wife, had offered a sanctuary she'd needed.

"Why didn't you go back to Fall River?" I'd asked her one day while we were raking for littlenecks in Katama Pond and she was finally telling me something about the divorce.

"To my family?"

"Yes."

Zee had raked a bit before answering. "I don't know if you'll understand this, but my mother was on Paul's side. He's a charmer, and she figured that if he was leaving me I must have deserved it. I didn't need that. Aunt Amelia and Uncle Ray were on my side."

I ran that through my computer while I dug two littlenecks out of my rake and dropped them in my basket. Littlenecks were selling at many pennies each in the Edgartown fish markets, and I planned on making a couple of bucks that afternoon.

"My mother died when I was young," I said, "so I don't know what she'd have done when my wife and I split up. I'd like to think she'd have been on my side."

"You and your ex still get along," said Zee. "Paul and I don't. Your mother wouldn't have had to choose; mine did. She chose the doctor. To understand that, you have to understand her. She came from the Azores, from a poor family in a poor town. Over there a doctor was almost like a saint. He was the most important person in town. He had education, money, and usually owned the biggest house in the area and had a car. He was the one people went to when they had problems. He gave advice, helped them write letters to America, helped them with government paperwork."

"The Godfather."

"Yes. My mother got to America only because she was sponsored by a cousin in New Bedford. She didn't speak English at all, but she learned it. She married my father, a man a lot like herself, and they raised us kids in Fall River. They worked hard. She cleaned houses, he was a handyman. Finally they saved enough money to open their little store. Muleto's Market, specializing in Portuguese foods. All us kids worked there from the time we were little. My parents did that with no education, but they made sure my brothers went to college and they were even proud when I decided that I would go too.

"When I met Paul in college and my mother learned that he was going to be a doctor, she was completely overjoyed. Her daughter and a doctor. A Portuguese boy, to boot. He was charming, she was in love with him, and I fell in love too." She glanced at me as she dropped a littleneck into her basket. Her voice was clinical and detached. "Paul and I made plans. I stopped studying the liberal arts and switched to nursing because we knew that when Paul was in medical school I'd need a good job. We were married the June after graduation, and my mother was in heaven. Of course we couldn't afford children. Six years later, in the middle of his internship, he found someone who didn't know about his less-attractive side. A wife always knows about that side of her man, but other women don't. His new love didn't. My mother didn't. She still doesn't. But she knows about mine. And after all, Paul is a doctor and I'm only a nurse. They still write and they visit when he's in Fall River. I think he's her favorite son."

"She still doesn't see the warts, eh?"

"Only mine. Aunt Amelia sees mine too, but she knows that everybody's got them, so I came down here where I could be with her if I needed to. And I did need to."

"As you no doubt are aware," I said, "before my modesty obliged me to forbid public use of the name, I was known as J. Wartless Jackson."

"Are you sure they weren't saying 'Worthless'?" asked Zee, discovering a large conch in her rake. "Whoops," she said and tossed the conch in a high arc so that it landed right in front of my nose and splashed me with a goodly splash.

It seemed a fair response. I spat out some salt water. "So your mother's still in love. Are you?"

"I was, but it seeped away. I was glad when it was gone."

"Love is good for you," I said.

"It can be pretty awful."

I thought of my own divorce. "Yes, it can." I had not thought of myself as a particularly loving person or as someone needing a lot of love, but when my wife left me I felt very bad for a long time. It had taken a while for me to find much joy in things. Probably, I thought, that's why, after being shot in Boston, I had taken my police disability money and moved to the Vineyard. Down here I knew I could do simple things that might heal me: fish, keep my garden, hunt ducks and geese and deer, be on the beach at sunup or sunset or midnight. And I didn't have to talk to people about the turns my life had taken: the loss of my wife, the addition of a bullet near my spine, my private encounters with the void.

And the island magic had worked. Prospero had waved his wand and made me better. Not perfect, but better. The sea is a great redeemer, after all. And then I'd met Zee and had gotten better still.

But now Aunt Emily thought it was time for Zee to start mingling with "proper society."

"What do you mean 'proper society'?" I asked, trying to act as if I didn't know.

"Aunt Emily thinks it's time I started mixing with men and women again. That it's time to leave Paul behind and get on with my life. Aunt Amelia thinks so too. She's had to do the same thing since Uncle Ray died, and she says that divorces and deaths are a lot alike for the survivors. I think she's right."

So did I, having experienced both kinds of loss. Joy was still possible, but you had to seek it and then open yourself up to it. You had to take a chance on suffering other losses, because that was better than living in old sorrows. I believed that the Buddha was right when he said that life is suffering, but I had never liked people who dwelt on their own. They had some kind of self-pity in them that was distasteful to me. I considered myself an expert on self-pity, having engaged in more than my share from time to time.

Zee said, "Of course Aunt Amelia and Aunt Emily don't agree at all about who I should be mixing with. Aunt Emily wants to introduce me to some very proper people who will be at the big event on Saturday. Aunt Amelia thinks that you're more the type for me."

Good old Aunt Amelia! I brightened inside.

"You've helped me more than anybody," said Zee, surprising me. "You and Aunt Amelia. You're both proliving, antideath people. A lot of women like me feel guilty when things go wrong in our lives; we think we're to blame. My mother's that way, but Amelia doesn't think that and neither do you. Because of you two, I'm beginning not to think it either." She turned her head and smiled at me. God, she was beautiful.

But I was uneasy with such talk. "Everybody gets knocked down sooner or later," I said. "Some get up again and some don't. You did. Your Aunt Amelia's right. Now it's time for you to forget Dr. Jerk and move on."

"Yes, it is."

"Tell me about the emeralds."

"Ah yes, the emeralds. Well, the fact is, I don't know much about them. Aunt Amelia never talked about them, really, maybe because Uncle Ray, being the good Azorian man that he was, didn't have much place in his life for a wife with an emerald necklace. He and Amelia were both more interested in gardening and each other than in her past or his. She does have an old scrapbook with newspaper clippings and photos of when she was a young deb in Boston. That was before she left the debutante society to marry a Vineyard farmer. I never saw the scrapbook until after Uncle Ray died. There are some pictures and articles in there about the emeralds. Would you like to see them? I'm sure Aunt Amelia wouldn't mind. She likes you."

I liked Amelia too. She was one of the people to whom I took bluefish when I was catching them. I'd never thought of her as the owner of an emerald necklace.

"Yes," I said, "I would like to see that book."

"When we finish our tea, I'll phone her and find out when would be a good time."

"Meanwhile, I'll just ogle you," I said. "After Saturday night you'll be too sophisticated to mix with us hois and pollois."

"I'll be kind," said Zee. "Sometimes I'll think of you while I'm on my yacht. I'll have the prince bring the boat into Edgartown now and then."

"Of course you'll be anchoring in the outer harbor because it'll be too big to bring inside."

"Of course. But I'll send crewmen ashore with the launch and insist that they buy our fresh bluefish from only you. And now that you're a special policeman with a badge and everything, I'll insist on having you be part of the security that protects us from the common people."

"The autograph hunters and all . . ."

"That's right. And if we meet by accident in one of the finer shops downtown, I'll be sure to speak to you."

"You'll remember my name?"

"Of course. What was it again?"

4

Amelia Muleto owned a small truck farm off the West Tisbury road. When her husband had been alive the two of them had worked it and sold their vegetables at a farm stand, getting by in the good years, scrambling in the bad ones. My father had bought his vegetables there when I was a boy, and Amelia had delighted me with small, surprising gifts such as a seemingly normal apple that broke in two in my hands to reveal an apricot instead of a core, and within the apricot, where the pit had been, a strawberry. Her humor was the witty kind that had delighted both me and my father.

My father had liked the Muletos and had made a practice of taking fish by their house when he'd had luck with the blues or bass. Ray Muleto, like every Azorian I've ever known, and there are a lot of them and their children on the Vineyard, loved fish. His farm kept him too busy to catch them himself, so he was particularly happy to get them when they came his way. In exchange, he would give my father wine that he'd made. It was strong, red stuff. "Vigorous," my father had called it. The first alcohol I ever drank was Ray Muleto's vigorous wine. I sneaked it straight from the bottle and almost choked to death. After my father died, I took fish to Ray and Amelia and got red wine in return. Now that Ray was gone, I still took fish, but there was no more of that rich, dark wine.

Amelia now leased her farm to another truck gardener and worked at his stand part time. When not at the stand, she was at her small, neat, gray-shingled house, where she grew wonderful flowers and entertained her grandchildren whenever she could pry them away from their parents, Amelia's son and his wife, who had abandoned the island to live in

America, across the Sound, way out west in Worcester, in fact, where, in the modern style, they both worked to support their family.

"The grandchildren have gone home," said Zee, as we drove up. "Pre-school shopping and all that. Their mom must take them to the malls, and there are no malls on Martha's Vineyard."

Amelia Muleto was a tall, slender, Yankee-looking woman whose silver hair was cut short and touched with blue. She was in her gardening clothes when we arrived: jeans, a loose shirt that had no doubt belonged to her late husband, and sandals. She came walking from her front rose bed as we pulled into her driveway. She and I had aged together. Long ago when, as a boy, I'd first come to her house with my father, when I'd been five, she'd been in her mid thirties and I'd thought of her as old. Now she was in her mid sixties and seemed pretty young to me.

She kissed Zee and gave me her hand and we went into the house. Amelia sat us down on her couch. On the coffee table in front of it there were scrapbooks and photo albums.

"There you have it," said Amelia. "There's a Stonehouse family genealogy too, but I think Emily has it. That sort of thing means much more to her than to me, I'm afraid. Look those things over while I bring us some coffee. Or would you prefer beer?"

Coffee would do. She went into the kitchen, and I opened the first of the photo albums. It was filled with pictures from the late twenties and the thirties, many of two little girls growing up. The adults seemed to wear a great deal of white, and there were large houses and lawns and lakes in the shots. As Zee and I turned the pages, the girls and their parents grew older. Photos of early formal dances in large halls appeared. Nowhere was there any evidence of the Great Depression which had swept the world. The people in the pictures were happy and attractive. Uniformed servants could be seen in attendance. Young men were also on the scene, in sporting or formal clothing as the occasion demanded. There were pictures of healthy young people sailing, rowing, playing croquet.

The next album was more somber. A severe-looking father, serious young women. Young men in uniform. Fewer pictures of lawn parties. World War II had taken center stage. The girls, the Stonehouse sisters, Amelia and Emily, now in their late teens, were shown in the uniforms of nursing aides. The family was doing its share.

Then it was the mid forties and the young men had come home from the war and there were parties. Debutante balls in Boston. I recognized the old Copley Plaza. Then there were photos, some in color, of the emerald necklace, magnificent against a bed of silk, glowing against the skin of Amelia and Emily's mother as she stood with her daughters in their daring, low-cut gowns at the foot of a great stairway, seeming to shimmer as she danced with her husband and the girls danced with perfectly groomed and formally attired young men at some ball.

Then there were photos of Martha's Vineyard in the forties, and suddenly the young face and form of Raymond Muleto began to dominate the pages of the album. Raymond leaning against a fence, Raymond grinning, with an arm across Amelia's shoulders, dozens of pictures of Raymond. Then a single snapshot of Amelia and Raymond standing with a man in shirtsleeves before a building, a house, perhaps, upon which there was a sign which, I guessed, read JUSTICE OF THE PEACE. Later, a series of pictures showing stiff-looking Stonehouses seated with an equally stiff-looking Raymond Muleto. In the last pages of the album there were pictures of a pregnant Amelia laughing as she sat at the beach, wearing a maternity bathing suit. And then there were baby pictures.

"I thought you might be interested in the sort of life my family led before I was married, but I didn't think you'd want to look at ten thousand pictures of our son." Amelia, who had brought in coffee and said nothing until I'd finished looking at the albums, smiled. "Let me help you go through the scrapbooks. Most of what's there has nothing to do with the emeralds. It's just more family stuff."

She came and sat between Zee and me and opened the first book.

Yellowed articles from newspaper society pages; notes of business successes with references to Eugene Stonehouse, the latest Stonehouse entrepreneur; clippings of weddings; of the birth of the Stonehouse sisters; of balls and travels. Mr. and Mrs. Eugene Stonehouse home from Africa, home from Paris, home from a world cruise.

"This is what you're after," said Amelia.

An article from the society pages of the Boston *Post,* complete with blurry photographs, about the fabulous Stonehouse Emerald Necklace. I read it carefully, noting the breathless style of the writer, the strategic vagueness with respect to just exactly how the jewels first came into possession of Jacob Stonehouse, the discreet fawning over the then-current Stonehouse family and its social set.

It was a more detailed version of the summary tale given to me by the Chief. While the American colonies were separating themselves from England between 1776 and 1783, Jacob Stonehouse, an ex-officer in the British army described in the *Post* as a "gentleman adventurer," was employed by one Mohammed Rashad to train and lead a rebel army against the then-Padishah of Sarofim. Here the writer provided a parenthetical description of a Padishah as a king, more or less.

Sarofim was a small kingdom mostly consisting of sand but commanding a strait that lay on the sea route between East and Middle East. The Padishah's fortresses overlooking the strait and his corsairs roaming it brought considerable wealth back to the Padishah, if not to his nomadic people, who benefited little if at all from their ruler's commercial successes. Mohammed Rashad, an intelligent and ruthless camel herder with lofty aspirations, noting that the Padishah's cannon and parapets faced the sea, where his enemies could be found, attacked from the desert, his ragtag army trained and led by Jacob Stonehouse.

Here the narrative became diplomatically obscure. The revolution was a success. The old Padishah's head was placed on a stake outside the main city gate. Mohammed Rashad became Padishah, and his sons and grandsons followed him to the throne. The Rashad dynasty still ruled Sarofim.

Jacob Stonehouse, ever an opportunist, reappeared in England with mysterious wealth, which he invested in companies producing goods for the British army and navy. During Napoleon's wars he made magnificent profits and earned a minor title from a grateful monarchy. It was at this time that the famous emerald necklace first came to public view. Stonehouse adorned the neck of his wife with the emeralds on the occasion of a royal ball and, when pressed for the story of the jewels, hinted that they were the gift of an Eastern potentate, given in thanks for a "bit of work" he had performed.

Stonehouse, already wealthy, added to that wealth by shrewd investments in land and in ships carrying on the East India trade. Then, suddenly and without particular fanfare, he moved to America, where he continued his investments in trade but added whaling to his business interests. He grew old and richer and built his great New England houses. The now-famous emeralds dazzled New England society on the necks of Stonehouse women.

Jacob Stonehouse's grandson, upon inheriting the family fortunes, was the man who hired a Dutch jeweler to make the almost equally famous pastes of the original emeralds and to duplicate their setting. He, Nathaniel Stonehouse, was a New England Yankee in every sense, frugal and far-sighted. He did not fancy risking the real jewels to some low (or even high) thief, what with the migrations of "foreigners"—the Irish in particular—to Boston.

The emerald necklaces, both the real one and its copy, were placed in the vaults of a great, gray Boston banking and insurance company (Stonehouse, Chute, Cabot, and Adams) and thereafter, save for very rare, very special occasions, the Stonehouse women wore only the pastes, which, in time, took on a fame of their own.

The real jewels appeared so rarely that one generation passed without their being worn at all. Unwilling for *that* to happen again, the Stonehouse women prevailed upon the men and the representatives of Stonehouse, Chute, Cabot, and Adams to produce them for social events at least once every decade.

There was a dim photo of Mrs. Eugene Stonehouse before a large vault. Beside her, looking owlish and humorless, were four men in severely conservative suits. In front of them on a table were two wooden cases lined with silk, one holding the emerald necklace, the other the paste copy.

"Mom," said Amelia. "With Stonehouse, Chute, Cabot, and Adams, I imagine. No . . . Actually, I think all of them were dead by then. She was like me. She didn't really care much for jewels. Here's the next generation." She took a second scrapbook and leafed through it. "Here we are."

The photo was of her and her sister in front of the same great vault, flanked by four different but equally solemn men. The same cases and necklaces lay on the table.

"It's our official introduction to being Stonehouse women," said Amelia with a little laugh. "We get to go down and be photographed with the keepers of the sacred jewels. I think Emily's daughter did the same pose several years back."

I thought two of the men looked familiar. They were the youngest of the four.

"I saw their pictures in your photo album," I said, pointing.

"You have a good memory. I imagine it came in handy when you were a policeman in Boston. Yes. The tall one is Willard Blunt and the short one is Jasper Cabot. Willard and I actually dated a time or two before and after the war. We were both considered a bit wild, if you can imagine that. Rebellious youth, our parents thought. We had been exposed to dangerous views. I at Radcliffe, he both at Harvard and off in the Middle East, where they posted him in the war. They considered our political and economic views to be absolutely radical. Of course to our parents, Roosevelt was somewhere left of Lenin and Marx. Willard and I both later became rather stodgy, I'm afraid. Still are, for that matter. He has informed me that he'll be down this week to see to it that arrangements for the transfer of the necklace are proper. You will meet him Saturday night, I'm sure. Jasper Cabot and Mr. Willard Sergeant Blunt have been guarding the Stonehouse emeralds for almost fifty years; Willard insists upon personally overseeing their transfer to the Padishah. Good riddance of them, I say. I am no admirer of the Padishah of Sarofim, despicable man that he is, but there may be some justice in the emeralds going back to the place where old Jacob stole them originally." She rose and went to her mantel. "If you really want to know something about Sarofim and the Rashads, you should probably have read this." She brought back a book and handed it to me. There were also letters in her hand.

I took the book. *Free People,* by Hamdi Safwat. The subject was Sarofim. The print was small, and there were no pictures. It seemed to be a combination of history and political theory. A very gray book. I didn't know if I wanted to know that much about Sarofim or the Rashads.

Amelia gave Zee the letters. "Mail these for me, will you, dear? Since they moved the post office out by the triangle, I have to drive through that traffic jam in front of the A & P in order to mail anything. I hate it. But you're going by there anyway, so would you be a darling . . . ?"

"Aunt Amelia, I hope you're getting something out of this necklace business," said Zee.

"Something? Oh yes. Quite a lot, according to Willard Blunt. But not anything public. Transferred funds from the Padishah's Swiss accounts to the Stonehouse Boston accounts. Frankly, I can use the money. Father was a sweet man who knew much about many things; unfortunately, money was not one of them. The same was true of my husband and is true of me as well. Happily, Willard Blunt managed to prevent Father from spending everything before he died, my sister married wealth, and Raymond and I never needed more than we had. What more could any of us have asked?"

"It sounds okay to me," Zee said. "But now you'll be well off for a change. I'm glad."

"As am I. Willard Blunt sent me quarterly checks for forty years. A trust of some sort, set up by some Stonehouse who properly doubted that his children would be as shrewd as he was. That money helped Raymond and me stay afloat on farmers' wages, but now it's run out, so this new money is just fine. The emeralds mean nothing to me, and I'm only sorry that Raymond isn't here to enjoy the money they're finally bringing. Not that he would live any differently. He was a man who always did what he wanted to do. He wanted to be a farmer and he was. He'd still be a farmer."

Most people don't like to talk about their money. There are exceptions, of course; usually people who have just made a lot of it and want you to know about it. Most other people don't discuss it because, I guess, they think they'll either embarrass you or embarrass or endanger themselves by whatever they reveal. Amelia Muleto seemed indifferent to the psychological issues surrounding money. She used money seriously but didn't take it seriously.

I said this to Zee as we drove away.

"Uncle Ray was the same way," said Zee. "Money was like air or food or shelter to him. He knew you needed a certain amount of it, but he never went after any extra. He appreciated the checks from Willard Blunt, but never thought about them very much. He was interested in his vegetables and wine and his family. Money was only a tool. As long as he had enough, he was satisfied. I doubt if he ever imagined that he might die and leave Aunt Amelia a widow without income. I doubt if she thought about it either. When it happened, of course, she dealt with it, because that's the kind of person she is."

"She'll be going to the big Saturday bash, though."

"In formal gown, looking splendid, you may be sure. She even has a role in the drama. She will accept the paste necklace on behalf of the Smithsonian while Aunt Emily presents the real thing to the Padishah. Aunt Amelia is still a beautiful woman. She dazzled high society when she was a debutante and now she'll dazzle it again for one night. And then she'll come back to her little house and live a life without grand balls or Padishahs or any of the other adornments that Aunt Emily thinks necessary."

Zee quite apparently favored Aunt Amelia over Aunt Emily. That was good news for me because my economic system was more like Ray Muleto's than Edward Damon's. And I had to do without a trust fund, too.

"Did you notice the name of the royal family of Sarofim?" I asked.

"I thought I saw you twitch a little when you read the name. Do you imagine what I'm imagining?"

"That the jerk who nearly ran over us is the Padishah of Sarofim being passed off as a mere 'Mister' Rashad? Yes. And that Standish Caplan's job is to make sure he's entertained and keeps out of trouble while he's over here."

"And that Colonel What's-his-name is his bodyguard?"

"Nagy. Yes. And the boat belongs to your Aunt Amelia's brother-in-law."

"Did anyone ever draw it to your attention that life is sometimes ironic?"

"You've been reading your philosophy books again. I can tell."

I took Zee home so she could get some chores done before she changed for work. She was on the graveyard shift at the hospital. "For obvious reasons, we don't use that phrase," Zee had once explained, a bit testily. Zee had wonderful full red lips, which I could still taste as I left her West Tisbury house and drove back to Edgartown to find Manny Fonseca, the Portagee pistoleer.

▪ 5 ▪

Manny Fonseca had a lot of nicknames, all of them tied to the old West, which fascinated him. He was a gun lover and he considered it to have been his great misfortune to have missed every war fought by America in his lifetime. He had been too young for World War II and Korea and too old for Vietnam. Although the United States government had undertaken several undeclared and officially secret military operations while Manny was doing his turn in the army, and although Manny had done his best to be assigned to those activities, he had been stationed instead in Mississippi and been forced to content himself with becoming the camp's small-arms expert. Manny had brought back home to the Vineyard his interest in shooting and now, in his mid forties, he was one of those guys who shot up a great deal of his income at the target range at the Rod and Gun Club. His wife and kids seemed pretty normal in spite of Manny's mania. Manny himself wasn't all that odd, either, even though he was constantly trading guns, buying guns, selling guns, shooting guns, talking guns, and reading gun magazines. He belonged to the NRA, had progun bumper stickers on his truck, was pretty far off to the right on most issues if he ever thought about them at all, but was only openly prejudiced against the Wampanoag Indians up in Gay Head. He called the Wampanoags "Japanese Indians" because of the imported trinkets that were sold in the shops at the top of the Gay Head Cliffs.

I stopped at his house and was told by Helen, his wife, that he was still at the shop. The shop was a clean white building in Edgartown, out toward the yacht club tennis courts. I drove down there, parked, and went in.

Manny was a woodworker. A fine finish carpenter. If it

could be made out of wood, Manny could make it. He was a man you could trust absolutely to do good work, on time. A rare commodity on Martha's Vineyard or anywhere else. His shop smelled of woods, oils, and paints. There was sawdust on the floor and in the corners of the rooms.

Manny was about to close up when I came in. He raised an eyebrow.

"How?" I said, holding up an empty hand.

"No jokes," said Manny. "I haven't had my evening whiskey yet. Besides, I don't even want to think about those savages up there. 'Professional Indians' I call 'em."

Actually, he loved to think about them. Whenever he wasn't thinking about something else, he fussed and fumed about the Wampanoags. But I hadn't heard the "Professional Indians" phrase before.

"What do you mean 'professional,' Wyatt?"

He smiled, pleased to tell me. "I just thought it up. Those injuns up there are all professionals. A professional is somebody who does something for money. Those people up there weren't interested in being Indians until they found out it paid. For a couple of hundred years they didn't want to be Indians. They just wanted to be like everybody else. But once they found out that this stupid government of ours would give them half of Gay Head if they were real Indians, they got busy and got themselves declared official redskins. They're all a bunch of Professional Indians. It's a damned crime!"

I hadn't thought about it that way. I had my own complaints with Gay Head, the Vineyard's westernmost township, the principal one being that there was no place to park up there to go fishing. Gay Head's roads were lined with not only NO PARKING signs, but NO PAUSING signs as well. Gay Headers didn't like other people using their beaches, apparently. I took this to be a sign of general unfriendliness toward out-of-towners, of which I was one. I wouldn't have cared except that Gay Head is a beautiful area, famous for its colored clay cliffs and for its fine shore fishing.

"Professional Indians, eh, Wild Bill?"

"You've seen those signs they've got up there at their so-called Tribal Council headquarters? 'A federally recognized tribe.' You think the Utes or the Navahos or the Apaches have little signs saying that they're 'federally recognized' tribes? You bet they don't. But these professional Wampanoags have 'em all over the place so everyone will know that they're sure-enough Indians." Manny, who as far as I knew had never seen a Ute, Navaho, or Apache, took a deep breath. "You know how you get to be an official Wampanoag?"

"No."

"You're a direct descendent of somebody who was a Wampanoag back in 1860 or something like that. You got an ancestor who was a Wampanoag, you're a Wampanoag. What do you think of that?"

I didn't want to think about that and said so. "I didn't come here to talk about Wampanoags. I came to borrow a pistol."

Manny brightened. "What kind of a pistol?"

"One I can wear under a suit jacket without anybody knowing I've got it. My old service .38 is too fat. Besides, all I have is a belt holster. I think I need something else."

"Follow me home," said Manny happily.

I did and we went down into his basement. He unlocked the door of his gun room and we went in. The place was an armory, with pistols, rifles, and shotguns in cases along the walls, a neat workbench with tools and gun parts laid out upon it. There were scopes, boxes of shells, containers of powder and shot, bullet molds, scabbards, holsters, and gun cases stored or hung around the room. The smells of cleaning agents and oils permeated the air.

"I gather that you don't want anybody to know you're carrying," said Manny.

"I just don't want to make an issue of it. I also don't expect to use it."

"Better to have it and not need it than need it and not have it," quoted Manny. He looked me up and down and side to side. "You got any preferences? You prefer something heavy? Something light? Forty-five? Nine mm?"

"No preferences. Like I said, I don't expect to use it."

"You got a permit to carry?" Manny was a law-and-order man.

"Yes."

"You have big hands. You want something you can get a hold of. I got just the thing." He unlocked a case and took out a pistol. "Here you go. A Colt Mark IV Series 80. Forty-five caliber. Load her up with 200-grain CCI Lawman slugs. Thousand feet a second. Mucho oomph. Take it."

I took it. It was heavy but nicely balanced. Manny rummaged around in another cabinet and brought out a holster. "Top-grade cowhide. You can wear it on your belt or under your arm. You'll want it as a shoulder holster. It will fit that weapon like a glove." He unlocked cabinets, tossed me a box of ammunition, and dug out some man-shaped targets, earplugs and shooting glasses. "Let's go up to the club."

The club was the Rod and Gun Club, which had a newly renovated shooting range. From my house I could often hear the popping sounds of the Rod and Gun Club shootists at their play. It was Manny's favorite spot on the island. We drove there, unlocked the gate, and went in. We parked and walked down to the table at the twenty-five-yard mark, and Manny got me into the holster and adjusted it to his satisfaction.

"You ever wear one of these rigs?"

"No."

"Well, when you draw you just pop off the thumb strap and yank her out. I'd carry one in the chamber with my piece locked and cocked. It's plenty safe."

No gun is safe as far as I'm concerned, but I just nodded. Manny loaded two magazines and put one in the gun. "You know anything about this pistol?"

"I've shot a revolver."

"This is different. Safer, actually." He jacked a bullet into the firing chamber. "Now she's ready to go. Here's the safety." He ran smoothly and patiently through the prefiring actions, with a strong emphasis on safety, then put the pistol on the table. "Put the plugs in your ears while I set up the targets." When the targets were set, he came back.

"Watch."

He put plugs in his ears, donned his shooting glasses, raised the pistol in both hands, and rattled off a series of booming shots. Cartridge cases streamed into the air and arced to the ground. Sudden silence rang. We walked up to the targets. The left-hand one had a tiny cluster of bullet holes right where the nose of a real man would have been. Manny looked satisfied. We walked back.

Manny showed me his grip, right hand gripping the pistol, left hand supporting the right, right arm locked stiff. I loaded the pistol and shot off a clip of bullets at the right-hand target, aiming at the widest part of it. The .45 jumped less than I expected, and all of the bullets were in the black.

Manny was pleased. I shot up the rest of our bullets, and after I made a few practice draws from the shoulder holster, we went back to his house.

I paid him for the bullets we'd used and for another box of them.

"You want to buy that weapon," said Manny, "I'll give you a good price."

"No thanks, John Wesley. I'll have it back to you on Sunday."

"Lemme know how it goes," said Manny enviously. Then, "Where you going to be, anyway? What's going on?"

I couldn't resist. "I've been hired by the Wampanoag Tribal Council to be a security guard at their Saturday-night meeting. They don't want any interruptions by white-eyes from out of town."

"Get outa here!"

I got. Actually, of course, the prospect of me working as security for the Padishah of Sarofim was no more outlandish.

On Thursday the Chief called me in and made me an official Edgartown special police officer. At home again, I called Vineyard Haven, ordered a tux, and told them to charge it to Edward C. Damon.

Zee was still working the night shift and sleeping days, so I went fishing alone. Up to Norton Point on the north shore, in hopes that maybe the blues that weren't down off Chappy anymore might be up there instead. I know a guy who lives off Lambert's Cove Road who lets me use an old road on his land to get to the beach. When my father was young there were still a lot of people up island who would let fishermen use their driveways to get to prime fishing spots, but over the last twenty years, as off-island people have bought up Vineyard land and built new houses where there were never houses before, the driveways and old roads have been closed to fishermen and hunters. There seem to be fewer available fishing spots every year. I felt lucky to know somebody who would let me in.

I wasn't so lucky with the fish. I worked up and down the shore for most of the late afternoon but got nothing for my efforts. Still, it was a nice day. A fine August sun, The Elizabeth Islands across Vineyard Sound, pretty water between them and me, with boats of all kinds going west with the falling tide or east against it. Everyone was doing fine, since the wind was southwest and behind the people fighting the tide and the tide was with the people beating into the wind. I imagined myself in Jeremy Fisher's catboat, going west toward Menemsha or over to Tarpaulin Cove across the Sound on Naushon or on west to Cuttyhunk. Of course in my imaginings, it wasn't Jeremy's catboat, it was my catboat.

In the old days the local fishermen used catboats for all kinds of fishing, and there was no reason why I couldn't too. Some world champion bass had been caught long ago just off Cuttyhunk, and I might just go over there in my catboat and see if there were any more around. After the bass came back and the moratorium had been lifted, of course.

I got so dreamy about catboating around the south coast of New England that even if I'd managed to hook a fish he probably would have gotten off, and I got home too late to invite Zee to supper. I found some of the last of last fall's scallops in my freezer, lettuce in my garden, and leftover rice in the fridge, and while the scallops were thawing in a pan of hot water, made myself an Absolut martini and called Zee anyway.

"What would you say if I told you I landed an eighteen-pound bluefish this afternoon at the change of the tides on Norton Point?"

Her voice was suspicious. "Did you?"

"No. I was going to invite you over for supper to help me eat it, but since I got home too late to invite you and didn't catch it anyway, I'm inviting you to lunch tomorrow instead."

"Tonight's my last night shift, and I'm sleeping in tomorrow, so I'll pass on the lunch. After four, though, you can pick me up at my house and take me to Amelia's. She's going to take a couple of tucks in my gown so I'll look particularly fetching Saturday night when the Padishah proposes."

"Well, I know he's wild about you, and I certainly want to aid the advancement of true international love," I said. "I'll see you at four."

"I'd drive myself, but this way I'll have a chance to see you."

"I can pick you up again afterwards and then you can really see me."

"Not tomorrow night. After Amelia does my dress, she and I are going to go out to eat together. After that, she'll drive me home. It's all arranged."

"Rats."

"And you won't see me Saturday, either, because Amelia and I are going to dress at her house in the afternoon, and then one of the Damon cars is going to pick us up and take us to the party."

"Double rats."

"However, after the party you can drive me home!"

"That's after the Padishah proposes to you?"

She adopted her Scarlett O'Hara accent. "A lady gets many proposals, but she doesn't accept them all."

"I'll make you one you can't refuse."

"Oh, how you talk . . ."

I made a lettuce salad and mixed up a bit of honey mustard dressing for it. By then the rice was reheating and the scallops were melted in their plastic bag. I made a not-too-thick roux flavored with garlic, sautéed the scallops in a bit of butter, and poured the scallops and sauce over a plate of rice. Delish! I washed everything down with a half bottle of Vinho Verde, a wine I like even though it never makes the food columns in the *Globe*. Afterwards: Cognac. As the poet once rhetorically asked, what can wine sellers buy that is better than what they sell?

The next afternoon I picked up Zee and a large box with a bit of white satin hanging out between the bottom and the lid.

"For innocence," said Zee, tucking the bit of cloth back in out of sight.

"Screw that," I said. She laughed.

As we pulled up at Amelia's house we found another car there before us. A large, dark, expensive car.

Zee's eyes lit up and she clutched my arm. "That's Willard Blunt's car! Remember him? You know, I wonder if he's wooing her! She's a widow and he's an old beau and he's been here a couple of times this week already! Whee!"

Women, for all their complaints about men, love a romance, real or imagined. So do I, for that matter.

"I'm going to sneak in there," said Zee in a whisper, clutching the box. "Maybe I'll hear something!"

"Maybe they'll catch you at the keyhole and give your ear a twist. Serve you right!"

"Shhhh!" Zee grinned and scuttled up to the front door. She glanced back and put a finger to her lips. In the spirit of adventure, I cut the ignition. Zee waved thanks and eased open the front door. I thought I heard voices; then they stopped and Zee stood and spoke and Aunt Amelia appeared, kissed Zee, and waved at me. I waved back and drove away.

The next day, at 9:02 in the morning, after giving my name and showing my brand-new badge to a guard at the gate, I was on the Chappaquiddick estate of Edward C. Damon, political fat cat and ambassador-to-be to Sarofim. As I drove in and parked my rusty LandCruiser, I looked things over.

The house was one of those originally built in the early part of the century when a few wealthy families moved themselves, their servants, and perhaps a cow or two for fresh milk to Chappy for the summer holidays. As the years passed, the Damon house had had wings and taller roofs added, until now it stood wide and high just south of the narrows that link Edgartown Harbor to Katama Bay. It was a great wooden structure, gray shingled, many windowed, balconied and chimnied, with a round tower rising from one corner. Below the house was a boat house and a long dock, alongside of which was tied the family yawl, sixty feet or so of traditional wood and brass, built in the days when, indeed, if you had to ask how much a yacht cost, you couldn't afford it. A polished catboat and the cigarette boat lay on the other side of the dock.

On the three sides of the house away from the water there were wide lawns sprinkled with large oaks. A tennis court and a green for croquet were set back near a barn that once might have housed the family milk cow but now, I was soon to learn, was storage for an antique car and for the various machines and tools needed to maintain the grounds. On the second floor, in a converted hayloft, was the apartment of the couple who constituted the permanent staff for the estate, a Mr. Outside and his wife, Mrs. Inside. Around the perimeter of the grounds was a well-maintained stone fence and a thick hedgerow entwined with roses, a completely satisfactory barrier to keep in whatever the Damons wanted to keep in and to keep out what they wanted to keep out. The entrance road came through a gateway between two standing granite stones from which a heavy gate was hung.

All in all, I was impressed. My old Toyota looked a bit out of place, and I guessed (rightly, it turned out) that my house would fit into Damon's dining room.

There was a collection of men and women standing near the front door of the house. I knew some of them. I walked over. Some Vineyard cops and several people with a city look about them. Security folk all, both locals and imports. A man with a list stepped out and stopped me. I gave him my name and showed my badge again. He checked his list, said "You're late," and waved me into the group.

Standing on the porch in front of us was a tall man in his fifties wearing a dark summer suit with a faint chalk stripe in it. I had never seen a summer suit with a chalk stripe before. On Martha's Vineyard the only people who wear suits in the daytime are the lawyers who do business down at the courthouse. You can spot a Vineyard lawyer at two hundred yards.

This was not a Vineyard lawyer, though. It was Jason Thornberry, head of Thornberry Security. Just after I had become a Boston cop, he had left the force to start his own PI and corporate security business. That business was now very big. Thornberry looked smart, smooth, and tough, but for some reason was wearing one of those thin little mustaches that were so popular with movie stars back in the thirties and early forties. I thought it made him look a bit shady, but maybe he thought it made him look like Errol Flynn.

He gave me a hard look, glanced at the man with the list and got a nod in reply, and spoke. His voice was that of a certain kind of doctor: calm, rational, detached, commanding. The voice of authority.

▪ 6 ▪

Thornberry coolly explained the importance of the occasion. An international event of significance to both the Middle East and the West. He emphasized the need for alertness, cooperation, and discretion on the part of all security personnel, both uniformed and in civilian dress. He wanted each of us to know everything about the physical layout of the estate and the house.

He took us on a slow walk around the grounds, pointing out the locations where uniformed guards with radios would be located: at the gate, along the waterfront, both inside and outside the hedge and stone wall. I thought the security may have been overdone, but said nothing.

He took us into the house and went through it floor by floor, basement to tower, pausing to point out stairways, doors, windows, closets, balconies. Servants—again, I recognized a few locals—were busy in the kitchen or polishing silver or laying out linen cloths on tables. They stood back as we passed by them or interrupted their work, for Thornberry exuded dominance that no maid or butler could withstand.

He led us finally to the great library. Its walls were lined with leather-bound books on dark shelves. The walls between the bookcases were hung with portraits of, I assumed, past Damons. There were tables and reading lamps and leather chairs, and, in a far corner, an ancient steel safe topped by a statue of some goddess or other carved in the late-Victorian style. Two crystal chandeliers, long ago converted from candles to electricity, hung from the high ceilings. A huge Oriental rug, worn thin here and there, but rich and exotic nonetheless, covered most of the floor. The room didn't look like a place where anyone had ever actually done much reading. Not lately, at least.

At the front of the room rows of chairs had been arranged facing a screen, a large television set, and a VCR. Behind the chairs was a slide projector. We sat down, the lights dimmed, pictures appeared on the screen, and Thornberry spoke, first giving a brief history of the necklace and of its significance on this occasion, then turning to the evening's scenario.

"There are only four ways for guests to get to or from the estate: by ferry from Edgartown, by boat, by four-wheel-drive vehicle along South Beach, or by helicopter. Because of the limited access to the house, only one hundred guests will be in attendance." Thornberry paused. "Of course it is also possible to arrive by parachute or hang glider or to both arrive and depart by swimming. However, should you encounter anyone traveling by those means, you may assume the individual is uninvited and act accordingly."

His mouth flicked up and down, and the security people he had brought with him from Boston tittered quickly, recognizing Thornberry humor. He went on. "The invited guests will arrive by car and boat and are scheduled to be here by six. Naturally there will be delays. The Padishah and his party will be upstairs in the north wing of the house as guests of Mr. Damon. At seven the Padishah and his party will descend the main staircase and he will be greeted by Mr. and Mrs. Damon and Mrs. Damon's sister, Mrs. Muleto. The Padishah's party and the Damon party will then join the other guests in the ballroom for champagne.

"Dinner will be served at eight in the dining room and on the terrace. Immediately after coffee, at nine-thirty precisely, if everything goes smoothly, which it rarely does at such events as this . . ." A pause, the quick flick of Thornberry's mouth, the respondent titter from his hirelings. He continued. "Mrs. Damon will go with Mr. Willard Blunt to the master bedroom where both the real and the paste necklaces have been locked away since yesterday, when

Mr. Blunt brought them here from Boston. Mrs. Damon will put on the paste necklace, the safe will be locked, and Mrs. Damon will descend the stairway on Mr. Blunt's arm. There will be applause. She will then remove the necklace from her own neck and present it to her sister, Mrs. Muleto, who will accept it in the name of the Smithsonian and afterwards place it here"—he pointed to the safe—"for safekeeping.

"Mrs. Damon will return to the master bedroom, this time with both her husband and Mr. Blunt. She will don the real necklace, and the three of them will then descend the main stairs to the ballroom, where they will be met by the Padishah. There will, of course, be more applause. Mrs. Damon will waltz first with her husband and then with the Padishah. Her husband will then remove the necklace from her neck and formally present it to the Padishah, who will accept it on behalf of Sarofim and give Mrs. Damon, in return, a diamond tiara. Afterwards, wearing her tiara, Mrs. Damon and her husband will lead more dancing in the ballroom. The dancing will go on until one o'clock or until the Padishah tires. Whichever comes last."

Pictures had flashed on the screen as he had spoken, showing the scenes of his narrative. Thornberry paused. "If you think all of this is theatrical, you are right. The Padishah is fond of American films, and Mr. Damon has hired a Hollywood producer, a friend, I'm told, to make the event properly dramatic. It was Wilde, was it not, who observed that only shallow people do not judge by appearances?" Thornberry's mouth again flickered in what I assumed was his version of a smile.

Unsure about how to respond to Wilde wit, his audience did not, and Thornberry, after a moment, went on as photos of various people appeared and disappeared from the screen.

"The firm of Stonehouse, Chute, Cabot, and Adams has for many years been entrusted with both the emeralds and the pastes. This is Mr. Willard Blunt, who is overseeing the necklaces' transference from the Stonehouse estate: one to the Padishah and the other to the Smithsonian. The necklaces are, as you know, now under guard in the safe in the master bedroom. Our people are stationed at the doorway of the bedroom, and others are outside the window on the balcony. The windows are locked on the inside, and the door has been locked and will be unlocked by Mr. Blunt himself. Another one of our people will be at the end of the hall leading to the master bedroom. These are the faces of the men guarding the room. Remember them."

Faces appeared, lingered, and were replaced. I recognized members of our group. They looked like ex-cops. Thornberry liked to have trained people working for him. Pictures of the master bedroom, the hall, and the balcony appeared and disappeared.

"Because the master bedroom contains the safe, Mr. and Mrs. Damon will be dressing farther down the hall in a guest room. Once the transfer of the necklaces has taken place, the firm of Stonehouse, Chute, Cabot, and Adams is no longer in any way responsible for their security. Thornberry Security is responsible until the Padishah and his party depart the country with the jewels. After the emeralds have been presented to the Padishah, they will be returned to the master bedroom, where they will remain under our guard until the Padishah's departure from the United States.

"Here are faces to remember. Mr. Damon, Mrs. Damon, Mrs. Muleto . . . the Padishah [yes, indeed, it was the helmsman of the cigarette boat]; his wife; Colonel Ahmed Nagy, the Padishah's personal bodyguard [with a face like a hatchet]; Dr. Mahmoud Zakkut, the Padishah's personal physician and political advisor; Dr. Omar Youssef, the curator of the National Museum of Sarofim and an internationally known expert on gems who has, by the way, already seen the emeralds and certified that they are the real thing; Mr. Marks and Ms. Johanson, my chief aides . . ." Zee's picture appeared on the screen, was identified, and went away. There were no pictures of me. "Uniformed personnel will be on duty outside under the supervision of Mr. Marks. Inside the house we will be formally dressed, unobtrusive but alert. Ms. Johanson will be in-house supervisor and will help you in any way she can. Remember one thing: an order from Mr. Marks or Ms. Johanson is an order from me."

The slide screen went blank and the television screen lit up. Thornberry's voice changed a tone or two. "I expect no problems tonight, but there is something you should know. The nation of Sarofim is politically unstable at the moment. The Padishah has enemies. Representatives of the opposition are said to have arrived on Martha's Vineyard, and an embarrassment to the Padishah would serve their cause. There has been violence in Sarofim and in Europe. This is a film clip of men and women thought to be members of the Sarofim Democratic League, one of the organizations believed to be responsible for revolutionary activities against the Padishah." The screen flickered and Middle Eastern faces, youthful and laughing, appeared. Another cut showed faces in a crowd on an American street. "Those were taken two weeks ago in Weststock, Massachusetts, where they are students," said Thornberry's voice. "Now they have disappeared, probably by moving in with Sarofimian students studying in Boston. The intellectuals of Sarofim are often supportive of the SDL. Keep your eyes open for these people and for others like them. Sarofimians are not necessarily easy to spot. Be alert and suspicious."

The television went off, the lights went on, and Ms. Johanson took charge of me and my fellow insiders and explained where she wanted us during the evening's festivities. I got to be in the ballroom, with roving opportunities elsewhere on the ground floor. I was a downstairs person.

"You come on duty at five," said the efficient Ms. Johanson as she dismissed us. She looked at me. "Can you arrange a ride with somebody else? That car of yours looks terrible."

Ms. Johanson wasn't a bad-looking woman. "How about with you?" I asked.

Ms. Johanson did not smile. "There's a spot about a hundred yards outside the gate. You can park there. Hide that machine in the trees if you can."

She went away and so did I. Off to Vineyard Haven to collect my rented tux. On the way I looked for revolutionary Sarofimians but didn't see a one. I suspected that I might be on their side, if I ever happened to find their side.

7

The northeast wind that had blown in the clean dry weather had gone away, and the day was muggy, with a thin overcast of high clouds. Undaunted by the paleness of the sun, the August people were out on the beach between Edgartown and Oak Bluffs, making the most of the warm weather. There were kites in the sky, surf sailors just off the beach, children and adults in the warm summer water. Out on the Sound the sailboats moved between the Vineyard and the dim haze that hid Cape Cod, and there were fishermen on the Jetties and kids diving from the bridges into the channels that linked Anthier's Pond to the sea.

In Oak Bluffs there were boats anchored near the ferry dock, with fishermen trying for bonito. It didn't look like the fishermen were having much luck, but none of them seemed to be complaining. And no wonder: fishermen think going fishing is usually better than anything else you might want to do; besides, if you actually hooked a bonito you would really have a good time. Bonitos give you a real fight. I even know some guys who no longer go bluefishing because they like bonito fishing so much better. Personally I do not subscribe to that radical view.

On the far side of Oak Bluffs I passed the hospital where Zee was not working that day. She was busy getting herself and Aunt Amelia properly gussied up for the big event that night. Why so much time? I should have asked just to make trouble. A man wouldn't understand, she'd have said, me in particular. True.

I drove on into Vineyard Haven, hoping but not expecting to find a parking place not too far from the store that was renting me my formal duds. Vineyard Haven has the worst driving and parking conditions on all of Martha's Vineyard. The dreaded T, where the Edgartown road intersects the State Road and left turners routinely are backed up for eternities, is second in frustration only to the infamous Five Corners downtown where the ferries unload and traffic is routinely complete chaos.

Vineyard Haven natives are no doubt used to such messes and in no hurry to do anything about them, but those of us who live elsewhere dread our visits there. It is a paradox too obvious to merit comment that most of the traffic on and off the island goes through Vineyard Haven and that the town houses the Vineyard's best stores and that therefore we often have to go there whether we like it or not. I mean it's not like Gay Head, which is a place you only go to because you choose to. You *have* to go to Vineyard Haven sometimes.

I found a parking place right on Main Street. Another sign that there is a God? Inside my store the salesgirl and I looked each other over as she got my tux.

"We don't get many calls for this size," she observed in what I took to be an approving tone. She ran her eyes up and down while I did the same.

I smiled modestly and didn't tell her that I'd ordered the jacket a size big to allow Manny Fonseca's hefty pistol to hang less obviously under my arm.

She wore a diamond on her left hand. The hand touched my arm. She was a nice looking young woman. A college girl, I suspected, about ready to go back to the books and not above a last flirtation. "You're a big guy," she smiled.

I tapped her diamond with a forefinger and raised a brow.

"Oh, that," she said, leaving her hand near my arm. "Don't mind that."

"I'm tempted, but like you I'm already taken," I said. "Oh, if only I were free."

She took back her hand and sighed then grinned. "Oh, well."

I took my tux and left, thinking that I was probably old enough to be her father although I didn't feel that way.

I drove home and fixed myself a late lunch. Precombat food. Carbohydrates. Pasta with pesto made from my own basil. Since neither Thornberry nor Ms. Johanson had mentioned food for the security folks and since both had ordered no drinking on duty, I washed my pasta down with lots of good cheap red jug wine, just so I wouldn't waste away to nothing before the evening was over.

I ran off several Bad Bunnies who were snooping around my garden fence, then weeded the garden for an hour (about my weeding limit on my very best weeding days), gobbled up a few asparagus sprouts sneaking up through the seaweed I'd spread over the asparagus bed, admired my fine tomatoes, thinking I should can a few tomorrow, after the Sarofim emeralds were safely transferred and Manny Fonseca's pistol was back in his armory, picked two zooks that were threatening to get out of hand, and took a shower. Outside, of course. I have two showers, one inside and one outside. The outside one is much superior. It doesn't steam up the place, there's plenty of room, you don't have to clean out the drain because there isn't any, and you can walk directly from the shower to the solar-powered drier to hang up your towel. Only in the wintertime do I use my indoor shower.

I shaved, wondering again if I should grow a beard but once more deciding not to. How about a mustache, one with maybe waxed curls on the end? I placed a finger across my upper lip and looked at myself in the mirror. Nah.

A bit of toothbrushing, then into clean skivvies, pants, frilly shirt, cummerbund, and shiny black shoes. One thing the armed services teach you is how to shine shoes. The black tie was the snap-on variety, thank goodness. I can tie a bow tie, but I don't like to. It takes me a long time to get the ends even.

I strapped on the shoulder holster. It was the kind where the pistol hangs horizontal under your left arm. Under the other arm is a unit to hold extra clips. A real shootist's sort of rig, irresistible to a guy like Manny Fonseca. I made sure there was *not* a round in the chamber before I stuffed the .45 into the holster. I did not want to accidentally shoot a hole in anyone standing behind me if I actually had to draw the weapon. Manny would be disappointed with me if he ever found out, but I didn't plan on telling him.

I put on the tux jacket and admired myself. Not bad. You really had to look to see the lump under my arm. Very sophisticated. James Bond would approve.

I was tempted to phone Amelia Muleto's house to ask Zee if she wanted to change her mind and ride to the party with me in my LandCruiser. But I could imagine what she'd say: no, she would see me over there. Right now she was very busy, so goodbye. Click.

What do women *do* during these primping sessions?

I poured vermouth in a cold martini glass, sloshed it around and poured it out again, got the Absolut out of the freezer, and filled the glass to the brim. The perfect martini. Just enough vermouth. I had heard about an atomic scientist, out in Nevada in the bomb-testing days there, who had tied a bottle of Noilly Prat Dry to the bomb tower before the detonation and thereafter claimed to get exactly the right amount of vermouth from fallout. I preferred mine not *quite* so dry.

I drank my martini in elegant solitude, and when I was finished it was time to drive to Chappaquiddick.

The On Time ferry, so called, some say, because it has no schedule and is therefore always on time, carries three or four cars at a time and runs back and forth between the Edgartown town dock and the Chappy landing. After four o'clock the beachers were headed for home, so there were a lot of cars coming off Chappy and only a few going back. I drew a curious look from the ferry captain, who had never seen me looking so splendid.

"Dare I ask?" he asked.

"The Damon party," I said, glancing at my nails.

"You'd better park your car where nobody can see it, then." He brought the ferry smoothly into the Chappy landing.

A lot of people were picking on my car lately. I drove it right up to the Damon gate, showed the guard my badge and ID, and parked behind the barn where the rest of the help had parked their cars. Ms. Johanson could park *her* car down the road if she wanted someone to park there.

Inside the house I came face to face with Jason Thornberry. He was suave and comfortable in his tux. He'd come a long way from wearing blue on the Boston PD.

"J.W. Jackson, isn't it?" He put out a hand. I took it. His was still a strong one. "I thought your face was familiar when I saw you this morning. I remember offering you a job a few years ago, just after you retired from the force."

"Maybe I should have taken it."

"The offer is still open. Thornberry Security can always use a good field man."

"I spend more time on the beaches than in the fields these days."

"But here you are on security detail."

"Tomorrow I plan to be canning tomatoes."

His sharp eyes looked me up and down. "You wear formal clothing well. The same cannot be said for many agents. You have police experience, you have a college education, you were well thought of by your superiors on the Boston PD."

"You've done some digging."

He nodded. "I'm in the business of finding things out. Thornberry Security can offer a man of your qualifications excellent opportunities for interesting and remunerative work."

"I'll keep that in mind."

"Do. Good to have you working with us, Jackson."

He moved off, a tall, sophisticated figure with sharp eyes examining once again the physical layout of the house and the people who were responsible for house security. He had been one of the most youthful captains in the history of the Boston Police Department and had had a reputation for being honest, ruthless, and politically astute. Probably you had to be ruthless and politically astute to become a youthful captain in the Boston PD. I wasn't so sure about honest. I did know that a lot of people on the shady side of Boston life had breathed easier when he left the force to form Thornberry Security, Inc. Some of the remaining PD brass had not been as pleased when he siphoned off several of their best men to work for him.

I walked on into the house and into the ballroom. It was large, high ceilinged, and like the library, was hung with crystal chandeliers. At its far end, doors opened onto a veranda that overlooked the northern part of Katama Bay. Next door, also with doors opening out onto the veranda, was the dining room. I strolled there and found linen-clothed tables set with silver and summer flowers. The head table was opposite the doors to the veranda. I went out through the doors and found more linen-clothed tables. Not even the Damon dining room was large enough to hold a hundred guests. Some people would be obliged to eat in the open air. I wondered if they would mind. Personally I preferred the view from the veranda, but I imagined that many would consider that lovely vista of blue water and boats greatly inferior to one of the Padishah of Sarofim seated with various Damons at the head table.

In the library I found Ms. Johanson looking exquisite in an evening dress of blue, which set off her blond hair nicely. Gold gleamed from her wrists and throat. She would fit right in with the evening's crowd. She was reading something on a clipboard. Just as good pilots, before taking off, do not depend on their memories but on checklists, so Miss Johanson was checking off her duties. Having forgotten a lot of things myself, from time to time, I approved. She looked up. I raised a friendly hand. She stared, then looked down at her clipboard and up again.

"Jackson, yes?"

Alas. She'd had to read my name to remember it. On the other hand, she *had* remembered it after reading it.

"Jackson. Yes."

She looked me over and nodded. "Very good. Are you an island policeman, Jackson?"

"Only a special officer. I've retired from real work."

"Indeed?" She glanced at her clipboard and turned a page. "Ah, yes. You were once on the Boston PD, I see."

"Long ago."

"You were shot and you retired on a disability pension."

"I could never keep secrets from a woman like you."

"You are to be on duty in the ballroom, principally. Should anyone speak to you, be casual. Smile, move off as soon as you can. Keep alert to anything unusual. Drink only soda water. After the guests leave there will be food in the kitchen for you, should you want it." She glanced at a small golden watch on her left wrist. "The guests should begin arriving about six. Have you any questions?"

"Only one. Your first name."

She looked at me the way women look whenever some man is impertinent and stupid. "My subordinates address me as Ms. Johanson."

I waited. She frowned and looked down at her clipboard.

"Helga," she said after a moment, touching a hand to her hair. "My name is Helga. Now go to work, please, Mr. Jackson."

I went.

A few minutes before six, Edward C. Damon, his wife by his side, their daughter and her husband close behind, all gloriously yet tastefully attired and bejeweled, descended from their rooms upstairs. As they did, the front door opened and Amelia Muleto was bowed in by the butler. There were embraces between the members of the two parties, those careful kinds that occur when no one wants tulle crushed or makeup smudged. I was standing in the ballroom, half hidden by a marble statue of Nimuë that stood at one side of the doorway. No one saw me or my glass of soda with lemon peel. And I did not see Zee.

Amelia wore a dress of silver gray silk which was both elegant and simple. The gray sash at her waist matched her hair, and I saw her suddenly as a lady of high caste, quite a change from the vegetable and flower gardener I'd come to know over the years.

I stepped away from Nimuë, which was more than Merlin had been able to manage, and walked across the hall. Amelia looked up and saw me and smiled. She gave me her hand and lifted her head for a kiss which I, caught off guard but ever suave, gave her.

"You look splendid," I said. "But where is your lovely niece?"

She looked distressed. "Oh, dear. I tried to call you, but you weren't in. There was an emergency at the hospital. Zee had to fly to Boston with a patient. The hospital phoned me about noon. Poor Zee didn't even have time to phone me herself. She may not get back until Monday."

The front door opened, and the first of the guests was announced. Amelia and I were looking at each other. Suddenly Emily Damon was at Amelia's side, taking her arm, smiling vaguely at me. "Amelia, dear, do come and meet our very good friends the Leaches and the Alexanders. You'll excuse us, I'm sure, young man . . ."

I was distracted. "Of course," my voice said.

Amelia gave me a gentle look, briefly gripped my arm, and was gone.

▪ 8 ▪

Zee in Boston for the whole weekend. And I had a date to take her home after the party, too. Rats! I leaned against the wall while black-uniformed waitresses carrying trays of exotic appetizers brushed by me on their way to the celebration. I snagged a crabmeat canapé as it passed. Not bad. I felt lonesome. Then I felt sorry for Zee. It was going to be quite a party from the looks of things, and she was going to miss it. I decided to do my duty and enjoy myself too. It's a nice combination when you can pull it off. I wandered around a bit, trying to look unobtrusive. I seemed to be good at it. Nobody paid any attention to me. They were all busy discussing and looking at More Important People, of whom there were apparently quite a few.

By six-thirty, everyone was there awaiting the descent of the Padishah's party down the great stairway. The liquor had begun to flow freely. The guests were gathered in knots in the entrance hall, on the veranda, and in the ballroom and library. Among them I recognized the grandfatherly figure of a famous retired television newsman, two famous once-married but now divorced pop singers from up island, an actor who had become a star after his film portrayal of a comic-book hero, and a famous but secretive painter who preferred the fishing at Wasque Point and Lobsterville to the New York gallery scene and with whom I had shared coffee a few times during Bass and Bluefish Derby time when the winds were raw. I heard talk and saw sidelong looks that indicated that other celebrated folk were among the crowd, but since I did not own a television set and did not like or listen to popular music, most of the names and faces were unknown to me.

There were readily identifiable reporters and camera people circulating and recording the events of the evening while they liberally partook of champagne and hors d'oeuvres. All of them wore formal evening dress, I was glad to see. The reporters I know are not normally so properly attired. It was not hard to keep track of the hired security people: they were the only ones not drinking. The guests, like the reporters, were keeping the bartenders busy and were primarily there, I guessed, to see the famous emeralds. Until the emeralds appeared, they were still interested in seeing who else of importance was there and in having those important people see them. They took no heed of the dozen busy-eyed soda sippers who moved through and about the crowd trying to notice everything and hoping that no one was noticing them.

Helga Johanson, of course, *was* watching them to make sure that they were on the job. She had emerged from the library and was a graceful and alert figure who captured the attention of more than one admiring man or envious woman, but who slipped charmingly away from invitations for drinks or extended conversations so that she could better do her double job of watching for the bad guys while checking on her own people. Her dress was form fitting. Where did she carry *her* trusty Colt .45?

I went away into various rooms and looked for suspicious people. I found none. The most suspicious-looking people at the party, I thought, were those hanging closest to Edward C. Damon. They were a shifty-looking crowd. In a corner, apart from other guests, I saw Amelia Muleto talking with a tall, cadaverous man whom I recognized as Willard Sergeant Blunt. Was he really her wooer, as Zee had theorized? His head was bent toward hers. Lovers wishing they were alone? Could be, I thought.

I heard a sigh rise collectively from the ballroom and returned in time to see an entourage descend toward the Damons awaiting below. The Padishah, wearing an extraordinary military uniform, led the way and was the principal focus of attention. He was followed by a less brilliantly attired party of five. All of the faces were familiar to me from the morning's briefing. Colonel Ahmed Nagy, his personal bodyguard; his elderly and frail-looking physician and political advisor; his secretary; his number one wife; and the curator of the National Museum of Sarofim. I gave Colonel Ahmed Nagy a good look. His face still looked like an axe, and his hooded eyes went everywhere. When they reached mine, they stopped. Mine stared back. Finally his moved on.

I thought (correctly, I was later informed) that the Padishah's uniform looked modeled after those worn by generals in Hollywood films about the nineteenth-century British Empire. Medaled and feathered hat, very red coat very hung with braid and medals, very blue trousers with red stripes down the sides, very shiny black boots with spurs, and a very black belt and pistol holster.

The hat went to the secretary, and amid the flashes of photographs being taken, the guest of honor and his host and hostesses met.

There was no formal receiving line, but in the ballroom the Padishah took a position at the head of the room and accepted introductions of the guests, who were awed perhaps by their first sight of official royalty. The ladies curtsied; the men bowed and briefly shook the royal hand. The Padishah bestowed the kingly smile and made small talk. He had been educated in England, according to the gossip I had overheard in my wanderings, and knew how to murmur the right things. The wife of the Padishah was not included in the formal introductions, I noted.

When the handsome young man who had portrayed the comic-book hero in films was introduced, the Padishah, overcome by the appearance of a genuine movie star, welcomed him with even more enthusiasm than he had shown for some of the younger ladies, over whose hands his own had lingered longer than absolutely necessary. The young man only escaped after laughingly agreeing to consider making his next comic-book film in Sarofim. The Padishah seemed overjoyed by the prospect.

I discovered Helga Johanson beside me. She gestured toward the guest of honor. "Do you suppose he likes boys best?"

"I hear he has a collection of women."

"People who collect women don't necessarily like women. Is everything going smoothly?"

I said that it was, and she was gone. Shortly afterward dinner was served. On time, too. Whoever was orchestrating this event was doing a good job of it.

I'd seen the work going on in the kitchen. No rubber chicken was served. Instead, a delicate cold soup; a choice of lamb, shelled lobster, or a fragrant vegetable dish native to Sarofim; champagne and vintage wines to wash everything down; and a cordial-soaked tart for desert. Coffee and brandy and more cordials to end the meal.

If there were any dietary laws in Sarofim, they were not revealed by the Padishah, who ate and drank everything offered with regal gusto.

I had another soda with lemon at the bar so I wouldn't drool all over my shirt while everyone else was eating. As I sipped, I thought about cordial-soaked tarts. I'd known a few in my lifetime, and they were generally not bad women at all.

Thinking of this, I heard, over the drone of voices at the dining tables, the sound of distant shouts from down toward the Damons' dock. I walked out onto the veranda and found some diners standing and looking toward the water. Shadowy figures ran down the hill and joined other figures on the dock where the Damons' boats were tied. Shouts and yells floated up to the house. Some were in slurred English, but others were in a tongue I did not know.

"Drunks," a man nearby said, sitting down. "College kids trying to crash a party." He grinned. "Wrong party, guys." The others at his table laughed.

I watched the figures outlined against the lights dancing on the water. Maybe it really was a bunch of college kids out for a night of late-summer fun. Maybe not. The voices rose and fell and then fell some more. Calmer voices sank from my hearing. Slowly some sort of order was restored. I heard an outboard motor start up and saw a boat, crammed with more people than it could safely hold, move away from the dock out into the narrows. From it, derisive voices again were suddenly raised just before the outboard roared and the boat blundered away into the night.

I stared down there awhile and saw figures slowly coming back up over the silvery lawns. Then, as I turned to go back into the house, I heard a rattle of popping sounds off by the south fence of the estate.

"God," said the man who had just sat himself down, "what next?"

"Firecrackers," said the woman next to him. "These kids!"

I didn't wait to hear the rest of their theories, but moved into the shadow cast by the wall of the dining room and stared at the corner of the house beyond which the pops were popping. The figures that had been slowly returning to their posts from down near the water began moving faster, in a crouch, coming back uphill.

More popping sounds from the south fence. Voices from beyond the corner of the house. A floodlight went on, illuminating the south lawn. I turned and walked back past the veranda diners to the north end of the house. I waited in another shadow, staring through the darkness, watching for movement from this side.

"What's going on, for God's sake?" asked a voice behind me. "All this commotion."

"Nothing," I said. "Just some college kids using up the last of their Fourth of July fireworks."

"Oh." The voice went away. I kept looking into the night.

Nothing happened. After a while a man in a uniform came around the corner of the house and along to the veranda. I recognized him when a window light touched his face.

"Grady Flynn," I said to him from the shadows. He started and raised his flashlight. "Don't turn it on," I said. "You'll worry the guests. It's me, J.W. Jackson. What's going on?"

He came close and peered at me. "It's nothing," he said. "I thought it was a damned Uzi or something. I never heard an Uzi, but that's what I first thought. Jeesus. You know what it was? It was firecrackers. Somebody tossed them over the fence and then ran off through the woods. Kids! Scared the hell out of me."

"Nobody got onto the grounds from there or from the docks?"

"No. Bunch of drunks down there. Lots of noise. They had a keg and wanted to join the party. They went off somewhere else. Be lucky if that damned boat doesn't sink out from under them. Must be a dozen people aboard. Harbormaster catches them, their asses will be in a sling."

A bit before nine, Edward C. Damon conducted male cigar smokers to the library, and various ladies withdrew to the house's many powder rooms. Willard Blunt and Emily Damon went up the grand staircase followed by the stares of the guests remaining in the ballroom. In not too long a time, the paste emeralds would make their appearance and the drama of the evening would approach its climax. My stomach was growling a bit, so I walked around and looked for college party crashers but found none. Manly laughter mixed with cigar smoke filtered out of the library. Royal or boardroom humor, no doubt. I couldn't find Amelia.

I expected the pastes to show up in about half an hour, a time span adequate, I thought, for the ladies to return from the powder rooms and for the gentlemen to finish their cigars.

I wondered why Zee had to be in Boston the whole weekend.

About fifteen minutes had elapsed when I happened to pass an alcove off a hallway and heard an angry voice that surely was Helga Johanson's. A man's voice, touched by British accents, responded. I looked in.

There was a Venetian etching by Whistler on the wall. In front of it the Padishah of Sarofim stood eye to eye with Helga Johanson, one of her wrists caught in his hand, his other arm hooked around her waist. He seemed to be of amorous inclination. As I appeared, he started, then glared at me.

"Out!" he said, with an angry nod toward the door. "We wish to be alone!"

His tone was that of a man used to having such wishes instantly obeyed. I stepped closer, and Helga Johanson turned her head and saw me. She turned back and said in a low voice, "Let me go."

He did not. Instead, his hand tightened on her wrist, and I saw her wince. He was not a small man.

"Get out!" he said to me, with another sharp nod of his head toward the hall.

Instead, I walked in. His eyes darkened with fury and surprise. I put a hand on his shoulder and shoved. He released Helga Johanson and staggered back, then, spitting out some word I did not understand, regained his balance and swung a bejeweled fist at my face. I caught it on my arm and put a short right into his body, just below the rows of medals that adorned his chest. The air drove out of his lungs, and he doubled over. I looked at Helga Johanson.

"Are you all right?"

"Yes. Look out!"

I looked back at the Padishah and saw him groping at the holster on his belt. He was having trouble catching his breath. I grabbed his wrist, twisted the pistol from his hand, and pushed him back against the wall.

"You'll thank me for this someday," I said to him, "because now you still have both of your testicles in working order. American women have knees as hard as their fists, and you remember how hard one of those can be. And just in case you're wearing your cast-iron jock strap, Ms. Johanson knows some other ways to make you walk funny for the rest of your life."

He glared, gasping for air. I dropped the magazine from his pistol into my pocket, added the bullet in the firing chamber, and dropped the pistol on the floor.

"I'll give your ammunition to Thornberry Security when I leave tonight. Meanwhile, I think we should all just forget this ever happened. After you, Ms. Johanson."

Helga Johanson gave him a shriveling look, rubbed her wrist, and brushed out past me.

"This is twice you and your women have laid hands on my person," he hissed.

"Let us hope there is not a third time, Your Majesty." I bowed and followed Helga.

I caught up with her in the ballroom. She said some unladylike words, then gave a thin smile. "I hope he believes I'm as tough as you said I am, because I am, even though I can hardly walk in this damned skirt, let alone defend myself." She took my arm, then, rather self-consciously, I thought, released it. "You got there just in time to save him, though I don't know what you did for friendly American-Sarofimian relations. I suspect he now regrets having sent his bodyguard away so he could be alone with me. Let's have a drink. Isn't this an interesting evening?"

At the bar we both had sodas with twists. I gave her the Padishah's ammo, and she put it into her little evening purse. I was glad that Colonel Ahmed Nagy had been sent away by his master. I was not sure that Helga could have handled him. For that matter, I was not sure that I could have handled him. Colonel Nagy did not have a merciful face.

"How did that slimeball corner you, anyway?"

"I was in there looking at the etching on the wall. He followed me in. I believe he has overindulged in spirits, as they say. Besides, he's used to being a Padishah. I'm personally inclined at the moment to throw my weight behind the revolution."

"Dangerous talk, woman. We're supposed to be busy here cementing international relations. The Padishah thinks of you as one of my women. What do you think of that?"

"He also thinks I should be one of his. He lives in a fantasy world. I advise you not to do the same." She glanced at the watch on her wrist. "Almost time for the pastes to make their appearance."

Most of the guests apparently agreed. They had crowded into the ballroom and were glancing openly up the stairway. The Padishah himself, accompanied by Colonel Nagy, had also appeared, looking regal and only slightly ruffled. He was careful not to look at Helga Johanson and me. Colonel Nagy, on the other hand, looked at us carefully, his eyes hooded, his face passionless. I stared back at him. Some sort of electricity tingled between us. I felt as though I had touched a hot wire.

A ripple of applause drew my eyes to the staircase. There, Emily Damon, arm in arm with the gaunt, dignified form of Willard Blunt, descended, a necklace of gold filigree and green stones glittering at her throat.

The ripple became louder, and Emily Damon smiled and waved a graceful hand. A few steps from the bottom of the stairs she paused and lifted both hands. The applause and voices in the room silenced.

"I want you to know that this is not the real thing!" She touched the necklace and smiled, and there was laughter. She gestured again, and silence returned. "This wonderful paste necklace will be placed in the collection of the Smithsonian Institution as a memento of the century and a half when the Sarofim emeralds were in the keeping of an American family, *my* family, and as a remembrance of the return of the emeralds tonight to their rightful owner!" Applause. Smiles from Damons and the Padishah. Silence once more. "And now, if you will help me, Willard, I will give this necklace to my beloved sister, Amelia, who will accept it on behalf of the Smithsonian Institution."

Blunt bent his tall frame and unfastened the necklace, and I saw Amelia come forward, smiling but pale. Emily Damon fastened the necklace about Amelia's neck, and the applause rose again. I left Helga Johanson and shouldered my way through the crowd. I heard Emily Damon's voice say, "There you are, my dear. And now, ladies and gentlemen, and you, Your Royal Highness, if you will be patient with me, I will return in a few minutes."

I was wondering if Amelia had heard something about Zee. Was that why she was so pale? I got close to her and found her surrounded by women admiring the necklace. She saw me and gestured, and I found her arm. She smiled at the ladies and allowed them to touch the famous pastes, but then put a hand to her stomach.

"You will forgive me, friends, if I allow myself to be conducted to the library by this young man. I'm not feeling well and I must lock away these glass jewels so that they're not humiliated by the real thing." Expressions of sympathy emanated from the women and men nearest to her. Smiling and nodding, her arm in mine, she moved toward the library. A sort of path opened before us as the crowd turned its attentions back to the stairway. Helga Johanson, wearing a concerned frown, joined us as we left the room.

"Are you all right, Mrs. Muleto."

"There's a loo just this side of the library, I believe. I've got to make a quick stop."

"I'll go in with you, Mrs. Muleto," said Helga.

"Thank you, my dear. Don't worry, J. W., I've just got a bit of a bellyache. Too much champagne, probably. We'll be right out."

They passed into the room, and I leaned against the wall and thought that men and women surely had different attitudes toward going to the toilet. For women it's a social event. They go together, chatting and making an occasion of it. At a party or a restaurant a woman will say, "I've got to go to the ladies'. Would anyone else like to come?" And all of the other women at the table will jump up and say, "Yes, yes, we'll come too." And off they'll go together. For a man, going to the toilet is a lonely bit of work. Men do not invite other men to join them in the john. I was still weighing this curiosity of gender when Amelia and Helga came out again.

Amelia smiled. "I'm much better now. We'd better hurry this necklace into the library safe so we can be back in time to see Emily's grand entrance!"

We opened the library door and went in. The smell of cigar smoke was still heavy in the air though the room was empty. Amelia waved a hand as if to fan the odor away as we crossed to the safe. She opened the small silver purse she carried and took out a scrap of paper.

"The combination," she said. "Edward entrusted it to me for the occasion." She knelt and spun the dial on the ancient safe. I admired the statue on top of it and noted that it was not of a goddess at all, as I had earlier guessed, but of Pandora looking dreamily at a small box in her hand.

The safe door swung open. Amelia lifted her hair from her neck. "If you will, J. W."

I undid the clasp, and the necklace slid into her hands. She held it for a moment, then placed it in the safe, closed the door, and spun the knob. Then she rose, found matches by an ashtray, and lit the scrap of paper containing the combination. The paper flamed in the tray and became ash. Amelia smiled and we went out. "Just in time to catch Emily descending," she said.

But Emily Damon did not descend the stairs wearing the fabulous necklace. Instead, Jason Thornberry appeared at the top of the stairs and hurried down. Helga Johanson, seeing him, moved swiftly away from Amelia and me and met him. They talked and threw glances around the room. My eye caught hers and she gestured. I touched Amelia's arm and crossed the room. Helga's voice was low and urgent.

"There's been a robbery! The emerald necklace is missing! It was there when Mr. Blunt took the pastes out of the safe, but it's gone now!"

Thornberry's face was expressionless. "I don't want anyone to leave, and that goes particularly for any of these reporters. You take the front door and make sure no one goes by you. Stay there until you're relieved!" He dipped his head and spoke into his lapel mike, giving orders to someone not at hand. Marks, the Outside Man? Then he and Helga moved away and I moved to the door and tried to look impressive.

The crowd whispered and looked confused. Across the room the Padishah was receiving a message from his secretary. *The* message, I took it from the look of consternation on the royal face.

"What's going on?" asked the grandfatherly ex-television anchorman. He still had a nose for the news.

I told him what I'd heard. He grunted, and his eyes lit up. "Better than the average party." He grinned and walked away. At the top of the stairs a man wearing clothes at least as nice as my own appeared and stood with crossed arms. The troops were being positioned.

Three reporters made gallant efforts to pass me, but were denied and rushed off elsewhere looking for unguarded phones or exits. I didn't have to shoot a single one of them.

• 9 •

There was a large crowd at the Damon place that night: a hundred guests, two dozen servants and as many security people, the reporters and camera people, a band, which had arrived just in time to be impounded, and, of course, Damons and Sarofimians. Fortunately, it was a very large house which could hold everyone and had no more exits than there were security personnel to guard them.

The upshot was that everyone was steered inside, where Edward C. Damon himself, too shaken to be truly ambassadorial, gave the news to them all (except, it turned out, two young couples who were discovered, in the subsequent search of the house, more or less au naturel, in dark corners of upstairs maids' rooms). The guests were shocked and thrilled at their host's revelation and were much abuzz as they rapidly tried to calculate which of them had been upstairs and therefore more or less near the emeralds sometime during the evening. Some of the ladies had, for several of the powder rooms were upstairs, and many thought themselves more a part of the drama because of that.

"Who'd have thought my bladder would be responsible for my practically being right there when the emeralds were stolen!" exclaimed a distinguished-looking dowager to her friend, paying me and my nearby ears no attention whatsoever.

"It's very exciting!" agreed her friend. "Do you suppose they'll *search* us? Gracious!"

I imagined searching her and decided I'd let someone else do it. On the other hand, I would be glad to volunteer to search Helga Johanson.

Jason Thornberry then was introduced, and both his appearance and profession provoked further small cries of interest. Chief of Security! Imagine! What a handsome man!

Thornberry explained himself and informed the crowd that indeed the emerald necklace was missing from its rosewood box in the safe in the master bedroom. His aura of authority combined with his distinguished appearance and calm speech was in sharp contrast to Damon's nervousness.

"Now *he* should be an ambassador," whispered one gentleman to his wife, and she eagerly agreed.

Thornberry explained that a thorough search of the house had already begun and that everyone, particularly those who had been in the upper rooms, would be asked to give statements to him privately in the library.

Everyone? *Moi?* Hands touched chests. Questioning looks were exchanged. Thornberry smiled comfortingly. Most would, of course, have nothing to contribute, but someone, perhaps, may have seen something of importance that could be of help. Often, witnesses were not even aware that they may have observed something, but a trained inquisitor could, by asking the right questions, sometimes produce valuable information that would otherwise be lost. Best to ask those questions immediately while memories were still fresh.

It was logical. It was also romantic. A robbery! And not an ordinary one, but theft of the Stonehouse emeralds! Thornberry strolled into the library, and a line of eager guests formed at the door.

A bit later, sirens were heard, adding to the drama, and almost as soon as they stopped, the door behind me opened and in came the Chief and a corporal of the state police. The Chief gave me an I-thought-I-told-you-not-to-let-this-happen look, and the two of them followed my pointing arm into the library.

An hour later, as the line crept forward, much of the good humor was gone. Some people's feet hurt, some were feeling the drinks they had had earlier. Helga Johanson, noting this, collected the band members and disappeared into the ballroom. Moments later the sound of music followed her back out into the hall. Tired eyes looked at her, and she stepped forward and took the grandfatherly retired newscaster by the arm.

"Come along, everyone," she said. "If we must wait, we can dance while we do it!"

And like the Pied Piper, she led them into the ballroom. Happy sounds replaced the unhappy ones. More champagne appeared at the bar.

I stood at the front door without even another soda and twist. No one tried to escape. From time to time someone came out of the library and someone else left the ballroom and went in. The corporal of the state police went upstairs. Smart Thornberry had put guards around the veranda and allowed the dancers to go out for air. Below them the water glimmered with lights reflected from the far shore and from the boats, now moored for the night. I reckoned that from the water and the houses across the bay it must have seemed that the Damons were having quite a party.

People appeared at the top of the stairs. The corporal, Willard Blunt, other men in tuxedos, women in party dresses. The search committee, their faces indicating that they had found nothing. Actually, they had found the two young couples but had decided to leave them where they were after searching both their rooms and their clothes, which latter were mostly not being worn by their owners. The searchers were not in the morality business at the moment.

I thought about the upstairs layout of the house and remembered that from the window of the master bedroom you could see the upper reaches of Katama Pond and the narrows leading into Edgartown Harbor.

I wondered if anyone had told Thornberry that in the old days people used to swim their cattle across those narrows so they could pasture on Chappy for the summer. I guessed not.

I had been most impressed by the unexpected decorations on one of the bedroom's walls: a display of the souvenirs of some Damon fond of collecting primitive weapons in far off places. The wall was hung with dusty assagais, dark bows and long reedy arrows, wooden shields, crude machetes, blowguns and darts, slingshots, shark's-teeth swords, and similar hunting and fighting weapons. An exotic decor for a master bedroom. Maybe the Damons were more interesting people than I had thought.

A Thornberry guard had stood outside the locked bedroom door, and two others had been on the balcony outside of the locked windows, one to watch the rooftops and one to watch the balcony door. (Each to watch the other?) Yet another guard had stood at the end of the hall that led to the bedroom. Inside the room, inside the locked safe, inside their rosewood boxes, had lain the necklaces.

I imagined Emily Damon and Willard Blunt passing the guard at the end of the hall, passing the guard outside the door, entering the room. I imagined Willard Sergeant Blunt opening the box holding the pastes, and Emily Damon donning the necklace. (Where? Before a mirror? Bending her neck to allow Willard Blunt to fasten the catch? Did it make any difference?) I imagined the two of them locking the safe, then leaving the room, Willard locking the door, the two of them walking to the top of the stairs and descending. And then I didn't have to imagine what happened, because I'd seen it.

But later Emily Damon had repeated her trip upstairs, this time in the company of both Willard Blunt and her husband. What had happened then? Presumably Blunt had opened the safe and then the box supposedly containing the genuine emeralds and had found the necklace missing. Either he hadn't opened that box when he and Emily had gone for the paste, or the real necklace had still been there at that time. Otherwise the alarm would have been sounded earlier.

Unless, of course, he had stolen the emeralds himself. I looked at his craggy Yankee face as he came down the stairs. He looked unhealthy and was leaning on the polished railing as he descended. I had read of doctors who could diagnose diseases from the mere appearance of a patient, but I was no doctor, alas. As if suddenly aware that he was revealing some weakness or distress that was inappropriate, he straightened and released the railing and seemed to grow taller, stronger. The evening clothes, which moments before had hung on him as on a scarecrow, now were revealed to be custom fitted and subtly splendid. He wore them with casual old New England grace that would have bordered upon grandeur had he not insisted upon being gray and respectable instead.

I had a hard time seeing him as a thief, but who else was there? I had never been good at locked-room mysteries. Could, perhaps, a trained ape have stolen the necklace? What would Poe have imagined?

It was one in the morning before the last person in the house had been interviewed. Thornberry came forth from the library with a weary Edward C. Damon, the Chief, the state policeman, and a petulant looking Padishah of Sarofim, who did not bother to put on a happy face for his public. Damon mounted the bandstand and announced that the inquiries had ended and everyone could go home, but that the police might wish further interviews later.

I left the door and went into the library. Helga Johanson was there, leaning over a plan of the house.

"What did Blunt have to say?"

She was tired and not in a generous mood. "I don't think you need to concern yourself with this matter anymore. Your job is over when the last guest leaves this house."

"I'm a police officer," I said. "Are you withholding information from a police officer?" That seemed an unlikely ploy, but instead of laughing she shrugged.

"He said the jewels and the pastes were in their cases when he left Boston and that they were still there when he examined the cases and locked them in the safe in the master bedroom. Dr. Youssef concurs. He testified that he and Blunt examined the gems together, in their cases. Blunt put the pastes into the safe while Youssef verified the authenticity of the emeralds. Then Youssef himself put the emeralds in the safe and locked it. Blunt says that the only people who entered the room after he and Dr. Youssef left were himself and the Damons. And none of them were in there until this evening, when they went in to get the necklaces. The guards agree."

I ran times through my mind.

"When did Blunt bring the jewels to the house?"

"Early Friday afternoon. One-thirty or so. He came in by corporate jet to the airport and from there by one of the Damon cars. The cases were in a briefcase cuffed to his wrist. A guard was with him."

I really didn't know what I was trying to find out. "And afterwards the bedroom door and windows were locked? Could the guards have gotten inside?"

"The windows have inner bolts. Blunt kept them locked."

"The door?"

"Locked.' Her mouth curved into a brief ironic smile. "No secret passages, I'm afraid. No trap doors. No hidden stairs."

"So no one got inside?"

"Someone did."

"You mean a fourth someone, someone besides the Damons and Willard Blunt? Why look for a fourth suspect when you have three good ones to start with?"

She gave me a cold look, then focused her eyes beyond me. I turned as eight men came into the library: the Padishah, Colonel Ahmed Nagy, the Chief, the state police corporal, Damon, Thornberry, and two men who looked federal to me.

"You can go, Jackson," said Thornberry. "The evening has ended. Your check will be in the mail tomorrow. Thank you."

I looked at the Chief, who nodded and gestured toward the door. I felt two pairs of Sarofimian eyes on my back as I went out.

I didn't sleep well. I dreamed that Zee had some guy on the hook that I didn't know about. I woke up and thought about the Padishah of Sarofim, whose father kidnapped women and kept them in his harem and gave the uncooperative ones to his secret police. Later I had more bad dreams.

Early the next morning, while I waited, fuzzy headed, for other people to get up and get going, I went fishing. The sea's rhythms are indifferent to our fretting and can bring us back from inner chaos. I fished until early mass was over. Manny Fonseca always went to early mass so afterwards he could be the first one at the Rod and Gun Club shooting range. He was already popping caps when I drove through the club gate, which he had left open. I walked down the track to the range, then stopped to watch him shoot. He was very quick and sure. I wondered how he would do if one of the targets was shooting back. I knew I hadn't done so well when I had shot at people shooting at me.

When he had emptied all his clips and was reloading, he finally noticed me. I put the borrowed pistol and harness on the table holding his weapons and shooting paraphernalia. Manny always shot several guns on Sundays.

"Thanks, Jesse."

"Don't give me any more of that crap about working up at Fort Wampanoag, J.W. I heard you were over on Chappy last night. What went on there, anyway?"

I'd not heard of Fort Wampanoag before. Manny had been working on his vocabulary. I told him about the Damon party, and he almost threw his favorite shooting hat on the ground and stomped it. "Damn! I miss everything interesting that ever happens on this bleeping island!"

"You didn't miss much, Sundance. Not a shot was fired. Tell me, is Fort Wampanoag all of Gay Head or just the Tribal Council headquarters?"

He grinned, happy about something, at least. Having missed the big robbery, he could at least insult the Wampanoags. "The whole damn town. Injun country, I call it. A man has to be ready to pull himself into a circle every time he goes up there.

"Here." He handed me earplugs, glasses, and a pistol unlike any I had seen before. "Try this. Most of it's plastic. Gun of the future. Glock 17. Nine mm. Go right through an X-ray check if you happen to want to hijack a plane, ha, ha."

I wasn't interested in hijacking any airplanes, but I did shoot the pistol. The bullets went out fast and pretty straight. Shooting something made me feel better.

"Not bad," said Manny. Then he shot the Glock, and my shots seemed pretty wild by comparison.

I had to shoot two more pistols before I could leave without hurting Manny's feelings. I didn't mind at all. I might have stayed longer, but I wanted to see if Amelia Muleto had heard anything more from Zee. I was irked because it was possible that Zee might even have phoned me and that I'd have been home for the call if I hadn't gone fishing. But I *had* gone fishing, so now I wanted to see Amelia.

▪ 10 ▪

Amelia was on her knees by the flower bed. She got up and came toward me, pulling off cotton gloves. "J.W., I've been trying to phone you, but nobody's been home. Have you heard from Zee?"

A little cold spot formed somewhere inside of me. "No. I was hoping you had."

"Come inside. I'll fix us some tea. I don't know, it's just not like Zee not to phone and tell us, you know, when to expect her, at least."

Amelia looked distressed. "She'll probably call later," I said. "Maybe she was up all night and is getting some sleep."

Amelia was heating water in the kitchen. "That's probably it. It's too bad she had to miss the party. She was looking forward to it. Her dress looked lovely when she was here Friday."

She brought in the tea. "It seems so long ago . . . So much has happened since. We spent the afternoon together, and the three of us ate down at Martha's. Willard was quite taken with Zee and she with him, I think. We had a fine time together. Afterwards, he insisted on driving her home."

"Lucky man."

Amelia smiled and patted my knee. "You should definitely be jealous. Zee is worth it. She took her dress with her so she could do a bit of last-minute stitching we hadn't managed during the afternoon. I remember she said she had to get some sleep because she had a lot of work to do on Saturday, prepping for the party. We laughed about that. Little did we know how much work she'd end up doing!"

"That's for sure. Who called you about her going off-island?"

"The hospital. About noon."

"What'd they say?"

'Oh, that there'd been an emergency and that Zee was flying to Boston with a patient and wanted me to know what she was doing and why she wouldn't be here for the party."

"What was the emergency?"

"I didn't ask. I'm sure you can phone the hospital and find out. What with all the goings-on at the party, maybe she won't be sorry she missed it."

High times on Chappy. "And she'll be back Monday?"

"As I understand it. I'm surprised she hasn't called . . ."

"Must be some kind of a private case to keep her away that long. I know she had the weekend off . . ."

"Zee has a kind heart. I imagine it was important and they were shorthanded and called her, and she, being Zee, couldn't say no. More tea?"

I thought she might be right about her scenario. "No. I have a date with my garden. I'll call you if I hear from Zee."

"And I will do the same for you." She smiled. She seemed a bit more content than she had when I'd arrived.

I couldn't say the same for myself. I looked inside to find out why and after a while dug out the answer: I was mad at Zee for not calling. I was like a parent waiting in growing vexation and worry for an overdue teenager to come home at night. But I was not Zee's father and Zee was a grown-up woman who didn't owe me any explanations about anything, and my anger seemed so childish that I decided it would be better directed at myself, where it more properly belonged. So I worked on that as I drove home.

During the afternoon I picked and canned tomatoes. I burned a hand because I wasn't paying attention to what I was doing. When I was through, I had enough tomatoes to last all winter, but more were still growing on the vines. It was almost as bad as trying to keep up with the zucchinis, an impossible job. I had about a million zucchini recipes and someday was going to write the definitive zucchini cookbook for all of those people whose zucchinis are about to overwhelm them and conquer the world. The working title for the book was *The Attack of the Zucchini Monsters.* So far I hadn't written one word. I didn't get started that afternoon, either.

That evening two interesting things happened. The first was an anonymous phone call. The calling voice was muffled and male.

"Mr. J.W. Jackson?"

"Yes."

"I've been trying to phone you all day. You don't know me, but I hope you will listen carefully and take what I say seriously. There are some people on the island who are making plans to harm you. Seriously harm you. They are of foreign nationality, and the attack, should it come, will come soon. Within days. Be on your guard, Mr. Jackson. The best advice I can give to you is to leave the island for a week or so. By that time, I believe the danger will be over. Do you understand me, Mr. Jackson?"

"Yes. The only foreign nationals who might be mad at me just now are from Sarofim. Are they the ones? And who are you?"

"You have a friend, a Mrs. Madieras. I have been trying to telephone her with the same warning I've just given you, but I cannot contact her. If you know where she is, please tell her what I've told you."

"She's off-island right now."

"She is in danger, just as you are."

"She's been gone since Saturday and won't be back until tomorrow. Do you have a name?"

There was a silence at the other end of the line. Then the voice said, "It would be better if she stayed away longer. I suggest that you make that recommendation if you can contact her."

"I don't know how to contact her. Who are you?"

Another silence. Then, "Well, do advise Mrs. Madieras of

this warning when she returns. Meanwhile, Mr. Jackson, you be careful. Leave the island if you can."

The phone clicked.

The second interesting thing was a shooting on the bluffs overlooking the bathing beach just west of Wasque. The victim was Willard Blunt. The shootist was good at his work. Willard Blunt died instantly.

11

I got the news the next morning by phone from Amelia, who had gotten it from her sister.

"I almost fainted," she said. "I had to sit down."

"You never struck me as the fainting type. Are you okay?"

"I'm all right. I think that it was just that everything has piled up so. The robbery, then Zee being gone, and now this. Besides, I'm probably still tired from being up so late. I'm usually asleep by nine, you know, so I can be up with the sun and have a little peace before the cars start going by."

"What happened?"

"It's not completely clear. Willard was at the Damon place. Early in the evening he borrowed Edward Damon's Jeep and he and Colonel Nagy drove to town. A meeting with the FBI man in Edgartown, apparently. Then he came to visit me. I never guessed it was the last time I'd see him. I . . . Willard had originally planned on flying to Boston with the Padishah's party yesterday afternoon, but those plans changed because of the theft. The Padishah's party flew up there by helicopter this morning, instead.

"When Willard didn't return to the house last night, the Damons got worried. He was elderly, after all, and had been under considerable strain. They called the police. Then this morning when it got light the Trustees of Reservations people found the Jeep in the parking lot there on reservation land. They found Willard in the driver's seat."

"Shot?"

"Once in the temple. The gun was in his hand."

"Suicide?"

"I guess his wallet was there and nothing was missing, so suicide seems the best bet."

"Any note?"

"No."

"Where'd he get the pistol?"

"I don't know."

"How are you doing?"

"I'm all right. No, I'm not; but I will be."

"Do you want me to come over?"

"That would be nice."

"Have you heard from Zee?"

"No."

"I'll be right over."

So I drove over, picking up the Boston Monday papers en route.

We met at her door, and I put down the papers and held her in my arms. Strong Amelia looked almost frail. We sat in the living room, and she talked about what a wonderful man Willard Blunt had been, while I listened. After a while she suddenly took a deep breath and got up.

"All this time and I haven't even offered you tea. Now where are my manners?"

While she was in the kitchen, I wandered her living room, feeling nervous, picking up this, looking at that. Her mail was lying on an end table, waiting to be taken to the post office. A package lay with three letters. One of the letters was to her son out in western Massachusetts. The package was being sent to Professor Hamdi Safwat at Weststock College. I remembered the name.

Amelia came in as I was looking down at the package. She set the tea tray on the coffee table. "Hamdi Safwat. You saw his book the other day before all this dreadfulness took place. I met him after the war when he was an undergraduate studying in Boston. Wonderful man. About to retire now. We've kept in touch. He's very knowledgeable about the riddles of the Near East. Perhaps you'll be kind enough to mail the package and those letters for me. It's on your way and it will save me a trip to the post office." She sat down a bit heavily. "I'd appreciate it. I really don't want to go into town today."

"Of course."

"Have you heard from Zee?"

"No."

"It's surprising that she hasn't called . . ."

"She'll be home today and tell you all about it."

"Yes. She's very sensible. Dear me, what a weekend."

I offered her the only distraction at hand: "Let's see what the papers have to say." I gave her the *Globe* and took the *Herald.*

For some reason the *Herald* gets more late-breaking news into its morning editions than does the *Globe,* which otherwise I'm prone to favor. This morning not even the *Herald* had much to say because no one really knew anything. The paper compensated in *Herald* style by having a blazing front-page headline over file photos of the Stonehouse emeralds and various celebrities.

We traded papers.

I realized that my mind was only half focused on the newspapers when I found myself rereading what I'd just read. At that moment, Amelia put her paper down and got up.

"I'm going to phone the hospital and find out when Zee is expected back."

She went into the den and I heard her voice. I couldn't catch the words, but after a minute the tone changed. Some quality in it brought me to my feet. A moment later she came back into the living room. Her face was gray. I stepped quickly forward and took her arm.

"What is it?"

She gave me a haunted look. "The hospital doesn't know anything about her. There was no emergency on Saturday. No patient was flown off-island. No one at the hospital telephoned me. What's happened to Zee?"

A coldness clamped on my heart. I sat Amelia down on the sofa and went to the phone. The voice at the Martha's Vineyard hospital repeated the message it had given her. I rang off and phoned the police. Whoever was at the desk was no doubt caught up by the death of Willard Blunt, compared to which a woman unaccounted for for a couple of days was not of primary concern. He told me what I already knew: that missing people usually showed up and that it was too early for me to be really worried, but that they'd get on it right away. Had anyone checked her home?

I hadn't and felt like an idiot. I gave him her number, then hung up and dialed it myself. It rang and rang. I hung up.

I needed something to do with my hands. Choke the policeman on the desk, perhaps? I picked up Amelia's mail.

"The police are on the case. I'm going to drive up to her place. Will you be okay? I'll stay longer if . . ."

She shook her head. "No. You go. I'll be fine. Call me from her house."

"Yes." I saw Zee lying on the floor of her own house. Dead? Hurt? Lying there for three days while I hadn't even had the sense to go up to her place and see if she was okay?

I drove away, thinking of the times I'd taken Zee home and dropped her off at the little house she rented amid the green foliage on the line between Chilmark and West Tisbury, the Vineyard's prettiest townships. I had often invited Zee to live in Edgartown with me, but she had declined just as she had declined my several suggestions that we marry. On the other hand she had never told me not to darken her doorway again, so she lived up island and I lived down island and we visited a lot. For me, it had been better than it might be, enough for me to keep my hopes up. Now my hopes were not so high.

I found myself in West Tisbury and didn't remember how I got there. I went to Zee's house and saw her little Jeep in the yard. I found the spare key hidden under the flowerpot and went inside. Zee was not there. I felt a rush of relief followed by another of despair. I went through the house very carefully and found nothing unusual. The box containing Zee's party dress was lying on the living room sofa as though it had been casually placed there. I phoned Amelia and the police and told them what I'd found.

I drove home past the fairgrounds, past the field of dancing statues, and, suddenly remembering Amelia's mail, as people often think of trifles in the midst of crisis, stopped at the general store, where I posted it. Then I drove past the millpond with its geese and swans and on toward Edgartown, thinking. A few miles down the road there was a new pond on the right surrounded by open space lately cleared from the woodlands. Some developer's latest brainchild, I guessed. I wondered if he would point out to prospective clients that his handsome properties lay directly under the flight approach path to the county airport. I reckoned not. The caveat emptor principal at work once again, even on the beautiful island of Martha's Vineyard. All Edens have serpents.

I thought of Willard Blunt. He had been an actor in two puzzles: the theft and Zee's disappearance. I was ignorant and needed information. I also needed distracton.

The Edgartown library is open on Monday afternoons, so I drove there. Libraries are favorite places of mine. Not only are they mines of information, they have librarians who will help you dig if you ask them to. I found encyclopedias and an atlas. The atlas showed me where Sarofim was located: east of Oman, west of Ahmadabad, nestled on the coast of the Arabian Sea, blessed by one fine, easily guarded harbor. Swamps were between Sarofim and Pakistan, and there were desert wastes along its border with Iran. The encyclopedias gave me rudimentary information about the country. Obviously, in the minds of the editors, Sarofim did not merit extended commentary even though it meant a lot to Edward C. Damon and, apparently, the United States government.

I eventually found out why the last two thought so much of it: not only was Sarofim rich in oil, but its harbor was deep enough for navy ships and a portion of its flat desert lands could easily be transformed into landing fields for military aircraft; moreover, its government, made nervous by Islamic militancy in neighboring countries, was lately interested in establishing mutually beneficial relationships with Western nations, to wit, defense and economic alliances between Sarofim and the United States. The United States would get a deep-water port for its naval vessels, air bases for its planes, and access to Sarofimian oil, and Sarofim would get American dollars, weapons and military protection, and political support for its ruler, Ali Mohammed Rashad, the Padishah himself.

However, the treaties and associated agreements leading toward these ends had yet to be negotiated, thus the importance attached to good relations between the countries. No wonder the disappearance of the emerald necklace was such a bummer to Edward C. Damon and the Padishah.

I went to the card catalog and sought in vain for more information about Sarofim. I then went to the fountain of information itself: the front desk. Librarians know almost everything and they know how to get any information they don't already have. The woman I spoke to was no exception. She listened to my problem, frowned slightly, then smiled.

"The *National Geographic,*" she said. She put a finger to her lips, and her forehead wrinkled slightly. "Now when did that piece about Sarofim come out? Was it last year sometime? Just one moment."

She got up and walked off. Not much later, she returned, a copy of the *National Geographic* in her hand.

"Here you are. We only have room to keep the latest copies of our magazines out here, so we have to store earlier issues elsewhere. When you're through with this, I'd like to read it myself. Mr. Damon, over on Chappaquiddick, is going to be ambassador there, you know, and I really should know something about the place."

I took the magazine and went back to my chair.

The *National Geographic* has been a favorite magazine of mine since I was very little. Its photographs are properly world famous, and its writers travel to the farthest corners of the earth. It was, until the publication of *Playboy,* the magazine that showed young boys their first photos of naked breasts, usually those of dark-skinned jungle women in tropical places.

While the photos in the *National Geographic* are always interesting, the writing is often very restrained, especially when its subject is a totalitarian state. The magazine carefully avoids direct condemnation of even the most wretched of current leaders, contenting itself with hints at the political or cultural conflicts within their realms. The writers are much better at writing about the distant histories of the places they visit. The photo story of Sarofim was a typical *Geographic* effort, with fine photos, a well-written short history of the nation, and an examination of its current state, including a few careful hints of current political conflict within its borders.

The story was entitled, "Sarofim: Modern Times in an Ancient Land." I thought it very *Geographic*ish.

The photos showed a desert country with treeless mountains; a bright blue harbor holding both rusty ships and modern yachts; Gwatar, the capital city, a minor metropolis of general shabbiness but occasional walled houses evidencing great wealth; the ancient fortress with its cannon pointing toward the sea; a market street, new construction, oil wells, shepherds, women with golden rings in their noses and ears, children with laughing mouths, the Padishah, businessmen, students, and camel drivers. Closer examination showed sores and sewers, poverty and eyes without laughter.

The history of the nation, illustrated with photos of books and paintings, was one of trade and war between religions, with Islam in a mutant form eventually establishing itself as the dominant faith and a dynasty originating in Afghanistan positioning itself in the late Middle Ages as a trading and raiding power on the sea route between India and the Persian Gulf.

This dynasty was finally overthrown in the late eighteenth century by the revolution led by Mohammed Rashad with the aid of ex-British army officer Jacob Stonehouse, who made off with a good portion of the royal treasury as the war ended and the Rashad dynasty began.

I was pleased to find a photo of a drawing of Jacob Stonehouse done by some Sarofimian artist, apparently just before Jacob escaped with the family silver. Stonehouse was portrayed as a tall, lean fellow with fair hair and blue eyes. He was wearing one of those brilliant uniforms favored by military officers of that day. It was buttoned to the chin and

must have been uncomfortable on the deserts of Sarofim, bu
Stonehouse showed no sign of sweat. His clever eyes looke
out at me over a long nose and slightly smiling thin lips.

Beside his picture was a color photo of his most famou
theft: the Stonehouse Emerald Necklace. It looked wel
worth stealing, I thought. For that matter, to me, the paste
had looked worth stealing.

The Rashads took up their predecessors' practices of trade and piracy and putting down occasional revolutions. Nothing much changed in Sarofim until World War I, when the country's harbor caught the eye of the great powers and the then-Padishah was obliged to curb his corsairs and establish alliances, none of which he kept longer than necessary, with those powers. Encounters with the great powers also brought closer contact with Western cultures, including French and Italian food and American movies, all of which fascinated the royal family and led it to send some of its sons to Western universities to learn more of such modern creations. Then, shortly before World War II, the great change came: oil was discovered on the wasteland of desert that made up the greater part of Sarofim's territory, and the Rashads no longer were obliged to plow the sea in search of a livelihood. They were instantly made rich by international industrial coin.

But with wealth came troubles, for oil was the lifeblood of industrial nations, and Sarofim was once again the focus of the attention of competing powers both in the East and the West. World War II erupted before the Padishah was obliged to choose yet another alliance, but that same war brought new concerns since Sarofim was a convenient stopover point for Western forces moving to the East to confront the empire of Japan. Western ships paused in Gwatar's harbor, and a crude military airfield was imposed upon its desert just outside of the city. The Padishah, unsure for a time about who was going to win the war, officially maintained a neutrality and invited all parties to use his facilities: in practice, though, they were used only by the British and Americans. One of the latter, I recalled, was the late Willard Sergeant Blunt.

At this point the writer became coy. Postwar Sarofim, its rulers made richer than ever by the spoils of that war, was an uneasy place. The wealth from the oil fields had not filtered down to the people whose sheep and camels grazed among the wells, who walked barefoot beside the highways the Padishah had built for the limousines of his family and aristocratic friends, and who still bought fly-covered food in open markets while the great families flew their cuisine in from Paris and Rome. Sons of the great families were educated in Britain, daughters in Switzerland; but the common folk remained largely illiterate.

Political activity of a revolutionary nature was hinted at but not overtly detailed. There were photos of the national university, of intellectuals discussing economics, and of young folk studying in Western universities, but these were balanced by cautionary comments about the conservative thought of the nation's leaders and photos of the national police in full military garb.

When I finished reading the article, I thought about things for a while. The Padishah, as the Chief had suggested, was not universally popular among his own people. But then neither was I among mine. On the other hand, I had never been accused of butchering people. I looked again at the photo of the Padishah. There, just off his left shoulder was, sure enough, the face of his bodyguard. Colonel Ahmed Nagy was with him both at home and abroad, it seemed. The Colonel's face was as I remembered it: watchful but otherwise expressionless. A ruthless, dispassionate-looking man. Just the sort you'd want as your bodyguard if you needed one.

I looked again at the fine photographs, pausing at one of the Padishah's harem taken inside the royal palace. It was a genuine harem, complete with concubines and wives, all smiling at the camera. How did he keep so many women content when I couldn't even manage one at a time? Did he have eunuchs with scimitars guarding the doors? According to the caption on the photograph, two of the wives were Americans. That probably shouldn't have surprised me, since from time to time a story is printed of some American man having many apparently happy wives living together under a single roof. Still, I am always a bit perplexed by such reports since the American women I know don't seem to be inclined to share their men.

I gave the magazine to the librarian as I went out. She smiled. "Well, J.W., how does it feel to be Edgartown's greatest authority on Sarofim?"

"The ancient sages were right," I said. "Wisdom is swell."

"Spoken like a true savant."

I went to the police station and went inside. The Chief was there. He took me into his office and told me that the island police agencies had all been alerted and that he'd talked to Amelia. Then he looked at me.

"Did she have any other boyfriends?"

It was a logical question. Crimes against women are often the work of actual or would-be lovers. When a woman is beaten up or killed or missing, the first suspects are the men in her life. I wondered if some man I didn't know had done something to Zee and had then faked that phone call from the hospital so no one would start nosing around for a few days. I felt the chill of fear and rage.

"I don't know," I said. "I don't ask her about what she does when she's not with me."

"She's a beautiful woman. She must have attracted a lot of eyes."

"Yes." I hated that thought, but knew it was true. I felt sick with fury and frustration.

The Chief chewed on his pipe. "Go home. The wheels are turning. She'll show up."

I had an extra martini or two that evening, and neither of them had much effect. The supper I made tasted like sawdust in my mouth. Afterwards I tried Cognac, but that too was flat.

Zee had been missing for three days. I thought of my anonymous phone call, of what I'd been told about the Padishah and women, and of what I'd seen of him and Nagy, and my eyes drifted toward the gun case across the room where I locked up my long guns and the .38 I'd carried in Boston.

I tried to read, but found myself looking at the same paragraph over and over. I found a radio station playing country and western music and listened to the twang of guitars and the voices singing of guilt and, sometimes, redemption. Somewherc along the line I went to sleep.

At three o'clock in the morning the phone rang.

▪ 12 ▪

Jeff. It's me."

Zee! My heart soared. "Where are you? Are you all right?"

"I'm home. Can you come up right away?"

"Yes. Are you all right? Is anybody there with you?"

"I . . . Yes, I guess so . . . No nobody's here . . ."

"Stay there! I'm on my way!"

I drove through the night. The dark trees whipped by. Left on Barnes Road, right past the airport. The old Toyota rattled through West Tisbury toward Chilmark, found Zee's driveway, and roared in.

The front door of her house opened as I braked to a stop, and there she was. I took her in my arms and wept. Then I was furious, then not furious. I held her and held her and then slowly let her go and looked down at her face. She had a crooked little smile and was very pale. I pulled her inside and shut the door.

I held her at arm's length. She brushed aside a strand of hair and let me examine her. She looked fragile. She was wearing the clothes she'd been wearing when I'd left her at Amelia's on Friday. They were dirty and wrinkled.

Where in the hell have you been? I raged inside. "Where have you been?" I asked.

"I don't know." She touched her forehead. "I've got to wash my hair. I'm a mess . . ."

"Yes. Let's get you out of those clothes."

I took her into her bedroom and got the shower going while she undressed. Then I put her in the shower.

After a minute, I stripped and got in with her. She stood under the stream of warm water and let it wash over her. I found soap and a sponge and washed and rinsed her down fore and aft, high and low, then I found shampoo and washed and rinsed her wonderful long thick black hair until it squeaked. Then she watched me wash myself off and did my back and then kissed me and put her arms around me and her wet head on my chest. I held on to her. Sometime later, the water began to grow cold.

"Jeez," said Zee. "It stays hot in the movies." I looked down at her and she was grinning. Not her greatest grin, but a grin. "I think I'm going to live," she said. "Hey, it's getting cold. Let's get out of here!"

I found two big beach towels, and we rubbed ourselves down. Zee wrapped her hair in another towel and found a robe for herself and the spare one I keep at her place.

The sky was brightening. I was starving. I went into the kitchen and fried up bacon and eggs and made toast and coffee.

"Cholesterol City," said Zee, sitting down at the table. "Let's eat!"

We did. I felt terrific. When the meal was eaten, I pushed back the dishes and looked at beautiful Zee while I drank another cup of coffee. I put down the cup, and words began to pour out of my mouth.

"Where have you been? I want to know. I know you don't have to tell me a thing, but I insist that you do. I won't let you not tell me. I won't let you out of the house until you tell me. And it had better be good, because if it isn't I think I'll wring your neck . . ."

"Stop." She smiled. "I want to tell you. You don't need to ask." Then her smile went away and she put her hand on my wrist. "I was kidnapped. I know that sounds strange, but it's the truth. And I don't even know who did it or why. Or why they let me go again."

Kidnapped? "How? When? Did they hurt you?"

"No, I'm fine. I was never . . . I was treated as well as a kidnapped person can be treated, I suppose . . . I mean, I got dirty, but . . ." She pursed her lips and shook her head. I saw a glint of the old humor in her eyes. "You'd be surprised,

Jefferson, to know how hard it is to talk about your recent kidnapping in a way that gives your audience the slightest idea of what it's like!"

A red anger flickered somewhere inside me, and I felt a simultaneous coldness of heart toward whoever had done this to her. Cold heart, red anger; a bad combination. I thought I might later enjoy seeing where it led. I took her hands in mine. "Tell me what happened."

"All right, but there's not much I can really tell you. It happened Friday night. Willard Blunt brought me home from Aunt Amelia's. I'd only been inside for a minute when I heard a knock on my door. I thought it was him, come back for some reason, so I opened the door, and somebody yanked a sack down over my head before I could see a thing. I yelled, but I doubt if anybody could have heard me. Then I swung a couple of elbows—I think I hit somebody—and I tried to yank the sack off, but just then somebody grabbed me around the knees. I reached down to whack whoever it was, and somebody else grabbed me around the waist and pinned my arms. Then we all sort of fell over onto the ground, and in no time at all they had me taped up. Duct tape. I still had some wrapped around me when they brought me back here this morning. It's strong! They taped my hands behind me and taped them to my waist and they taped my legs and then they carried me off and put me in a car and took me someplace." She looked at me. "I don't know where we went, but when they got there they eased the sack off of my head and taped my eyes before I could see anything. They kept me there until this morning. Then they brought me here and cut some of the tape off so I could get loose and drove away. I haven't the slightest idea what it was all about or who did it!"

"Nobody hurt you?"

"No. The worst part was not being able to see or move. They kept me blindfolded and all taped up. At night they put me on a bed. And when I had to go to the bathroom, someone took me there and helped me because I didn't have any hands. I hope it was a woman, but I don't know. It was pretty awful. I lost track of time. I didn't even know what day it was when I called you this morning."

"So there were several people involved."

"Yes. There were four or five at least, I think. Enough to tie me up in a rush, anyway."

"And you think one of them might have been a woman."

"I'm not sure. But I think so. Maybe there was more than one woman. Whoever it was knew what to do for me in the bathroom. I thought it was a woman. Maybe it was a perfume or something . . ."

"What did they say to you?"

"They never said anything to me. Not one word. And they never said a word to each other, either. At least not while I could hear them. I could hear them move around the room or house or whatever. You know, doors opening and shutting and that sort of noise, but never any voices. And they played pretty loud music all of the time. Rock and roll, heavy metal, that sort of thing. Maybe they talked when the music was playing so I couldn't hear them. They kept the music turned up. I tried to talk, to ask them who they were and what they wanted, but all I ever got was a spoonful of soup or a piece of pizza. Never a word."

"What could you hear? Cars? Voices from outside? Surf? Anything?"

"Just that music. I'll tell you one thing, I never want to hear the Gits again in my life. I must have listened to that Gits tape ten dozen times."

"The Gits?"

"You know. The Gits. The band. Rock and roll with some metal overtones."

"I don't do rock and roll or metal," I said. "I'm a classical and C-and-W man. Remember? I never heard of the Gits."

"Yeah, well I don't care if I never hear of them again, either. I'm all Gitted out. I'd have died for some Eagles."

"How long did they drive after they grabbed you? Could you tell?"

"No. Quite a while. The last part was over bumps. I think

that means we went off of the main road, but I don't know where."

You can't go too far on an island only twenty miles long, but even the Vineyard has a hundred square miles or so of land area, so it provides a lot of hiding space.

"How long to bring you back here?"

"Half an hour, I guess. I don't really know. It took a long time."

The house where they kept her could be next door. They might have been driving in circles for twenty-five minutes. On the other hand, a half-hour drive could take you to any part of the island except Chappy.

"What did your nose tell you?"

"My nose?"

"You couldn't see, you couldn't hear. Could you smell anything? You mentioned perfume. Did you smell that? Or cologne, or dirty diapers? Anything?"

"Food. Pizza, when they fed it to me. Soup smells, when they made it. Some spices I didn't recognize. Let me think. I thought there was a woman there, so maybe it was perfume of some sort, but I can't think of what it was. I'm not being much help, am I?" She yawned.

I felt a surge of almost paternal love for her.

"You don't need to be of any more help. You're here and you're safe and that's all that's important. The rest of it doesn't matter now. I think you should get some sleep. Some rest will do you a lot of good. I doubt if you've slept too well for the past three days." I stood and pulled her up. "I'll phone Amelia and the police and the hospital and tell them you're okay."

"Yes, sir," she said. "Thank you, sir." She leaned against me. "Why don't you come too?"

That seemed like a grand idea. I didn't want to be apart from her. "Go on in," I said. "I'll be there as soon as I make those calls."

I called the Chief and told him her story and that we'd see him later in the day. Then I called Amelia and told her that Zee was home safe and sound and was resting and that we'd tell her the whole story later. Amelia, I thought, had enough concerns at the moment and didn't need to worry about a kidnapping too.

When I finished telephoning and went into her bedroom, I found that Zee had closed the blinds to the bright morning sun and was fast asleep. She looked like an innocent child. Her hair made a black halo around her face. I got out of the robe and slid in beside her. She smiled and tucked herself against me, her body warm and smooth against mine. I put an arm around her and felt glad and good. For a while I lay balanced between gratitude for her return and deep anger at whoever had taken her. Finally I drifted away from the world of kidnapping, suicide, and thievery and was asleep.

When I woke up, Zee was leaning over me, her naked breasts grazing my chest. Her hands moved over me. "Hey," she said as I opened my eyes. "I'm awake and so is part of you. How about the rest of you joining us?"

She no longer looked like a child, and I didn't feel the least bit paternal. I put my lips to her throat, right where she liked to be kissed. A little shudder went through her. I ran my hands over the smooth curve of her hips, then cupped a breast to my mouth. Her breathing grew deeper.

Half an hour later we lay tangled in each other's arms, sweaty and satiated. "Not bad," she said. "I believe I've almost recovered from the weekend. You're better than bluefishing, even."

"Thanks a lot," I said. "Bluefishing's been lousy lately and you know it."

"Now don't fret," she said. "A while back I read a book about how the Germans trained some of their spies in World War II. They were trained to use sex to get people to lust after their bodies and reveal state secrets in bed. You know . . ."

"No. Yes. I guess so."

"No matter. The thing is that the spies were trained by these very scientific types in the tricks of the seduction trade, and I read all about how to do it. It's got nothing to do with feelings, it's all just a matter of properly stimulating your partner's primary and secondary erotic zones. You don't have to be emotionally involved at all. The scientists taught the spies how to do it. I thought it was a very Germanic approach."

"Just a matter of properly stimulating the primary and secondary erotic zones, eh? Sounds pretty cold."

"Doesn't make any difference. It works, that's what's important. So even though right now you look like you couldn't get it up with a crane, by properly stimulating your primary and secondary erotic zones I could soon have you rearing like a stallion. If I wanted to, that is."

"I'll bet you can't do it," I said.

It was a good bet. There were no losers.

It was early afternoon. We felt lazy and safe. Out of our second shower of the day, Zee rubbed her hair with a towel. "Let's complete the cure," she said. "Let's go catch some fish."

"First, the cops," I said.

"Second, the cops," she said. "First, the fish."

"That's what I said," I said, "First, the fish, second, the cops. Why do you have to argue about everything?"

"It's just my way. You have to learn to put up with it." She kissed me.

"Well, all right . . ."

13

Just because August on Martha's Vineyard is occasionally a not-so-good fishing time, does not mean you don't go fishing. In those days you drive up and down the beaches a lot, carrying both light tackle for bonito and regular gear in case you run into a bass or a bluefish who decided not to make the trip north. The bass seem to be coming back after a few years when they were getting very thin, and some people like to catch them and let them go again just so they can be catching something, at least until the bonito show up.

It's illegal to keep any bass under three feet long, and I disapprove of going after the bigger ones, because they're the old females who lay the eggs that will someday—soon, perhaps—replenish the sea with lots of bass, which I'll then be glad to catch. I think a lot die even if you let them go, so I don't fish for bass at all unless I want one for supper, in which case I keep the one I catch whatever size it is, illegal or not. A no doubt dangerous confession for a policeman (only a special one, admittedly) to make, but there you are . . .

It was Tuesday, and Zee and I were fishing the Chappaquiddick beaches. We had cast in vain at Wasque Point, tried again at Bernie's Point, tried for bonito at the Jetties, tried under the cliffs at Cape Pogue and had tried at the Cape Pogue Gut. We had gotten not even a swirl or a nibble. The sea had yawned at us, and the fish were asleep off in some fish motel. We drove back to the Jetties and found Iowa there making casts with a Swedish Pimple, which is usually a good lure for bonito. It is local wisdom that bonito won't take a lure if it's on a leader, so all of us tie our lures onto our lines. Zee and I had our own Swedish Pimples so attached, of course, and we began fishing without high expectations, beside Iowa.

There were boats anchored or drifting about two hundred yards off the beach. Iowa looked enviously out at them.

"Look at those guys. Catching fish while we're here catching nothing. I'd like to spend just one day out there!"

Fishermen are very inclined to think the other guys are doing better than they are. Many a fisherman had abandoned a perfectly good spot for a worse one because he thought the rods over there were bending more than his was here. In this case, the guys in the boats weren't catching any more than we were. I pointed this out.

Iowa was not about to change his mind. "I'd like to spend just one day out there!"

It was a lovely, lazy day, with blue skies, a hazy horizon that hid Cape Cod, and a gentle southwest wind which was easing sailboats up and down the Sound. The worst day of fishing is, as the bumper stickers say, better than the best day of working, so even though we had seen no fish, Iowa and Zee and I were content.

"There's a helicopter," said Iowa, looking toward the Cape Pogue lighthouse as he reeled in.

I followed his gaze. There, indeed, was a helicopter. It was coming over the Sound toward Edgartown. We watched it without much interest. As it came closer, we began to hear its engine, and shortly, as it went between us and Edgartown, I recognized it as being the very helicopter that I had seen on the Damon lawn. The helicopter seemed to be headed there again. We watched it disappear behind North Neck.

Just then a fish hit Iowa's lure. Iowa, half-turned so he could watch the helicopter, spun around so fast that he lost his hat. "Hey!" he yipped.

A bit later, after a good tussle, he landed a nice Spanish mackerel.

"Not bad," he said. "Not a bonito, but not bad."

Zee and I could not but agree.

Iowa got a five-gallon plastic bucket from his pickup,

filled it with water, and put the mackerel in it head down, throat cut so it could bleed.

A while later I got a hit but lost it. Then Iowa got another mackerel and landed it. Then Zee got one and landed it. There was life in the sea after all. I could see that Zee was beginning to feel pretty good. The shadows of the weekend were being pushed away from her. Fishing can do that for you, especially if the fish are hitting your lure.

"Let's go, Jefferson," said Zee. "We'll catch your fish for you if we have to, but you'll have a lot more fun if you catch your own."

I finally hooked a mackerel and actually landed it. Zee patted me on the back. "Good boy," she said. "I knew you could do it."

"Watch it," I said, "or I'll grab one of your zones."

"Oh, you silver-tongued devil, you. You aren't just sweet talking me, are you?"

I faked a grab and she faked one of her own. Iowa pretended to ignore us.

We fished there all afternoon and had a lot of fun filling up our buckets with Spanish mackerel. Then, right before dusk, Iowa got the first bonito I'd seen all season.

"Hot damn!" he cried. "The good times are here again!"

So they were. Within an hour Zee and I also each had a bonito. I looked at Zee. She had a good healthy smile. The therapy had worked. "What do you say?" I asked. "Shall we go see the Chief?"

"One more cast."

She made her cast and reeled in. "Okay," she said.

Iowa was going to stay awhile longer.

"Don't worry," I said to him. "When I get into town and show those poor lads who stayed at home what a bonito looks like I'll be sure to tell them that you actually caught the first one."

"Sure you will," said Iowa. "I know I can depend on you not to lie about a thing as important as that."

We kept two of the Spanish mackerel because they are fine eating, but sold the rest of the catch. For my share I got almost as much as I'd spent for gas, which for a surf caster is not bad.

Then we drove to Edgartown's brand-new police station and actually found the Chief in his office. He was getting ready to go home. Instead, he gave Zee a steady look, seemed satisfied at what he saw, and got out a tape recorder.

"Do you mind if I tape us? Later I'll have a transcript made."

We sat and Zee told her story. The Chief asked her the questions I'd asked her and got the same answers. Then he got out his pipe, leaned back, and studied her face. "You look pretty good, Zee. You seem to have put this behind you pretty well."

"With a little help from my friends." She threw me a smile.

"Good. You have no idea what this was all about?"

"No."

"Do you, J.W.?"

"Maybe." I told him about my anonymous phone call.

Zee looked at me with surprise. "You never told me about that."

"I thought you had enough to think about. Anyway, you know now. The thing is," I said, "that the guy seemed confused when I told him you'd been gone since Friday. That caught him off guard, somehow."

"You recognize his voice?"

"No. He'd muffled it somehow or other."

"Any accent?" asked the Chief. "Anything odd? No? Who do you think he was talking about? You aren't the Vineyard's man of the year, but what off-islanders might want to do you wrong?"

I told him about the incident with the Padishah in the Cape Pogue Gut and about the one in the alcove the night of the party.

"So you think it's him? The Padishah?"

I shrugged. "He's the only guy I can think of. Zee hit him and shoved him overboard. I broke up a play he made for Helga Johanson. He's used to having his own way, especially with women, and has the reputation of being pretty ruthless with people he doesn't like."

"In Sarofim, maybe. But this is the U.S.A."

"That's right. But the guy on the phone also said that everything would probably be all right if Zee and I just dropped out of sight for a week. I don't know how long the Padishah is planning to stay in this country, but maybe it's for another week."

The Chief scribbled a note. "I'll find out. Just to be on the safe side, it might be nice if the two of you actually did go away for a while. They tell me that Nova Scotia is a lot like the Vineyard was twenty years ago . . ."

"The point is," I said, "that the people who kidnapped Zee were obviously not the ones who, according to my guy, want to hurt her. If they were, they'd have done it. So we've got some kidnappers and we've got these people my guy says want to hurt Zee and me. And they're not the same people."

"Even I, a simple small-town policeman, understand that," said the Chief. "But look at it this way. If you two go off for a week, I won't have to worry about you and I can maybe shake a man or two loose to try to find out what's going on. Why don't you do that? I'd really appreciate it."

"I have to work," said Zee.

"I have to work too," I said.

"No you don't," said the Chief.

"I want to find out what the hell is going on."

"I'm your boss," said the Chief. "I can order you not to snoop around."

"You can have your badge right now," I said, reaching for my wallet.

"Now hold on, J.W. You may want that badge before you're through. Just settle down." I settled down. "Look," said the Chief, "Zee already got grabbed once up at her place. And that was by people who didn't want to hurt her. If there are people who do want to hurt her, what's to keep them from kidnapping her too?"

"Put an officer on guard. Let somebody ride around with her."

"I don't need anybody riding around with me!" said Zee. "I can take care of myself!"

"No you can't."

"Yes I can! If I know I have to be careful, I can be careful."

"Like you were careful on Friday night!"

"On Friday night, damn it, I didn't know I had to be careful. Now I do. Don't you try to play those 'Protect the Little Lady' games with me, Jeff Jackson! And I'll tell you something else. I'm not going to let anybody scare me away from my work or my house or this island. I'm going to live my life the way I want to live it!"

"But—"

"No buts!"

I looked at the Chief. He looked at me. "So much for Nova Scotia," he said. "But I'm going to arrange to have people check up on you when they have time, Zeolinda, so don't get your nose out of joint if a cop comes by now and then to see if you're still in one piece. The same goes for you, J.W."

"I can take care of myself."

"Sure. You and Zee can both take care of yourselves. Tell me this: Why do you think that the people who snatched Zee never talked to her?"

"Because they were afraid she'd recognize their voices?"

"Can you think of any other reason?"

"No."

"Neither can I. This whole kidnapping thing is odd. They grab Zee, keep her for three days, then let her go. No rape, no ransom note, no talk, no anything. It doesn't make sense. Jake Spitz is still on the island working on the jewel theft. I'm going to talk to him. The FBI knows more about kidnapping than I do. Maybe he can figure it out."

"Maybe they had some plan and then changed their minds," said Zee.

"What plan? Ransom? Do you have any relatives with money?"

"No. Aunt Emily has money, but she's Aunt Amelia's sister. She's not really related to me."

"What, then?"

"I don't know. Maybe they thought I was somebody else and found out I wasn't and let me go."

"I'd like to hear what Spitz thinks," I said.

The Chief reached for his phone, looked gratified when his call went through, and arranged to meet with Spitz the next afternoon. "One o'clock. You're both welcome to join the party," he said, hanging up.

"I have to work tomorrow," said Zee. She looked at her watch. "And right now I have to get home and iron a uniform." We all stood up.

"I'll feed you first," I said. "And I'll be here at one, Chief."

At my place I sent Zee out to the garden to chase away the Bad Bunny Bunch and pick a salad while I filleted the mackerel, unwrapped a loaf of Betty Crocker's white bread (made with the recipe in the *old* red-and-white cookbook), and put a bottle of Chablis in the fridge and two martini glasses in the freezer beside the Absolut. One always keeps one's vodka in the freezer so it will be cold enough to drink whenever one wishes. While I was working I had a bottle of Yuengling in celebration of the arrival of the bonito. When Zee came in, we rinsed the lettuce, sliced the radishes, cukes, and a baby zook and tossed it all in a bowl.

Zee's fine nose sniffed toward the bread I'd unwrapped.

"Bread!" she said. "You are a devil. You know I'm a sucker for homemade bread."

"True," I leered, rubbing my hands together. "Now, my dear, if you'll just slip out of those clothes for half an hour or so, all of that loaf will be yours, heh, heh."

She gave me a kiss instead.

We had slices of bread and butter for hors d'oeuvres, and washed it down with ice-cold Absolut. When I am wealthy enough to afford Absolut, I rarely corrupt it by adding vermouth or tonic. I use those adornments only when my wallet dictates that I buy the cheap stuff.

"Not bad," said Zee, patting her flat belly, then holding up a restraining hand. "No more bread right now. It's murder on my waistline. Besides, didn't you fillet a Spanish mackerel?"

I went into the kitchen and got the oven going. Three-quarters of an hour later, we pushed our plates back. Zee touched her lips with her napkin. "Another fine meal at the Jackson place. I believe I detected mayo, dill, and Grey Poupon in the sauce, Chef."

"But of course, madame. An old family recipe. We will now have coffee and Cognac. No dessert tonight, in deference to your figure."

"Thank you."

Before I drove her to her house I asked if she wanted my pistol. "I think you should have it," I said.

"No thanks. I don't like pistols. Besides, I'm sure I won't need one."

It was the answer I'd expected.

As I drove her home I found myself looking in my rearview mirror, but no one was ever there. At her house I went in when she did and looked around. No bad guys were hiding in the closets.

"I'll be fine," said Zee.

"Keep the windows and doors locked."

"I will."

"Maybe I should stay the night."

"Not tonight. Sooner or later I have to be on my own. I may as well start tonight."

"Maybe I'll park out in the yard all night."

"If you do, I'll call the cops. Go home, Jefferson."

"If anything odd happens, call me right away."

"Good night, Jeff."

Outside, I walked around the house once in the gathering darkness and then drove home.

I was doing the dishes when the telephone rang.

"Hello," said the caller. "Mr. Jackson? My name is Jasper Cabot. I'd like to talk with you."

Jasper Cabot. My brain clicked and whirred and photos in Amelia Muleto's album appeared. Jasper Cabot, one of the young men in Amelia's life when she too was young and later the coprotector with Williard Blunt of the Stonehouse Emerald Necklace.

"When?" I asked.

"This evening, if possible. I realize that it's late."

"Where?"

"Your place? I'm in Edgartown. I have a car."

I gave him directions.

I'd finished cleaning up when I saw lights coming down my driveway. I didn't hear any engine. Jasper Cabot's large car was the sort that muttered powerfully but quietly. It pulled to a stop in front of my porch as I went to the door, and a short, solid-looking man slid from behind the wheel. He looked to be sixty or seventyish. Nowadays I find it hard to judge people's ages, what with the benefits of cosmetics and exercise being popular and people wearing similar clothing, irrespective of their years.

"Mr. Jackson? I'm Jasper Cabot." He put out his hand and I took it. It was a medium-sized hand, firm and smooth. No calluses.

"Of Stonehouse, Chute, Cabot, and Adams."

"Yes."

We went inside, and Jasper Cabot's lawyer's eyes took the place in. Old, saggy, comfortable furniture. No TV. Bookshelves. Fishing rods hung across the ceiling. A bachelor's house. While he was doing that, I found two snifters and the Cognac bottle and put them on the coffee table. I poured two glasses and handed one to him and gestured toward the couch. He sat down, and I sat across from him. He cupped the snifter in his hand and swirled the Cognac under his nose. I did the same. Good Cognac has a wonderful appley aroma that I love.

"I like your place."

"The rug came from the dump. My lawn mower and vacuum cleaner and some other of my stuff came from there too. It used to be the greatest store on the island. We called it the Big D. Now you have to pay for everything you take there, and they've got a machine that buries everything as soon as you unload it. No more recycling of good stuff. The environmentalists have seized control of the world and the golden days of dump picking are a thing of the past."

He nodded. "And the dump had a one hundred percent guaranteed refund policy too. You could always take it back if you weren't completely satisfied. We used to have one of those dumps up in Maine where I summer. It's a rich town, like this one, and the people in the big houses were always throwing away things that were perfectly good. The local folks said they could build and furnish a house with what the summer people threw away. I think they were right." He paused and gave a small smile. "We Cabots were summer people in a big house, of course."

I lifted my glass. "Here's to the summer people. You didn't come here to talk about the Big D."

"No. Amelia Muleto suggested I talk to you. She thinks you may be the man I need to assist me in an inquiry I'm making." He swirled his Cognac. The eyes in his smooth, plump face were sharp and evaluative. "Amelia told me that you were a policeman in Boston before you retired down here. She told me that you and her niece are friendly and that you are trustworthy and"—here he dropped his eyes politely before raising them again—"free to do some work if we can agree that you are the man for the job."

"If you mean that I'm unemployed and therefore have time to do what I please as long as it doesn't cost very much, you're right. What job do you have in mind?"

"You do not live in the style of a man with a great deal of money. I can offer you an honest wage for your work."

"I can always use an honest wage. Or an extravagant one."

Again that brief smile. "The Cabots did not accumulate their fortune by paying extravagant wages to their employees, Mr. Jackson. The wage will be fair, if we agree that you're the man for the job. I want to investigate the theft of the Stonehouse emeralds and the death of my colleague and friend, Mr. Willard Blunt. I need an island operative to assist me since I will be working primarily in Boston. Are you interested in the work?"

"I'm not a private detective. Why don't you hire a professional?"

He nodded. "A professional agency is already working on the case. You know of them, I believe. Thornberry Security, an excellent firm."

"They weren't so excellent that the emeralds weren't stolen."

"True enough, although there is some question as to exactly when the emeralds were stolen. Perhaps they were stolen before Thornberry Security was hired to protect them. Your face suggests that that possibility has occurred to you. I advise you not to try making a living as a poker player, Mr. Jackson."

"It's the face of innocence," I said. "I am without guile."

"I certainly hope that is not the case, Mr. Jackson. I want my agent to have a bit of the fox in him."

"Why not trust Thornberry Security? They're a big outfit. They have the operatives and the money to do the job. Besides, there are a lot of police on the case too."

"Thornberry Security is working for Stonehouse, Chute, Cabot, and Adams. You would be working for me. I need an experienced man with local knowledge, one who has time to do the work. The local police have all of their usual responsibilities to occupy them and limited funds, to boot. Similarly, for the state and federal investigators these crimes are only two of the many that will be occupying their time and sapping their resources. Finally, Thornberry Security, for all of the firm's expertise, lacks the local knowledge that I think necessary for a proper investigation of these crimes. I need a man who is discreet, focused upon his work, trustworthy, and—I hope this does not shock you, Mr. Jackson—not tied by official rules of evidence. Do you understand me?"

I sipped my Cognac and looked at him over the brim of my snifter. He mirrored my action. I ran the weekend crimes through my mind.

"You think that the theft and Blunt's suicide are tied together."

"Yes. If, in fact, it was suicide."

"Do you think it wasn't?"

"The coroner has not officially announced the cause of death."

"Why do you really want a private agent working on this case?"

We looked at each other. After a moment, he nodded.

"My interest is more than simply professional. Willard Blunt was not only my colleague, but my friend. I am interested both in his death and in securing the reputation that survives that death. Mrs. Amelia Muleto is also a friend who may be hurt if this matter is not resolved, and I am concerned with defending her interests. Finally, you must understand that I watched over the emeralds for the best part of my life and have a personal interest in their fate. That will have to satisfy you for the moment, Mr. Jackson."

I was surprised to hear a kind of passion in his voice.

"Maybe it will," I said. "When did you talk to Amelia Muleto?"

"This morning. I drove down from Boston this afternoon."

"Did she tell you about her niece being missing for three days?"

"She did tell me that. But she said the girl had reappeared and was all right.'

"Yes. That's what I told her this morning. In fact, her niece was kidnapped." He looked at me steadily. I told him about the abduction and about the phone call I'd received. "There may be some tie between the things that interest you and the things that interest me, but I have my own agenda. I couldn't care less who stole the emeralds or why or what the consequences may be for relations between Sarofim and the United States. In fact, like a lot of people, I'm inclined to think that people who wear their jewels in public places more or less deserve to have them stolen. I never weep when I hear of somebody's million-dollar bracelet being lifted from her apartment in Palm Springs. I *am* interested in finding out who grabbed Zee Madieras and who wants to hurt her."

"It is my impression that we may in fact have some common objectives, Mr. Jackson. Perhaps the answers to your problems will be the answers to mine." Then he told me what he would pay, and the image of Jeremy Fisher's catboat sailed through my brain.

I sipped my Cognac. I could see no disadvantage to making some money doing what I was going to do anyway.

"Okay," I said, "I'll take the job."

▪ 14 ▪

"If we are to work together, we must be frank with one another," said Jasper Cabot.

"Yes." I recalled Dostoyevsky, who believed that even in our most secret thoughts we lie to create images of ourselves that we would prefer to believe.

"What do you know of Sarofim?"

I told him. He nodded. "Very good, Mr. Jackson . . ."

"My friends mostly call me J.W."

"I do not make friends hurriedly, Mr. Jackson. For the moment we are only business partners. I hope you are not offended."

"No."

"Have you ever heard of the SDL?"

"The Sarofim Democratic League?"

"You are more knowledgeable than I'd hoped.'

"What country doesn't have a national liberation front of some sort these days?"

"It is an age of revolution, Mr. Jackson. I believe, in fact, that a few years back your own island threatened to secede from Massachusetts."

"Indeed. We also tried to save the substandard bump, but that move failed too."

He frowned, as any off-islander would do. I explained that years before, the State Highway Department had decided, in its wisdom, that a section of the highway out by the airport, where the road dropped into a shallow dale, was too abrupt in its descent and constituted a "substandard bump," which was a hazard to motorists and needed to be corrected. Delighted by the phrase, islanders, particularly teenage boys who liked to make their cars temporarily airborne by racing them over the descent at illegal speeds, had immediately issued SAVE THE SUBSTANDARD BUMP stickers and launched a campaign to restrain the Highway Department from improving things. The Highway Department had prevailed and the once-interesting substandard bump was now only legend. "Another revolution gone astray," I concluded.

Jasper Cabot nodded, but was not to be distracted. "The revolution in Sarofim has not yet gone astray, although the issue is in doubt. The SDL is headed by intellectuals and radicals who wish to overthrow the Padishah and replace his government with one of another sort. A democracy with a socialist economy seems to be the choice of the majority of the membership, but others favor a Communist model. Needless to say, the Padishah and the members of the oligarchy controlling Sarofim, wealthy families all, have much to lose if the SDL happens to prevail. The secret police are therefore active. The university in Gwatar is routinely closed for weeks or sometimes months at a time. Writers and teachers and students 'disappear.' For many years Amnesty International annually listed Sarofim as one of the countries employing torture and murder as part of a national policy of quelling dissent. However, of late the opponents of the Padishah seem inclined to die of natural causes. Heart attacks. An unusual number of them. The government of Sarofim naturally denies any responsibility."

"Naturally."

"The Padishah's recovery of the necklace would significantly strengthen his image at home as a bold and decisive leader able to hold his own with a great power. The disappearance of the necklace this past weekend is an embarrassment to him, and in Sarofim an embarrassment to a beleaguered leader might just be enough to push him from power. For that very reason, the SDL would love to come into possession of the necklace. They would use it as a symbol of their own claims to power, a trinket indicative of their ability to outsmart both the Padishah and a great power such as the United States. A symbol is often more powerful than the truth, Mr. Jackson."

"Is it likely that the SDL pulled this off?"

"Not so unlikely a possibility as you might think, Mr. Jackson. Members of the SDL have been on the island for several weeks now. They were here the night of the Damon party and are still here. You may have unknowingly seen them yourself: college-aged men and women working in the hotels and restaurants. When not serving meals or cleaning rooms, they work to advance their political interests."

Even in Sarofim they apparently know it's easy to get work on Martha's Vineyard in the late summer when many of the young Americans who come begging for jobs in the spring give them up to go partying in mid August before going back to school in September. Foreign workers—young people from Britain, Ireland, France, and, it seemed, Sarofim—are more dependable than their American counterparts. They like the money, they are willing to live like dogs so they can save it, and they never complain, because they can't do as well at home. They dodge immigration officials who think they should have green cards and they won't get any flack from me for working illegally.

"What's the SDL doing down here?" I asked. "We've got dope runners and movie stars and academic types and other undesirables, but we're usually weak on revolutionaries."

Jasper Cabot's voice was dry and had just a hint of Maine twang in it. "My guess is that they learned about the plan to turn the necklace over to the Padishah at the Damon party."

"How would they have learned about that?"

He gave me the look of a Yankee peddler. "They have sources in Gwatar and here in the States too. Think of how many people know about even confidential matters. All it takes is one sympathetic person or one competent reporter to pass along the information."

Too true. No secret is secure when two people know it.

"Do you know if they were on Chappaquiddick that night?"

"No. That's why I've hired you. But someone caused those disturbances. The attempted landing at the dock. The firecrackers tossed over the wall. Very distracting activities, don't you agree?"

I agreed. "But none of those distracting people actually got into the house."

"Perhaps they weren't supposed to."

"A feint to capture attention while something else happened."

"Perhaps. Can you think of any other explanation?"

"High jinks. College kids having fun. Party crashing. Tweaking the noses of the rich and powerful. Using up left-over Fourth of July fireworks. That sort of thing."

"An hour or so later the necklace was missing."

"You mean that the guards on the balcony outside the bedroom might have been enticed into looking one way while something happened behind them. Some act by a colleague already inside the building, perhaps."

"I know nothing of how it might have happened. I leave such analysis to the professionals. To an amateur, however, it seems likely that a relationship exists between the theft and the distractions that took place."

I thought he was probably right. "I don't remember seeing any Middle Eastern types at the party. Except, of course, the Padishah and his party."

"Not every Sarofimian looks as you might imagine. There have been Eastern and Western ships calling at Gwatar for centuries, and the bloodlines are pretty mixed. When I was there I saw blue eyes and blond hair fairly often."

"I did see some blond hair and blue eyes at the Damon party. Helga Johanson, for example, has both. Do you know her? She works for Thornberry Security."

"I think you can omit her from your list of suspects, Mr. Jackson."

"I take it that you trust Thornberry Security."

He tilted his head. "They have always been completely dependable."

Death, taxes, and Thornberry Security. "Am I correct in guessing that Thornberry Security is still checking the guest list just in case some ringer got slipped into the party."

"I believe so. It is my understanding that Ms. Johanson is heading the island investigation for her agency. She is making her headquarters at the Damon home. I will inform her and the police that you will be working as my agent and ask that you all cooperate with one another."

I nodded. It wouldn't hurt to ask, but it was no secret that police agencies often distrusted one another, to say nothing of distrusting private agencies and, worse yet, civilians nosing around on their own.

"Where do these Sarofimian students live when they're not down here making life tough for the Padishah?"

"As you might guess, Cambridge has attracted a number of them. And Weststock has an active group."

"Who's their guru? What's their bible? I never heard of any group of true believers who don't have a saint or two and a sacred text."

Cabot raised a brow. "Are you a student of political movements, then, Mr. Jackson? I didn't know."

"The Christians have Jesus and the Bible, the Muslims have Muhammad and the Koran, the Communists have Marx and Lenin and *Das Kapital.* I imagine the SDL is no different."

"I'm not sure I'd throw all of those groups under the same umbrella," said Cabot, "but you're right. The SDL does have leaders. Here in America one of the most important is Dr. Hamdi Safwat. His book *Free People* is a major text for the SDL, and he serves as both a mentor to Sarofimian students in New England and as coordinator for exiled parties interested in overthrowing the Rashad dynasty. He is a professor of Middle Eastern studies at Weststock College."

"I've heard the name and seen the book. Could he have anything to do with the theft?"

He shrugged. "He was a friend of Willard Blunt's, so he is linked to this past weekend's crimes by that association at least."

"Yes. Do you know him yourself?"

"We've met. A charming man. Very gentle. Very moral. Not the revolutionary type at all, or so you'd think. An intellectual. Fine sense of humor."

"Would he help me find some of the local students, do you think?"

"Help you track down students who might, as a result, find themselves in difficulty with the authorities? Who might, because of that, be returned to Sarofim to face the secret police? Oh, I think not. Not at all. Many Sarofimian students over here are already worried that the new accords that are being arranged between Sarofim and the United States might result in the Padishah's political opponents being denied sanctuary or the opportunity to study over here. Dr. Safwat would certainly not cooperate with anyone whose activities might increase the risk of that eventuality."

"Would he talk to me at all?"

Cabot shrugged. "I can't say."

"Do you know anything about his friendship with Willard Blunt? How it started? Why? What sort of friendship it was?"

"If you learn as much from others as you are learning from me, sir, you should have this matter cleared up in no time at all. Yes, I can tell you something at least about Willard and Hamdi's friendship, although I do not see its relevance at the moment. It began back in World War II, when both Willard and I were in the army and were posted to Sarofim. Our job there was to maintain a rather crude airport for Allied planes headed east for Burma and the Pacific theater of war.

"Willard was immediately fascinated with the place and its people. So was I, but in no way to the same degree. Willard was blessed, as I have never been, with the gift of tongues and soon could speak the language fluently. It's an offshoot of Persian, incidentally. I could blunder around in it, but Willard was a master. He made many friends and soon developed a great sympathy for the poorer class of Sarofimians. We were invited to the houses of young people our age. One of them was the home of Hamdi Safwat, whose father was a teacher. Hamdi was only a boy, barely in his teens, but he was very bright. There was a sister who quite knocked poor Willard off his feet. A great beauty, worse luck for her." He paused, then went on. "The Padishah, the father of Ali Mohammed Rashad, our current Padishah, was infamous for his harem. He was also an absolute monarch, and one day his police simply took the girl. She was never seen again. The family protested. A few nights later the father disappeared. His corpse was found outside of Gwatar on a rubbish heap. He had been mutilated in unspeakable ways. I had never imagined such brutality.

"Willard was half-mad, but I restrained him. To understand his emotions you should perhaps know that both he and I came from Quaker stock, which inclines us to disapprove of war and led the two of us to noncombatant roles in the army. Willard was at once committed to personal nonviolence and filled with rage at what had happened to his friends. Fortunately, our tour of duty in Sarofim ended shortly afterwards and we were shipped back home. The Blunts are people of considerable influence, and Willard, being an only child and the apple of his parents' eyes, had no difficulty persuading them to arrange for young Hamdi and his mother to come to the States. Willard looked after them. Arranged for the boy's education. The mother died years ago. Hamdi has been here ever since, and he and Willard were always friends."

Cabot drew a watch from a vest pocket and snapped it open. It gleamed as only old gold can gleam. He looked at it and slid it back whence it came.

"Did he love the girl?"

He shrugged. "Who knows. He was far from home and she was beautiful. We were all young and full of ideals. After he had been home for a few months, he did begin to go out with other women. I thought for a time that he might marry Amelia Stonehouse, but then she met Raymond Muleto."

"If he was a pacifist, would he shoot himself?"

"A reasonable question. Some pacifists would not. Willard, however, approved of the Hemlock Society. Are you familiar with that organization?"

"I've heard of it. They support the right of terminally ill people to take their own lives."

"Among other things, yes. Willard approved of their ethics though he disapproved of the right of one individual to kill another. He saw no moral contradictions." Cabot put a card on the coffee table. "You may reach me at these numbers and addresses when you have something to report. Have you any other questions before I go?"

"A couple. Haw much are you willing to pay to get the necklace back?"

He named a handsome figure. "Of course I expect you to pay as little as possible, should you have the opportunity to pay at all."

Of course. The Cabots did not accumulate their fortune by paying extravagant amounts for anything, if they could help it.

"If I happen to find out who killed Willard Blunt, I assume that you want me to tell the authorities first and then you?"

"Yes." His lawyer's eyes were as expressionless as his voice. I didn't believe his answer reflected his desire. "I must go. I'll expect reports from you fairly regularly."

We stood, shook hands, and went out to his car. He turned it smoothly, and it purred away up my driveway. I watched until its headlights topped the rise in the road and disappeared and thought that I'd not like to have Jasper Cabot set his mind on discomforting me.

The August night was warm and sultry. I went inside, got my keys, and drove to the Fireside Bar in Oak Bluffs.

▪ 15 ▪

Oak Bluffs' main street is Circuit Avenue. There's a honky-tonk quality about it that contrasts sharply with the prim propriety of Edgartown's streets. It's lined with shops catering to day-trippers who come in off the boats from Hyannis and Falmouth and then get on the tour buses driven by highly imaginative drivers whose ignorance of the Vineyard in no way prevents them from spinning entertaining explanations about what their passengers are looking at. Back in Oak Bluffs once again after their tour of the island in their driver's mind, these tourists roam Circuit Avenue buying fast foods and souvenirs of their day on the island—brass trinkets, tee shirts, wood carvings of sea gulls on pilings, and other such New Englandish stuff, imported largely from Asia. Then they take the boat back to the mainland and tell their friends all about the Vineyard.

Mixed with these shops are bars that are largely filled in the summertime by young working people and college types. If there's ever a fight on Martha's Vineyard, it usually starts behind one of these bars and consists of drunken young men making loud combative noises while they swing at one another or roll around on the ground until the local cops come and PC them for the night. The Fireside is one of these bars. I found a parking place just up the street and went inside to find Bonzo.

Sometime before I met him, Bonzo was, I've been told, a promising young man. The only son of a widowed schoolteacher, he was the apple of her eye. Then, as occasionally happens to young men these days, he scrambled his brain with an illegal chemical additive, reputedly bad acid. He now earns a few dollars a day by performing menial tasks at the Fireside. He gazes out upon the world through sweet, empty eyes, and when not working, collects bird songs on his expensive recording devices and, now and then, goes fishing with me. He takes his work seriously and harbors no grudges against man or God. His mother lives in one of the gingerbread cottages near the Tabernacle and still labors in the academic halls of Martha's Vineyard High School. She loves innocent, blank-brained Bonzo without hope or self-pity. I take her fish from time to time, as Vineyard fishermen do to folks who cannot catch their own.

Bonzo and his mop and bucket were cleaning a spill back in the far corner of the barroom. The place was crowded with noisy people, mostly ten or fifteen years younger than I was, and the music was blaring in that mind-splitting mode that seems so popular with today's half-deaf youth. "American Bandstand" and I were born and raised together, so I am familiar with many a wretched, once-popular song and singer, but compared to the current awfulness, even Elvis, once a controversial figure, now seems sedate and bland. My advanced age did not seem to offend anyone, so I went to the bar, found a stool, and ordered a Sam Adams.

The Fireside was as alive with smells as it was with noise. The odor of beer, both fresh and stale, mixed with the faint fragrance of marijuana and the stronger scents of sweat and whiskey. Most of the customers seemed pretty cheerful, I thought, as I watched them in the mirror behind the bar. By and by I saw Bonzo spot me and come over. I turned on the bar stool as he arrived.

"Hey, J.W.," he said with his child's smile. "Good to see you again." He put out his gentle hand and I took it. "Do you think we can go fishing pretty soon? I sure like to catch those bluefish."

Bonzo was a tireless fisherman. He would stand on the beach with the surf sloshing his legs and cast and cast and cast, never stopping, rarely catching anything, delighted when I caught the fish his short, childish casts could not catch, alive with joy when he himself nailed some fish swimming close to shore.

"The bluefish have gone up north," I said. "They'll be coming back down again in September. We could try for some bonito, though."

"Bonito! That would be just fine, J.W.!" A faint frown then mingled with his smile. "Say, did we ever fish for bonito, J.W.?"

"I don't think you ever did, Bonzo, but we can give it a shot. You know those little boats that are anchored around the ferry dock lately? The guys in those boats are after bonito."

"Oh, yeah. Oh, yeah, I knew that!" He beamed and it was like the sun dancing on water. "You got a boat we can use, J.W.?" Again that frown mixed with his smile. "I haven't got a boat, myself, you know."

"I know you don't, but I've got my dinghy. That would be big enough on a calm day. I can bring it up in the Land-Cruiser and drop it overboard in the harbor and we can go out from there. I've got enough gear for both of us and I'll pick up some bait."

"Excellent! That will be just excellent! When?"

"How about the day after tomorrow? Early. I can pick you up about dawn, say five-thirty. That way we can get a morning's fishing in and you can still get back in time to go to work at noon."

He nodded soberly. "That'll be good, J.W. I got my job here and I can't just leave it. My work's important." He gave his mop handle a squeeze.

"Say, Bonzo," I said, "you're the kind of guy who keeps his ears and eyes open and knows what's going on, aren't you?"

He thought about the question, then nodded. "Yes, I am, J.W. I hear a lot, you know, because of my work. People talk and laugh and I'm right there and sometimes I laugh right along with them." He grinned, then stopped. "Sometimes they don't laugh, so I just be quiet and keep working. But I hear them and see them. You know what I mean, J.W.?"

"I know what you mean, Bonzo. Tell me this: Did you ever hear anybody in here mention the name Sarofim?"

I was not optimistic, but on the other hand the Fireside

was a popular hangout for young folks and it just might be that some lonely Sarofimian, tired of cleaning hotel rooms and planning revolutions, had dropped in for a beer and some company generally uninterested in politics.

To my surprise, Bonzo's blank face lit up. "Sure! I heard that word just the other day!"

It seemed too easy. "You did?"

"But not in here, J.W. In church!"

In church? My brain stopped, then started again. Why not? Some Sarofimians probably went to church just like other people. Maybe even Sarofimian revolutionaries went to church. A lot of revolutionaries think that God is on their side. "Who mentioned it, Bonzo?"

"Hey, you know who talks in church, J.W. The priest! Father Jim. He said it, Cherubim and seraphim. Two kinds of angels. Father Jim said the cherubim were high, but the seraphim were higher. Is that what you wanted to know, J.W.? I heard that in church, so it must be true."

I drank some beer and tried again. "I'm sure it's true, Bonzo. Now think carefully; did you ever hear anyone in here, not in church, mention Sarofim? It's the name of a country, and I'd like to talk to anyone from that country, if I can find somebody."

Bonzo's brow wrinkled then smoothed. "Gosh, a country with a name like an angel. No, J.W., I don't think I ever heard anybody but the priest say that name." He brightened. "But I'll tell you what I can do. I'll ask my friends. I got a lot of good friends here and they know a lot and I'll ask them. Then when you go fishing I can tell you what they tell me. Is that okay?"

I put my hand on his thin shoulder. "That will be a big help, Bonzo. One more thing. Did you ever hear of a musical group called the Gits?"

"Gosh, J.W., everybody's heard of the Gits. We got two Git songs on the box over there. Say, you want me to play that music for you? You can hear 'em clear over this noise. I tell you, J.W., the Gits are loud!" He grinned and reached into his pockets for coins.

The room was already a cacophony of voices and screaming electronic instruments.

"Louder than this, Bonzo?"

"Oh, sure. This is nothin'." He had his money out. "I'll play you some Gits and you'll see! They're really good!"

Ye gods! "No, no! I've got to go. Five-thirty the day after tomorrow. I'll pick you up. Okay?"

He looked at the coins in his hand, then slid them back into his pocket and smiled his sweet, dreamy smile. "Okay. I'll be ready. We'll catch us some bonito!"

I finished my beer and went out. Circuit Avenue was filled with walkers wandering between the bars and restaurants. Young people mostly, of all shades and shapes. Unlike lily-white Edgartown where many people still blanch at the thought of non-Caucasian neighbors, Oak Bluffs has for many years been racially integrated, so the flavor of the street inclines more toward Neapolitan than vanilla. It seemed the sort of street where a wandering Sarofimian might feel comfortable, but if I saw any, I didn't know it. I found my LandCruiser and went home. So far, I'd been held scoreless in the Sarofimian Bowl, but I had hopes for the morrow.

On the morrow I had a brisk get-the-day-going shower in my outdoor shower and, naked, toweled myself dry in the yard between my house and my garden. One of the advantages of living in a place hidden from other houses is that you can do things like that. The Chief's theory notwithstanding, no low-flying airplanes examined me during this procedure. Only two bunnies, who studied me between explorations for holes in my garden fence. In the garden, towel flung Hercules-style over my shoulder, I plucked a few weeds and picked a couple of zooks that, as zucchinis are apt to do, had grown hugely overnight and needed to be eaten before they ate me. On my way into the house, I paused to study Archie Bunker's chair. A little glue, a few well-placed wood screws, and some paint and it would be as good as new.

Inside, I judged the time to be right and telephoned Zee. I

was correct in my guess. Zee was between breakfast and departure for work.

"Just checking up," I said.

"Everything's fine. Do you plan on doing this every morning?"

"If you move in with me, I won't have to."

"I'm late, Jeff. I've got to go to work."

"Be careful."

"I will. You don't have to worry about me."

"Let's get married."

She laughed. "Not this morning, but thanks for asking."

"Goodbye?"

Another laugh. "Goodbye."

I chopped part of one of the zooks into a skillet with some butter and sautéed it while I dug out some eggs and grated some cheddar. Zook omelet and toast made from homemade bread, washed down with coffee. Not bad!

Then, since it was going to be another warm August day, I put on my thrift-shop shorts, sandals, a tee shirt, and my new hat—the baseball type with an adjustable plastic band in back and a logo on the front. Mine said HT-8 and was decorated with a picture of a helicopter and had my shellfishing license pinned over my left ear. Properly attired for detecting, I set off to Chappaquiddick to visit Ms. Helga Johanson, the well-known blond-and-blue-eyed private eye. I doubted if she'd be glad to see me.

Outside the gateway to the Damon house I discovered a uniformed guard. Grady Flynn, one of Edgartown's finest. On private detail. Big bucks for soft duty.

I suggested as much and he grinned. "It's a dirty job, but somebody's got to do it."

I told him I wanted to talk with Helga Johanson, and he pulled out his radio, talked into it, listened, and waved me through. The LandCruiser looked a bit out of place when I parked beside the house not far from the helicopter I assumed was the Padishah's. Another man, this one in civvies but with the unmistakable look of a cop—private, I guessed, in this case—opened the door at my knock and, after eyeing

me in general disapproval, led me into the library. There, i
seemed, Thornberry Security had set up war headquarters
General Johanson stood beside a table covered with papers
She was wearing a light blue blouse and a darker blue skirt. H
blue shoes had low heels, and her legs looked terrific. Her eye
moved over me from head to foot, and a flicker of suspicio
crossed her face. I, in reply, ogled her without shame.

"Blue is your color," I said.

She put out a cool hand. "Mr. Cabot has informed me tha
you are his agent and has asked that we cooperate with you
Naturally we're glad to do so."

"Naturally." I held her hand a moment after she attempte
to withdraw it, then let it go. "I'll tell you everything I know
in return for everything you know and a chance to go up t
the master bedroom."

"The master bedroom? I doubt if you'll find anything o
importance there, Mr. Jackson."

"Call me J.W. I'd like to look at it anyway. I was onl
there once and may have missed something."

"It seems very possible that you might," she said, "but
assure you that Thornberry Security did not."

"Come with me," I said. "You can guard the house fror
me and I can prove to you that I can walk and talk at th
same time. You can get away from these papers for a while
Do you good."

It was not a bad ploy. Who doesn't want an excuse to ge
away from a table covered with papers?

She hesitated, then nodded. "All right, Mr. Jackson."

"Great," I said, taking her arm. "You and me and the master bedroom. Sounds like a terrific combination."

She shook my hand away. "I haven't much time for yo
either professionally or personally, Mr. Jackson."

"Call me J.W.," I said and took her arm again. She shoo
her arm less vigorously and gave a sort of annoyed snort
But I hung on and smiled down at her, and after a momen
she relaxed. Together we walked out of the library.

▪ 16 ▪

A man came in as we went out. He was firm of step and purposeful. A Thornberry man, apparently. One of Helga Johanson's underlings, in that case. He looked slightly askance at her arm tucked in mine, but said nothing.

She gave him a stony look as I walked her past him. "We'll be in the . . . we'll be upstairs for a few minutes, George. The list you want is on the big desk."

"Yes, ma'am," said George.

We went up the grand staircase. She gestured down a hallway. "The Padishah and his people are there. That is to say, they are occupying that wing of this floor. At the moment I believe they're all in Washington, except for Colonel Nagy."

"Is the Colonel out checking up on the SDL?"

"What do you know about the SDL?" she asked sharply.

We were walking down a hall leading away from the Padishah's wing.

"Only what I heard from your boss and from Jasper Cabot." I told her what Cabot had said. "My master plan is to try to track one or two local Sarofimian types down and ask them some questions."

"The police are doing that now," she said. "You're probably just wasting your energy."

I smiled down at her. "I'll save some for the really important things. What's your theory about the missing necklace?"

"Thornberry Security prefers to work from facts, Mr. Jackson, not theories."

"Call me J.W."

"Oh, very well . . ."

"Good. I have a couple of ideas, Helga. Want to hear them? They're not much, but they're what I've got."

"I don't expect them to be much, Mr. . . . J.W., but I sus pect I'm going to hear them whether I want to or not."

We came to the master bedroom and went in. The roon was as I remembered it. The wandering Damon's dusty weapon collection was still hanging on the walls. I peeke into the adjoining bathroom. I didn't find the missing neck lace lying in the middle of its floor.

"Naturally you've searched the house thoroughly."

"Naturally. Water closets and all. You were going to tel me your ideas."

"Well, I figure there are a lot of ways the necklace coul have been stolen. First, of course, it might have bee stolen before it even got here. Willard Blunt is the obviou suspect since he's been in charge of the necklaces fo decades and afterwards apparently shot himself on th beach. Guilt, shame, and all that. Maybe he bought off Dr What's-his-name of the Sarofimian National Museum t just *say* he put the necklace in the safe. Or, second, mayb Blunt could have stolen it from the safe between the tim Dr. What's-his-name put the necklace in there and th night of the party. Who'd have suspected him? Trustwor thy old New England lawyer and all that. Maybe he jus carried it out in his pocket. Did anybody search him? don't know. Third, still on old Willard's case, maybe h passed them to a crony from here in this room. What d you think so far?"

"Naturally we have considered all of those possibilities Mr. . . . J.W. However, Mr. Blunt insisted on being searche that night and the guards on the tower also were searche and nothing was found. No one else could have gotten i there, unless, of course, you assume that someone in a rathe complex conspiracy bribed all of our guards or came acros the roofs and escaped the same way . . ."

"I'm willing to consider those possibilities. On the othe hand, there are a couple of better ways to get the necklace t some cohort." I gestured. "That slingshot. Open one of thes windows and wrap the necklace in, say, a handkerchief, an the right man could throw it clear over the far wall. Or if h was an archer he could have tied the necklace to an arrow and shot it off quite a ways. Remember the commotion at the dock and the fireworks. Which way do you think the guards out on the balcony were looking while all that was going on? Open a window behind them and they'd never have noticed it. Do you know how many arrows there were before the theft? Did you count them afterwards?"

"No. That's nonsensical anyhow. Look at these old bows. They'd snap if they were used."

"You an archer?"

"No."

"Neither am I. Was Willard Blunt?"

"I don't know."

"Could old Willard use a slingshot? He might have been a pretty handy sort of guy."

"I don't think it makes any difference. Mr. Blunt's reputation was impeccable and he had no motive."

The best embezzlers almost always have impeccable reputations. "Maybe old Willard had some motive you don't know about. Maybe he needed the money."

"Willard Blunt left a considerable estate. I assure you he had no need of money."

"Maybe he wanted to impress a lady friend."

"Please."

"Okay. He worked for Stonehouse, Chute, Cabot, and Adams. Maybe somebody in that outfit took it and somehow conned old Willard. Maybe Jasper Cabot did it."

"I believe that the owners and employees of Stonehouse, Chute, Cabot, and Adams are above suspicion. But inquiries are being made, of course . . ."

"Ah, that's why Thornberry isn't here. He's in Boston where the real action is."

She colored slightly. "There's plenty of action here, I assure you. We and the police are investigating the case thoroughly."

"Maybe one of the guards up here that night, or both of them, pulled the theft. Got inside and lifted the ice. Maybe Willard slipped him the combination of the safe . . ."

"You're really something. You can't get Mr. Blunt out of your head."

"Yes I can. I can think of several other people. How about the Padishah or one of his cronies? Or how about the SDL? Or how about you, for that matter."

She actually smiled a real smile. "You really are a cop, aren't you? You suspect everybody."

"Or nobody. It amounts to the same thing. You have to be careful about suspecting particular people too much; it can make you overlook other people. Now, Helga, you know my most secret thoughts on the matter, so tell me yours."

"Are you through up here? Let's go down, then. I do have work to do."

"Here you have me at your mercy in the master bedroom and you want to leave? What kind of a seductress are you, anyway."

"My God!"

"All right, all right. We'll walk and you can talk. Sheesh . . ."

We walked and she talked. "We're running checks on everybody who came to the party. That will take time. So far we have nothing. We're also checking the help who came in for that night. The caterers, maids, and so forth. Most of them are island people who never got above the ground floor. There were maids upstairs, but no one was allowed in the hall to the master bedroom. I don't expect to find the jewel thief among them, although we may recover a few pieces of silverware. We're also working the hotels and restuarants to find out if there are any Sarofimians employed there, our assumption being that any such people might be SDL members." She touched her yellow hair and looked up at me. "Jason is in Boston, as you know, and the police are working on Blunt's suicide. You can talk to them about that."

"You think the theft and the suicide are tied together."

"For the moment. Of course they could be unrelated incidents, but the coincidence seems too great. Willard Blunt was a key figure in the theft and now he's dead. A suspicious guy like you shouldn't have any trouble tying the two things together."

No trouble at all. " 'Once is happenstance, twice is coincidence, three times is enemy action,' " I said, wondering if I was quoting or misquoting and suddenly thinking of Zee's abduction as I did. Suicide, theft, kidnapping. Three crimes close together in time and space. Hmmmmm. "Do you have any leads?" I asked. "Any evidence I should know about?"

"You mean a clue, like in detective stories?" She seemed to be warming a bit.

"That's the word. I'm Theseus and you're Ariadne. Give me the clue."

"I know that one," she said. "As I recall, all she got for her efforts was being abandoned on Naxos."

"Your fate will be a kinder one," I said. "You can be abandoned on Martha's Vineyard."

"Abandoned is abandoned."

"And a clue is a clue. Do you have one?"

"Well, not really. Not yet. I think the guards upstairs that night are clean. They've been with the firm for a long time and they've been totally reliable. They say nobody else got into the room . . ."

"So Blunt didn't do it and nobody else did it either. And then Blunt shot himself. Do you know why?"

"You'll have to ask someone else about that."

"I will. Where shall I start?"

She waved a graceful hand in the general direction of Edgartown. "Out there. Talk to the police. The local guys and the state guys and the feds. We're all cooperating with one another."

"And with me, of course."

"Of course." We had arrived back at the library. George was at a table, talking into a telephone. Helga Johanson paused and looked at her fingernails. I looked too. They seemed all right to me. "Maybe we could discuss this further over dinner sometime," she said.

"Do you see yourself as the hostess or the guest?"

"I beg your pardon?"

"If you're the hostess, I know some terrific expensive places to eat. If you're the guest, it'll be pizza and beer."

She touched my chest with one of the fingernails she had just been examining. "It'll be on Thornberry Security. Business expense. Choose someplace where they won't let you in in those clothes."

"The tux was rented," I said. "This is the real me."

She smiled and shrugged. "Okay, pizza and beer it is. When?"

"On the other hand," I said, "I do own some red pants and a tie with little whales on it, so I can get into most places."

"Great. Wear your tie. When?"

"How about tomorrow night? Maybe by then I'll know something about this case and you'll feel more moral about charging the meal to the firm."

"Don't worry about my morals. You just tend your own. What time?"

"I'll pick you up at seven."

"Seven it is." She tapped that fingernail on my chest, turned, and walked to her desk. She had a nice shape. And blue was definitely her color.

17

It was almost noon. Zee was safe at work, and I was beginning to loosen up a little. The sun was hot, and I gave some thought to driving out to the Jetties and trying for bonito. Iowa was no doubt out there pulling them in. On the other hand, Jake Spitz of the FBI was meeting with the Chief at one, and I wanted to be there. As I rode the ferry across to Edgartown I imagined myself easing out past the Edgartown lighthouse in Jeremy Fisher's catboat. I didn't look too bad. People on the beach watched me enviously. Then, for the second time in two days, I drove to the brand-new police station over by the fire station on Pease Point Way. This time I paid more attention to it. The station was a thing of beauty, with an interrogation room, the Chief's new office, an armory, a lot more space than the old station had offered, and a computer with which Edgartown's finest could keep track of their records and reports. Today it was lacking only one thing, the Chief, who was down on Main Street trying to keep traffic moving. I walked down to find him.

Edgartown is a lovely village, but it wasn't made for cars. Most of its narrow streets are one way, and cars, especially those driven by tourists ogling the sights and looking for parking places, tend to move slowly if at all. This snail's pace is slowed even more by the notion visiting pedestrians apparently have that the streets are really just wide sidewalks and that the cars on them are make-believe. They pay no attention to the cars and look annoyed or at least surprised when one comes along and forces them to step onto a curb.

I found the Chief at the Five Corners. He was leaning on

the brick wall of the bank watching while a summer cop tried, not too badly, to sort out the walkers and drivers and keep all parties moving somewhere or other.

The Chief gestured at the street. "Automotive cholesterol. It clogs the town's arteries. The kid there is doing okay. When he came down here in June he couldn't keep water running. Now look at him."

"All thanks to you, Chief," I said. "It's people like you who make America great."

"What do you want?"

"What do you mean what do I want?"

"You never come downtown unless you want something. The rest of the time you hide up there in the woods or on the beach until after Labor Day."

"Look at the walkers," I said. "They think this place is Disneyland and that it's all just a big playground. Nothing is real to them. I'm amazed that they don't get run over by some car they probably think is just pretend."

"Fantasy Island," nodded the Chief. "The only useful store left on Main Street is the hardware store. The drugstore doesn't sell drugs, the post office is out of town, and the market, such as it is, is hidden behind a couple of places selling stuff for tourists. No wonder people are surprised that the cars are real. What do you want?"

"I got hired by a guy named Jasper Cabot to nose around Blunt's suicide and solve the mystery of the missing emerald necklace."

"I know. He phoned me from Boston. Just remember that if you use that badge, you're working for me and the law, not for Jasper Cabot."

"I don't plan on using the badge and I gave Manny Fonseca's pistol back to him, so I'm just a normal civilian."

"I don't know that I'd call you normal. I tell you, J.W., I've got more investigators around here than a dead fish has flies. There are feds and state cops and private cops and cops I probably don't even know about. They're crawling out from the woodwork. I just try to keep me and my people out of their way while they do their crime solving."

Sure. "How much have they solved so far?"

"They've found a couple of college kids from Sarofim working here in town. Both children of upper-crust parents who want them to get an American education and to work summers. We get a lot of kids like that down here. Those two just happen to be from Sarofim. The state and federal guys grilled them for a while, but decided that neither one was a revolutionary or even knew any revolutionaries."

"Of course a member of the revolutionary underground would want you to believe exactly that."

"Of course. The point is that neither of the two kids they grilled gave anybody any reason at all to think they're anything but what they seem. Besides, both of them were working the night of the Damon party." He shrugged and flicked his eyes up and down the street the way cops do because they don't like to miss things or be surprised. "Why do you think Blunt decided to kill himself way out there on Chappy instead of someplace else?"

"Jasper Cabot thinks it might not have been suicide."

The Chief glanced at his watch. "There's something funny about it, that's for sure. Pistol he used. Made for the Sarofimian army."

"I didn't know Sarofim had an army."

"Every country has an army."

"Blunt was stationed over there in the Second World War. Maybe the pistol was a souvenir."

"He did have a souvenir pistol, but he didn't shoot himself with it. He used a gun that wasn't even made back in the forties. His souvenir pistol was a Webley .455 revolver. Gun in his hand was a Beretta 7.65 mm semiautomatic. Modern pistol. Special order for the Sarofimian army."

"You know a lot about it for a guy who hasn't even got the coroner's report."

"That phone call from your boss Jasper Cabot. He was stationed overseas with Blunt when they were both kids. He knew the gun Blunt brought home. Went over Blunt's apartment. No pistol. Told me that he tried to call you before he called me, but you weren't home."

"I was over on Chappy."

"Thing is, the revolver's missing. Did Blunt bring it down here with him? And if he did, why did he use a Sarofimian pistol when he had his trusty Webley? And where did he get the Beretta?"

"Maybe he used the Beretta because he didn't have the Webley anymore."

"Maybe." The Chief sighed. "And then there's the other possibility . . ."

"That somebody else shot him with the Beretta?"

"Let's head for the office. Otherwise Spitz'll be there before we are." The Chief gave his young summer cop a final evaluative look before we headed up Main. "Thing about the Beretta is that it's too obvious."

I thought so too. Blunt, a suspect in the theft of the necklace, shot to death by a weapon made for the Sarofimian military. Obvious conclusion: he was shot by some Sarofimian military man. Who else but Colonel Ahmed Nagy? Motivation: revenge upon the man who robbed his king and country of its rightful jewels.

"Yeah," I said. "But if Nagy did it, wouldn't he have been smart enough to take the gun away with him?"

"If you thought of that," said the Chief, "I'm pretty sure Nagy would have thought of it too."

We found a cruiser parked in front of the courthouse and drove to the station.

"Tell me," I said. "Why is every police cruiser in New England a Ford LTD?"

"Because they won't give us Ferraris," said the Chief.

"Oh."

Jake Spitz came into the office at one o'clock sharp. He was a nondescript sort of guy, about forty or so, wearing neither snap-brim hat nor suit and tie, but chinos and a polo shirt. He did sport dark glasses, but who doesn't on Martha's Vineyard in August? I recognized him as one of the men I'd seen in the Damon library early Sunday morning.

The Chief introduced us and told Spitz why I was there

and who I was working for. Spitz did not seem put out by talking with a civilian. He had a firm handshake.

"I know who Jasper Cabot is. I've talked to him about this last weekend's crimes. He's been helpful."

"Jake, here, has talked to lots of people," said the Chief. "He's the one who told me about the Beretta."

"Funny business, that," said Spitz. He raised an eyebrow and gave a sidewise look at the Chief.

"J.W. knows about it," said the Chief, digging out his pipe. "He works for me too."

"I thought I saw you at the party," said Spitz. "On guard at the door."

"I didn't see you."

"Yes you did. You just didn't notice me. I take that as a compliment."

"Remind me not to play Sherlock Holmes for the next couple of days. I'm obviously out of practice."

"The only reason I've got a job is because I'm invisible," smiled Spitz. "It's God's compensation to me for being totally mediocre. What's this business about a kidnapping?"

I decided I would not bet the farm on his being mediocre. I told him everything I knew about Zee's abduction. He listened attentively.

"So," he said, "they grabbed her, kept her, and then let her go. No damage to her, no sex, no threats, no ransom, no nothing. They took her on Friday night and let her go on Tuesday morning."

"That's it."

"What do you think?"

"I think it's interesting that nobody ever said a word to her. Nobody asked her if she wanted to eat or drink or go to the toilet or answered her if she said anything. They tended to her, but they never talked to her."

"I agree. Anything else?"

"I think the music was loud all of the time so she wouldn't hear anything else. Maybe otherwise she'd have heard something familiar: a ferry whistle or a noon whistle or people going by."

"Yes. Anything else?"

"She mentioned spices used in cooking that she didn't recognize."

"Anything else?"

"I don't know. In general, I think they didn't want her to hear their voices or outside sounds for fear she might be able to identify them later. I haven't gotten much further than that."

"Except for the coincidences." Spitz gave me a sidewise look such as he had earlier given the Chief. Apparently it was a habit he had when he made a statement that was really asking a question.

The Chief had found his tobacco and matches and had lit up. I inhaled. Great smoke! Oh, for my pipe! "Coincidences," I said. "Yeah. I've thought of a couple . . ."

"The time she was held?" asked Spitz.

"That. The fact that Blunt dropped her off only minutes before she was grabbed . . ."

"That's it. Blunt took her home on Friday night. Whoever grabbed her was waiting for her. The next night she was supposed to go with her aunt to the party where her aunt was to play a role—a small role, but a role—in the ceremony, but now the aunt would go alone. The necklace was stolen. The next night Blunt was shot. Suicide, apparently. The next morning, Monday, nothing happened. On Tuesday morning she was released."

"Somebody wanted her away for the weekend?"

"Why would somebody want that?" asked Spitz.

"Because she knew something? Because she'd get in the way?"

"What did she know?"

"I don't know. Whose way would she get in?"

"Whoever was going after the emeralds?"

"The SDL?"

Spitz raised a brow. "The SDL, maybe. Maybe somebody else."

"Who?"

"I don't know. All I know is that when the weekend was over, they let her go."

"No they didn't. They kept her until Tuesday morning. The jewels were stolen Saturday night. If they just wanted her out of the way until the theft was accomplished, they could have let her go earlier."

"Maybe the theft wasn't the only thing," said the Chief. We looked at him. "Maybe Blunt's suicide is tied into this too."

"How?" asked Spitz. The Chief shook his head. "Okay," said Spitz, "let's say you're right. If you are, why didn't they release her Monday morning after he'd shot himself?"

"Because they didn't know he'd done it," I said. "It didn't become public knowledge until mid morning or later. Unless the kidnappers saw him shoot himself, they wouldn't know he'd actually done it until it was too late in the day to return Zee. So they waited until early the next morning . . ."

"We don't know if it was suicide or not," said the Chief.

"Suicide, murder, whatever. The public didn't know about it until it was daylight."

"Don't get chippy," said the Chief, blowing a smoke ring in my direction.

"It starts with Blunt and it ends with Blunt," said Spitz. "I think we've got ourselves a conundrum. Did I tell you that he and that Nagy fellow, the Padishah's bodyguard, came by to see me Sunday night? Phoned me from Chappy and came over to my hotel to discuss the case. Turned out none of us knew much. Afterwards, Blunt went off to see a friend, and Nagy—funny fellow, Nagy—said he was going to take a turn around town and then walk home. Said he used to walk in the desert at home when he needed to think things through."

"Blunt visited Amelia Muleto," I said. "Then I guess he went to Chappy."

"Anyhow, three hours later he was dead."

"I'll be interested in getting the autopsy report," said the Chief. "I think I know what it'll say. Death by gunshot. But at least it'll be official."

"If this really is all tied together, maybe it'll all come untied together," said Spitz.

I got up. "I'll let you know if I find out anything."

Spitz put out his hand. "Let's keep in touch. Be careful."

Be careful. I thought about that advice as I drove home. found a beer and phoned the Damon house on Chappy an asked for Helga. When she came on, I asked her who ha catered the Damons' party. She looked it up.

"Katama Caterers. Are you onto something?"

"I want to find out how they prepared that vegetable dis from Sarofim. It smelled terrific, but I never got any. I don' suppose that any of your detectives managed to come u with the recipe."

"I'm afraid there are no recipes in our files, J.W. Now really must go do some serious work."

"Our date is still on, I hope."

"Yes."

I phoned Katama Caterers and asked the voice that an swered if they had prepared the vegetable dish for th Damon banquet. They had indeed.

"Ah, you must mean the Sarofimian bhajji."

"Pcas, beans, carrots, onions . . . ?"

"Yes. That's it."

"I'd like the recipe."

There was a silence. Then there was hemming and haw ing.

"I'm a cook myself," I said. "I know that lots of cooks lik to keep their secrets."

"Well, then you understand that . . ."

"I'm also a police officer," I said. "I'm asking unofficially but I can make it official if you like. I'd appreciate your co operation. As odd as this may sound, the recipe may help i an investigation."

"Really?" The voice perked up. And why not? After all how many cooks can say that about their wares?

"Really." I asked if I could come down that afternoon an pick up the recipe. The voice said yes.

I found leftover salad makings and some smoked blue fish in the fridge. I mixed them together and slid the mixtur into a piece of pita bread. Then I went outside with a secon beer and sat in the sun and looked across Anthier's Pond a the beachers at the Bend in the Road.

The Bend in the Road is the first bit of sand you hit when you drive from Edgartown to Oak Bluffs along the beach road. It got its name because there's a bend in the road right there, and some keen-thinking Vineyarder took note of that fact and named the spot accordingly. I also call it Mother's Beach because there's a lifeguard there and the mothers of small children like that and the fact that they can park their cars right next to the sand, that the water slopes gently away, and that there's usually no surf, thanks to normally offshore winds.

There's a parking area at the bend which in summer months is usually filled by mid to late morning. Beyond it, all the way along the road to Oak Bluffs, other cars park by the side of the road next to the sand. It's a great beach for owners of two-wheel-drive cars because they don't have to lug all of their blankets and umbrellas and children very far. The cars stay there until late in the afternoon, when their beached-out owners head for the barn. Edgartown has the state's most convenient beaches. Unlike other towns on and off the island, it requires no special stickers and charges no parking fees for the use of its beaches. After you live in Edgartown you're insulted if you have to pay to go to a beach.

After thinking these provincial thoughts and finishing my lunch, I drove to Katama, found Katama Caterers, and got the recipe for Sarofimian bhajji. It looked pretty good. On the way home I stopped at the A & P and bought the ingredients. I phoned the hospital and left a message for Zee, who was busy helping bandage up another moped victim.

"Come to supper," I said.

She did.

18

Zee was met with Absolut in a chilled glass. I guided her out to a lawn chair, pulled off her shoes, and put her feet on yet another chair. I put crackers, cheese, and bluefish pate on the table beside her drink.

"This is the way it should be," she said, leaning back. "Maybe I'll arrange to have you travel around the country giving seminars on how men should greet their women in the evening."

"An excellent idea. You can travel with me and illustrate how the women can show their appreciation later that night."

"What are you, a professional man who wants to be paid for all services? All of a sudden I feel a headache coming on."

"No tit for tat, eh?"

"Is that what you call this welcoming ceremony? A tat?"

I hadn't thought of that pun. "Ha, ha. Just relax. You've had a hard day at the office, but old J.W. knows how to fix you up. I will ply you with booze and food and send you home a new woman, able to face the world with a smile."

I got my own Absolut and we sat and watched the evening deepen. She told me about her day at the hospital emergency room. Three mopeders had bitten the Vineyard dust, someone had gotten a metal filing in his eye, the police had brought in a drunk who had fallen out of the bunk in his cell and broken his nose. A normal victim list for a Vineyard summer day.

After a while I went in and finished the cooking: chicken baked in an orange sauce, white rice, and Sarofimian bhajji. I went out and invited Zee in.

As she came through the door, her nose twitched. Then

she thought and then she sniffed some more. I sat her down at the table and poured white wine. She looked at the bhajji.

"Say, I don't remember having this before. Looks delicious."

"An old family recipe. Let's dig in."

We did. Another excellent meal from the kitchen of J.W. Jackson. I am the first to praise my cooking when it works.

"Well," I said, "what do you think of the veggies?"

"I've never had this dish before, but there's something about it . . ."

"That's familiar?"

"Yes. It's not the vegetables. I've had all of them before. It must be the . . ." She leaned forward and sniffed the bhajji. Her eyes widened. "It's the spices." She looked at me. "I smelled these spices when they had me tied up!"

I felt happy. "Coriander and cumin. They use a lot of it in Middle Eastern cooking. Indian cooking. Sarofimian cooking."

"Sarofimian cooking . . . ?"

"Unless you have some other Middle Eastern or Indian types mad at you, I think you got grabbed by some Sarofimians. The Sarofimian Democratic League has my vote."

"The Sarofimian Democratic League? But why? I wouldn't know the Sarofimian Democratic League if I fell over it. What did they want with me?"

"I don't know yet, but I plan to find out. Are you sure about these spices?"

"Yes. I don't know if I ever smelled this particular dish, but I'm sure it was this combination of spices. But what did I ever do to the Sarofimian Democratic League? The only Sarofimians I've ever seen are that Padishah and his henchman in the boat." She shivered. "And I have a feeling that if either one of them managed to grab me I wouldn't have gotten off so easily."

"I think you're right about that, so I'm pretty sure it wasn't them. The only other Sarofimians that are on the island are students, so they're prime suspects. When I find the right ones, I'll find out why."

"Hey," said Zee, "easy now." She put her hand on my arm.

I saw that my hands were fists. I eased them open and willed away a tightness behind my eyes.

"They didn't hurt me," she said gently. She was dedicated to healing wounds, including her own. She smiled. "I don't need avenging."

"You're right," said my voice.

"Let's have coffee."

"Good idea." While we drank it, I told her of my conversations with the people I'd met.

"I can't believe Willard Blunt had anything to do with me being kidnapped," said Zee, when I was through. "He and Aunt Amelia have been friends for decades. He was a very nice man."

I'd thought so too. But then Caesar had considered Brutus quite a guy.

"If you spend the night, we can talk about this until morning."

"You're predictable and sweet," said Zee, "but I have to go home. You cook a great meal and you make a flawless martini, but I don't want to live with you. Yet."

Yet. "Yet?"

"At least yet. Are you mad at me?"

"Would it help if I was?"

"No."

"How about if I'm happy with you?"

"Are you?"

"Yes."

"Well, it helps, but not enough to keep me from going to my own house."

"Drat. Phone me when you get home."

"You don't have to watch over me, Jefferson."

"Humor me."

"What if I don't?"

"I'll come up and see how things are myself."

"I thought so! I'll call you."

She did. After I hung up I put out the thermos, made sandwiches for two, set the alarm for four, and went to my lonesome bed.

There isn't too much light at four in the morning in August, but by the time I made instant coffee, packed the sandwiches, collected light rods and a tackle box, and got some sand eels out of the freezer, it was getting brighter.

I drove down through sleeping Edgartown to Collins Beach, unchained my dinghy from the seawall, and loaded it in the back of the LandCruiser. Long ago, my father just pulled his dinghy up above the high-water mark and left it, but for years now no unchained dinghy has been safe, particularly during Regatta week. The gentlemen yachtsmen borrow them after late nights of drinking and go out to their million-dollar boats and then set the dinghies adrift. Now we keep all our dinghies chained up. So it goes.

I dropped the dinghy overboard in Oak Bluffs harbor and at five-thirty was outside Bonzo's door. Bonzo was waiting.

"Hey, J.W., here I am."

"There are already some guys ahead of us," I said.

"They won't get 'em all," he said confidently.

"None of us may get any. Bonito are harder to hook than bluefish and harder to keep, too."

"But we'll get one, won't we?" Bonzo never doubted that I could catch a fish almost whenever I wanted one. I couldn't bring myself to shatter that simple faith. I decided, as I always did, to let God do it, if it had to be done.

"We'll give it a shot," I said.

We unloaded the gear into the boat, and I parked the LandCruiser in the parking lot where the *Ocean Queen* loads and unloads its daily hordes of day-trippers from the Cape.

My trusty little Seagull kicked over as always, and we putted out through the channel between the stone jetties into the brightening east.

The sea was flat and dark. We hooked to the right and motored down to the dock where the big ferryboats landed. For reasons known only to bonito, the ferry dock is a good place to hunt them. We pulled around the end of the dock and found a half dozen other boats before us. They had the choice spots right next to the pilings. I found a place a little farther out and dropped anchor.

"Hey," said Bonzo, looking around. "This is neat."

It *was* neat. A cool morning promising to warm, flat water, a brightening sky, fish to be caught, and time set aside to catch them. Was there a fish pond in Eden?

We put sinkers on the lines and bobbers above them and sand eels on the hooks and we made our casts. Then we sat and watched the bobbers. Nothing happened.

No matter. The day grew lighter, and suddenly there was the sun, like a giant orange, rising from the sea. There were stringy dark clouds just above the horizon, and the orange ball of sun walked into the sky behind them. We sat and watched the new day being born. The dinghy rose and fell on tiny swells that bent the mirror of water beneath us.

My bobber dipped.

I waited a second and set the hook, then reeled in.

My hook was empty. Some wily fish had stolen my sand eel. I put on another one and cast out again.

In the next hour our bobbers bobbed and our eels were snickered away. The air grew warmer and we slipped out of our jackets. The sun rose above the clouds, and a small breeze ruffled the surface of the water. I felt lazy and good.

Bonzo yelped. His bobber was out of sight. He yanked the tip of his rod into the air. The line started cutting through the water. His reel zinged as the line ran out. I got my line in out of the way.

"Hey!" cried Bonzo. "Lookie, lookie!"

"Get him!" I said.

Other fishermen looked at us. Bnozo's line snaked away, slowed, then hooked back.

"Reel him in. Keep that line tight!"

Bonzo reeled like a madman as the fish raced toward the boat and then, at the last moment, peeled away. Bonzo's reel sang.

The fish turned back and Bonzo reeled. The fish went under our boat, and I tipped the Seagull up so the line wouldn't snag.

"Wow!" yelled Bonzo as the fish tore away from us and the line snaked off the reel once more.

I got the net. The fish was still full of beans, but was slowing. Bonzo reeled, and the fish flashed alongside the boat, in plain sight now. Then he was gone on another of those wonderful runs, but a slower and shorter run this time. Then he was under the boat again, and as he came up, I netted him and swung him into the dinghy. Bonzo fell over backwards and almost dropped his rod.

"A nice one!" I said, feeling a grin filling up my face. "A damned nice bonito!"

The hook was about one flip of the fins from being torn from his mouth, but it was too late for any escape now. Calls of congratulations came from the other boats.

Bonzo was as happy as a human could be. "Hey, I got one! I got him, J.W.!"

"Yes, you did! You got yourself a really nice fish. This is the only fish anybody's caught today! Hold him up so the other guys can see him."

Bonzo did, and the other fishermen waved and laughed and made statements about some people having all the luck. Bonzo grinned and waved and finally sat down.

"Now you get one, J.W.," he said. "Then we'll both have a fish."

"I don't know," I said. "You're outfishing me so far. Maybe you got the last one."

He thought and thought and finally remembered the fishing maxim. He grinned. "If you don't throw, you don't know," he said.

"You're right." I made my cast. I felt good.

We fished all morning, but that was the only fish we caught. I thought it was enough. As we putted back into the harbor at eleven, I asked Bonzo if he'd found anybody from Sarofim.

"No. Not one. I tell you what I did, J.W. If anybody talked sort of funny, you know, or maybe looked like they came from someplace else I don't know about, I went right up to them and said 'I think you're from someplace I don't know about. Are you?' I did just that, and, you know, they weren't mad or anything, ever. There was two people from a place called Kenya. That's in Africa someplace. There was three from Japan. But there wasn't any from Sarofim." He looked at me with a happy face. "You know what the funniest people said? They said they lived in a guitar! I laughed. I think that's pretty funny, don't you, J.W.?"

"Pretty funny," I agreed. He was full of pleasure about his fish.

"They been in there before, sometimes, but I never asked them anything before. But this time I said, 'You live in a guitar?' And they said yes, and we all laughed. And you know something else, J.W.?"

"What?"

"One of them is one of the people who like those musicians you like too. I think that is very funny, don't you?"

What musicians? We pulled up to the dock. "Tell me what's funny, Bonzo."

"Don't you get it, J.W.? The people who live in a guitar like the Gits! Guitar, Gits. You get it, J.W.? Gits and guitar are almost the same sound! Funny!"

I put a grin on my face. "Get your fish, Bonzo. Your mom is going to be very pleased."

"Yeah," he beamed. "Yeah, she will."

"Were the guitar people in the Fireside last night, Bonzo?"

His brow wrinkled, then smoothed again. "Last night? Yes, last night. They usually come in late, you know, just before we close up. The one girl, she puts money in the machine and plays the Gits. They all like the Gits, but she likes them best of all." He looked at me with his great empty eyes. "She likes the Gits just like you do, I guess, J.W. Say, when can we go fishing again? I like fishing for bonito."

"Sometime soon. You're ahead of me and I have to try to catch up."

I drove him home. His mother came out of her gingerbread house and admired his wonderful fish. Bonzo smiled his wide, bright smile, waved, and took the fish inside.

"Thank you, J.W.," said his mother.

"You should be proud of him," I said.

"I am. Oh, I am."

I drove back to the dock and loaded the dinghy into the LandCruiser.

The people who lived in a guitar liked the Gits. The people who lived in Gwatar liked the Gits, and one of them liked the Gits a lot. Zee's abductors played Git music until Zee was sick of it.

I drove up to the hospital, parked, and walked up to the emergency room door and peeked in. Zee was talking to a young doctor in a white coat. I sneaked back to my car.

I drove to Edgartown and chained the dinghy back in its place by the seawall. Then I went home for lunch. I felt like a hound who had finally picked up a scent.

19

I went down to the police station after lunch and stopped by the Chief's office. Naturally he wasn't there, so I drove on downtown and actually found a parking place on Main Street. After a half an hour on Main, a meter maid will come by and nail you with a ticket, but I thought a half hour should be enough. I found the Chief coming out of the courthouse. Policemen spend very little time catching criminals and a lot of time doing paperwork. We leaned on his cruiser, and I told him what Bonzo had said. When I was through, he grunted. "Now I imagine you're going to go up to the Fireside tonight and hope the Gwatar people come in so you can follow them home or some such thing."

"They didn't make you the Chief for nothing," I said admiringly. "I want to get in touch with Jake Spitz. How do I do it?"

He dug out his little notepad and read off a phone number. "I doubt if he's there," he said. "Why do you want to talk to him?"

"I want to find out what the Padishah and his bodyguard are up to. I don't even know if they're still on the island."

"Does it make any difference?"

"It might. My anonymous phone caller said some foreigner was out to damage me and Zee. The Padishah is the only guy I know who might fit that description, and I think Colonel Nagy is the man he'd send to attend to the job. The Padishah doesn't strike me as the type to do his own dirty work."

"Is that the only reason you want to know where they are?"

"You sound doubtful. You're becoming a suspicious old man."

"Is that the only reason?"

"No. Nagy pulled a gun when Zee pushed his boss overboard. I don't know guns as well as Manny Fonseca does, but it looked to me like about a 9 mm semiautomatic. I'd like to know if the Colonel still has his pistol or whether it's the one found in Willard Blunt's hand."

"Would you recognize it if you saw it?"

"I don't know."

"Too bad."

"I'll give Spitz a call."

"No need, if that's all you wanted to ask him. The Padishah is in Washington with Ed Damon and that Standish Caplan fellow. I think the idea is to glue this treaty together in spite of the necklace being stolen. He's getting the red-carpet treatment. Meetings with bigwigs in the Administration, Pentagon, and so forth."

"And Colonel Nagy?"

"Ah. He's back on Chappy. Came back from Boston by copter on Tuesday when his boss flew down to Washington. The Padishah's man in the hunt for the necklace."

"And how are the forces of truth and justice doing?"

"Not so good. There is some new information, though. The autopsy report on Blunt just came in."

"Death by gunshot wound to the head?"

"A 7.65 slug. One round fired from the gun in his hand, incidentally. The magazine was one short, so it was the round in the chamber. Went right up through Blunt's brain and lodged in the roof of the Jeep. Something else. Blunt was filled with cancer. Lucky to have lived long enough to kill himself."

"Is that right?'

"It is. Now maybe we know why he shot himself."

"Maybe. The bullet definitely came from that gun?"

"According to the FBI lab."

"You're a fountain of information today, Chief. I'm impressed."

"I'm tired of having half the cops in the world crawling around town. I want this case solved so I can get back to PCing drunks and listening to people complain about their parking tickets. I'm so desperate that I'm even talking to you."

"Parking tickets!" I looked at my watch. "I gotta go!"

I was just in time. The meter maid was one car away when I got to the LandCruiser. I gave her a big smile, and she, being a nice college girl, smiled back. She wasn't mean; she just had a job to do. I drove down and got in line for the Chappy ferry. I was giving them a lot of business lately. I decided I'd charge it to my boss, just like my father, who had been a radio-drama fan, told me Johnny Dollar used to do. Jasper Cabot could afford to give me an expense account.

There was still a cop at the gate to the Damon place, but he let me in. The helicopter was still sitting on the lawn. It costs a lot of money to keep a helicopter on hand like that, but the Padishah apparently had enough to manage it.

I got past the Thornberry man at the door and found Helga Johanson in thc library with George. The tables were still covered with papers, and George was on the phone. It was hard to tell whether they'd made any progress on the case.

"I'm looking for Nagy," I said.

"You're welcome to him," said Helga. "He hasn't done one thing to help solve this case. He's around here somewhere. Upstairs, maybe, in the Padishah's suite."

"I'll find him. How are you doing?"

"I'm ready for that evening out. We're on the last of the names on our lists. Not an honest suspect among them."

I told her about the autopsy. She hadn't heard.

"Cancer. I'm not surprised. He didn't look like a well man."

True. I told her about the Colonel's pistol. That interested her more.

"Does he still have his pistol?" I asked. "Would you know it if you saw it?"

"I never saw it," she said. "I saw the holster on his uniform belt and I figured he carried one under his shirt when he was in civvies, but I never saw it. It would be interesting if he didn't have it now, wouldn't it."

"I'm going to ask him about that right now. You want to come along?"

"I think I will," she said.

"By the way," I said. "I'd really like to know one thing. Last Saturday. Where did you carry your piece? I looked you over pretty well and I didn't see one bulge that didn't belong there."

She gave me a sweet smile. "None of your business. A lady has to have some secrets. Shall we go?"

We went upstairs and down the hall to the Padishah's suite of rooms. Helga knocked on a door, and after a moment the door opened and Colonel Ahmed Nagy stood there. He was wearing summer trousers and a short-sleeved shirt. His dark mustache split his hatchet face in two.

He raised a brow above an expressionless eye. "Yes?"

"Mr. Jackson has some questions," said Helga.

"Has he? Well, please come in." He stepped aside. His words were polite, but his voice was like his face, dark and cutting. A voice like a saw, like a knife, like his profession.

We went in. There were soft chairs near an open window overlooking Edgartown Harbor. Through the window I could see the Edgartown waterfront beyond the anchored yachts. The spire of the old whaling church was clear and white. A large yawl was leaning into a gentle northeast wind as it tacked out past the town wharf. That same wind was soft and cooling as it rustled the curtains at the window. We sat down in the chairs.

"May I offer you wine?"

"I thought wine was not drunk by Muslims."

"Ah, not by many, perhaps, but by me. Yours is said by some to be a Christian country, and though I see no great evidence of that save in the number of churches in your towns, perhaps I should quote your Saint Paul, who advised us to take a little wine for our stomachs' sake and for our oft infirmities. Or shall I cite the poet Khayyám, who held that since beautiful girls and wine were the promise of heaven they were also to be enjoyed on earth?" His hooded eyes were deep beneath his brows. "Or, perhaps," he said, "you would like coffee. I have that too."

"Nothing," said Helga.

"Nothing," I echoed.

"Then I will enjoy this vintage alone," said Nagy, bringing a decanter and glass to a table beside his chair. He gestured toward the window. "A lovely view. We have a few such yachts in Gwatar. They are like beautiful seabirds. What are your questions, Mr. Jackson?"

"You have a pistol. I'd like to see it."

His eyes floated toward Helga, then came back to me. "As you no doubt are aware, I have diplomatic immunity, Mr. Jackson. I need tell you nothing. May I ask why you're interested in my pistol?"

"Yes. Willard Blunt was shot to death with a 7.65 mm Beretta pistol manufactured for the Sarofimian military. It's not the sort of gun that's seen on Martha's Vineyard. If you don't have your pistol, it could be that yours was the one that killed Blunt."

"Ah. And I might be a suspect in the killing. A murderer, perhaps."

"Maybe. Can I see your pistol?"

He surprised me. "Of course." He got up and went through a door on one side of the sitting room.

"Adjoining bedrooms on both sides," said Helga, nodding at another door opposite the one Nagy had exited by. "I think that Zakkut and Youssef shared that room while they were here."

I nodded. Zakkut, the Padishah's physician and political advisor, and Dr. Omar Youssef, the curator of the National Museum of Sarofim. Both now with the Padishah in Washington, I imagined. Nagy came back to his chair and handed me a pistol.

It was a Beretta 9 mm Parabellum. I dropped the clip out. Full. I snapped the slide back and a round popped into the air. Nagy's hand flashed, and he caught the bullet before it hit the floor.

"It's dangerous to hand loaded weapons to people," I said.

"All weapons should be presumed to be loaded, Mr. Jackson."

True enough. I looked at the pistol, then replaced the magazine and handed it back. "Is this the pistol you were carrying when the Padishah nearly ran us down with his cigarette boat?"

"As I recall, Mr. Jackson, on that day you very gallantly stepped between me and the woman who had just pushed my master overboard. You had a look at my pistol then. What do you think now? Is this the weapon?"

"I don't know. I do know that this isn't one of the weapons that Beretta makes for the Sarofimian military."

"My master's private security force is a branch of the Sarofimian military. We are armed with the standard weapons, I assure you. With exceptions, of course."

"Such as this weapon for yourself?"

"Perhaps."

"How do you think Willard Blunt happened to have a Sarofimian pistol?"

"I'm sure you have a theory."

"Not really. Could he have stolen yours?"

"Stolen my pistol? Do you imagine that an elderly and ill man such as Blunt could steal my pistol?" Nagy's thin lips actually formed a smile.

"It's possible. There were some light fingers on Chappy last weekend. Did any other member of the Padishah's party carry a pistol?"

"Only the master himself and he, being a great fan of James Bond motion pictures, insists upon arming himself with a Walther PPK 7.65 mm. Sometimes he even carries it in a Burns-Martin triple-draw holster. It is a constant worry to me, as you might guess. Of course I need not tell you about his weapon, since you took it away from him only last Saturday night."

True. "You haven't answered my question. Is this the pistol you were carrying on the boat that day?"

"And if it is not?"

"Then Blunt may have been shot with your pistol."

"And I may be a suspect in that shooting."

"Not necessarily. If I were you and I wanted to murder Blunt and make it look like suicide, I certainly wouldn't leave my pistol in his hand. That doesn't make sense."

The Colonel turned his wineglass and held it against the light from the window. The wine swirled like a huge liquid ruby.

"I'd have used another pistol," I went on. "And not this one here, either."

"Indeed? And why not this one?" The Colonel sipped his wine.

"This one's brand-new. It can be traced to a dealer. It doesn't even look like it's been fired. I think you might have gotten it in Boston on Monday. Did you?"

"My dear fellow, I am impressed."

"I've been thinking," said Helga, adjusting her skirt to rid it of some imperfection of appearance that I could not see. "Blunt drove you into town on Sunday to meet with Spitz, the FBI man . . ."

"Yes. We met Spitz at his Edgartown hotel at seven to discuss the case. Afterwards, I told Blunt that I planned to walk home. Blunt went on to visit a friend. I stayed a bit longer with Spitz, then came back here, as you know."

"Arriving very late."

"Yes. I walked through the town for a time, stopped for a drink, then walked here from the ferry."

"Or from the parking lot where Blunt was shot."

Nagy's hand passed over the pistol on the table and took up the decanter. He poured himself another glass. "But, madam, the ferryman has testified that he brought me over and saw me walking in this direction."

"Yes, but perhaps Willard Blunt was waiting for you down the road."

He gave her an admiring look. "I have often advised His Majesty to employ more women in his secret service, but he is a child in many ways. He uses them or abuses them, but never appreciates their subtlety. Perhaps it is time that I told you the truth about that evening."

20

I am a peculiar fellow," said Colonel Ahmed Nagy. "I am sworn to defend and serve my Padishah with my life and will do that. But, I tell you, my young friends, my Padishah is a child in a man's body. He is willful, impatient, cruel, sometimes kind, ever in need of a father or a guide to advise him, yet resentful of that advice. He is well educated, yet is a man without thought. If he were not a Padishah, he would be a petty rug dealer, a seller of second-rate olive oils, a voyeur peeping through screens at other men's wives and daughters, a man of no consequence or potential.

"But he *is* the Padishah and is therefore a person of consequence, a person with enemies, a person, in this case, who needs to find that necklace and bring it home to Sarofim. And I am ordered to find it now that it is lost.

"Shall I tell you that although I have dedicated my life to serving His Majesty, I find my work on this planet to have no more meaning than that of a cloud moving across the sky or a great stone settling deeper into the dust? I am, like your Hemingway's Jacob Barnes, not capable of being engagé. Like Khayyám, my religion is to be free of belief and unbelief. Yet I have sworn to serve and am, thus, obliged to act as though my work is of significance while knowing that it is not. Am I making myself clear? No matter. I will now tell you the tale of last Sunday night.

"In the early evening I arranged to meet with the FBI man, Spitz, at his hotel. Blunt drove me there, and the three of us discussed the matter of the missing necklace. We had little information to exchange, but spent perhaps an hour considering the case. Blunt then said he was going to visit a friend. It was a beautiful moonlit night, as you will recall, and just as it has sometimes been my practice in Sarofim to walk in the desert while I consider problems arising from my work, so I determined to walk home to the Damon house while I considered the issue of the missing emeralds. On my way to the ferry, I strolled through the streets of Edgartown and even stopped for a glass of wine at a bar overlooking the harbor. Very lovely. One day, perhaps, the harbor at Gwatar will host as many fine yachts. But I digress.

"It was perhaps ten o'clock when I crossed to Chappaquiddick on the ferry and walked along the highway. The moonlight was bright on the water, the sand was silver. I thought of my wife, so far away, and wondered if she or our children ever thought of me. Then, ahead, on the side of the road, I saw a Jeep. It was Damon's Jeep, the very one that Blunt had driven when we visited Spitz. Blunt was in the driver's seat and he beckoned me to join him. I was rather mindless, I believe. I got in, and he suggested that we drive to a place overlooking the ocean and talk. I was agreeable, and we drove to that very spot where he was later found dead.

"Immediately in front of us was a short cliff. Beyond it was a span of sand and grass, and beyond that, the ocean. The sand was white, and the moonlight danced on the waves. I remember everything perfectly.

"Blunt said, 'Look out there,' and I did. Then I heard the sound of a revolver being cocked and turned my head and saw, indeed, an old-fashioned revolver in Blunt's hand. It was pointed at me. I recognized it immediately as a Webley .455 caliber. We have them in the national armory. Such weapons were once the standard officers' sidearms in the Sarofimian military. I was sure I was going to be killed. Would it interest you to know that I was very detached about it?

"I had my pistol under my shirt. Blunt took it from my belt. He said, 'Tell the Padishah that the necklace is beyond his reach. Tell him that I took it and that he will be strangled with it by his enemies. Tell him it is wergeld for a girl named Periezade.'

"I understood then that I was not going to die. He ordered

me out of the Jeep and told me to give his message to the Padishah. I walked along the roads to the Damon house, first over a sandy road, then along pavement, then over sand again. The moonlight was brilliant, and the shadows were fathomless. I was all alone. Never had the world seemed more beautiful to me, more mysterious, more alluring. It took me almost an hour to reach the Damon house. There, I told His Majesty what Blunt had said. He became furious, then almost hysterical. He ordered me to force Blunt to reveal the whereabouts of the necklace. He insisted that the FBI, the police, Thornberry Security, seize Blunt. I pointed out that the authorities would have only my word about Blunt's conversation with me and that, in America, respectable men such as Blunt could not be questioned with the same techniques as are sometimes used in Sarofim. Finally, Dr. Zakkut quieted him and gave him a sedative and they began to speak of the political consequences of the theft.

"In the morning we received word of Blunt's death, apparently by my weapon, and realized that even greater political complications might result from his use of that weapon. Zakkut immediately contacted young Standish Caplan, and we all flew off to Boston so His Majesty could go on to Washington. It was decided that I should return here to try to find the necklace. As you know, I have not found it."

Nagy turned his glass in the light from the window. He drank and looked at us with those hooded eyes. "Is that the story you want? Does that clarify any matters for you? You are perhaps pleased that your guesses were so astute?"

"You bought this pistol in Boston, then?"

"In my profession a pistol is necessary. You understand."

"Yes. And Blunt shot himself. You did not shoot him."

"I did not shoot him. Someone else may have."

"What about the revolver you say he had? It hasn't been found."

"No one's looked for it," said Helga.

"Indeed," said Nagy, giving her an appreciative look. "If I were to seek it, I'd not search far from the spot where Blunt's body was found."

"There's another matter," I said. "A little bird has whispered in my ear that some people from a foreign land have bad intentions toward Mrs. Zeolinda Madieras and me. You and your boss are the only people I know who might fit that description, and I want you to understand that I will take considerable umbrage should anything unseemly happen to Mrs. Madieras."

The Colonel almost smiled. "And what of yourself, Mr. Jackson? Should something unseemly happen to you, will you also take umbrage at that?"

"I can take care of myself."

"I have seen Mrs. Madieras only once, but my impression of her is that she too is quite able to take care of herself." The Colonel looked at Helga Johanson. "As are you, I understand. Such a country. Common men and women treating the Padishah of Sarofim as if he were no better than a beggar. Tsk. He is unaccustomed to such rejection. What is the poor fellow to think?"

"That Martha's Vineyard is not Sarofim."

"It is my understanding that His Majesty will be returning to his own country in a very few days." His eyes roamed about the room, settling here and there for a moment and then passing on. "Tell me about your little bird, Mr. Jackson. A cock or a hen? An owl? A hawk? A dove?"

"Only a voice speaking in my ear, Colonel. Perhaps you will whisper in His Majesty's ear that if he is one of the persons of whom my bird spoke, he might be well advised to change his plans about Mrs. Madieras."

Nagy's hand stretched across the table beside his chair again, passing over the pistol lying there. He took the decanter of wine and refilled his glass. "His Majesty is not always receptive to recommendations that he change his plans. He is, after all, a Padishah."

"One last thing. Mrs. Madieras was kidnapped last Friday night and released unharmed this past Tuesday morning. She was blindfolded all that time, and her captors never spoke to her. Do you know anything about that?"

Nagy actually looked interested. The hoods lifted momentarily from his eyes. "Kidnapped? Really? And not harmed? Not even raped?"

"No."

"Astonishing. Such a desirable woman. I confess I am surprised by this tale. I assure you that I know nothing of the matter at all." The hoods lowered again. "From Friday until Tuesday, eh? Much occurred between those times. Do you want my first thoughts on the subject?"

"Yes."

"She is lying about the abduction. The timing is too coincidental. She is involved in the theft of the necklace."

"She's not lying."

"Spoken like a man in love, Mr. Jackson. I am not a man in love. Calm yourself, sir. Surely you cannot believe that I intend to harm Mrs. Madieras and at the same time believe that I had her in my custody and did not harm her. You must choose one or the other of those theories, not both."

"I don't think you abducted her, but I think someone did. Who might that be, do you suppose?"

He shrugged. "Is she a foolish woman?"

"She is not."

"Then perhaps I'm wrong about her lying. An intelligent woman would create a more likely story to explain her absence. Do you agree?"

"Yes."

"Unless she is clever enough to know that we would think that."

"You live in a convoluted world, Colonel."

"Yes. I regret that I can be of no assistance to you in this matter. I will think upon it, however." He sipped his wine. "Oh, by the way, should any of the information I've given you become public, I will, of course, feel free to deny it."

I got up. "Of course."

"But of course you will tell your superiors."

"Of course."

Downstairs, Helga Johanson looked at me. "Well, that was enlightening. A kidnapping, eh? I hadn't heard of that. I'll telephone the police and give them Nagy's story. Maybe they can find that revolver. If they can, it will lend credence to the Colonel's tale. And there's this matter of the little bird whispering in your ear. I want to know everything. It might all tie together."

"So you're not going to leave this enigmatic stuff to us manly men, eh? Okay. I'll give you the details tonight while you're squandering your boss's money on me. I'll pick you up at seven."

I drove to Amelia Muleto's house. It was mid afternoon, and the sun was hot. No one answered my knock, so I went around the side of the house and found her out back weeding her vegetable garden.

"Just in time," she smiled, sitting back on her heels. "I'm ready for a cup of tea." She put out a hand, and I pulled her up. "Thanks. I don't suppose I could interest you in some tomatoes or zucchini . . . ? No, I thought not. Come in, dear."

Over tea we discussed Zee's adventure. "Spooky," said Amelia. "I can't imagine what it was all about. Thank goodness she wasn't hurt. I'm so grateful for that."

"Me too. Was Willard Blunt here on Sunday night about eight o'clock?"

"Yes. Poor Willard. He didn't look at all well. And just a few hours later he was dead. Quite shocking."

"The autopsy revealed that he had cancer throughout his body. Did you know about that?"

She nodded. "Ah. Yes, I did. He confided in me, but asked me to keep it to myself. He didn't want sympathy, you know. Said that he'd had a long and good life and had no complaints. He was in considerable pain, however, and that bothered me. He was on some sort of medication. That last night he seemed quite frail, I thought."

"What did you talk about?"

"Talk about?" She picked at a thread on her shirt. "Nothing, really. Looking back, I understand that he was making his last visit with me, but I didn't realize it then. He kissed me when he left . . ." She seemed uneasy at her recollections. "We talked of friends and—well, nothing notable. Small talk. You know . . ."

"Did he mention the theft of the necklace?"

"The theft? Well, yes . . . Of course we talked about it. Not that there was anything new to discuss . . ."

"Did he say he had stolen it?"

Tea sloshed from her cup. She looked at me with wild eyes. "What?!"

I told her what Nagy had told me. Amelia gazed at me as I spoke, and gradually the color which had fled her face returned.

"Are you sure about this, J.W.? Is that Nagy person to be trusted?"

"Willard never said any such thing to you, then?"

"Heavens no! What a remarkable notion!"

"Did Willard mention a girl named Periezade?"

She frowned at her teacup for a moment, then shook her head. "This Colonel Nagy gave you some very interesting information."

"Have you ever heard the name?"

"I . . . perhaps I have. It's a name I think I would have remembered had I heard it often. Who is it?"

"I don't know. It reminds me of Scheherazade. Do you have the telephone number of the professor who wrote *Free People?* You know, the book about Sarofim."

"*Free People.* Of course. Hamdi Safwat. He teaches at Weststock College. No, I don't have his number. I'm sorry. I still have his address . . ."

"That's okay. I can get his number. Maybe he can tell me if Periezade is a Sarofimian name. So Willard Blunt came by, you think now, just to say goodbye. You had no idea that he was considering suicide?"

Amelia had almost recovered her composure. "No, I did not. And he certainly did not confess to stealing the necklace. What an extraordinary notion that is!"

"He seems to have been an unusual man."

She looked thoughtful, then pushed back a strand of hair with her hand. "Yes. It seems that he was. Dear Willard . . ."

21

I showered, shaved, and dressed up in my most splendid Vineyard clothes: blue blazer, blue tie with little whales on it, Vineyard-red slacks held up by a belt decorated with sailing boats, and, to suggest that perhaps I just came off of one of the yachts anchored in the harbor, boat shoes with no socks. I admired myself in the mirror, got into the Land-Cruiser, and drove to the ferry. The ferryman was impressed for the second time in one week.

"You're becoming a very dashing fellow," he said. "First a tux and now this. What will the guys at Wasque think?"

"You working-class people will never understand," I said.

Helga Johanson was waiting at the door. She looked quite smashing, with her golden hair done up and a golden necklace at her throat above a black summer dress. I told her so.

"Thank you." She climbed into the LandCruiser without a single sarcastic remark, and we rattled back to the ferry.

The ferryman looked at Helga and bowed his head. "I didn't think it was possible, J.W., but I may have underestimated you all these years."

"She's my sister," I said.

Helga laughed.

We ate at the Shiretown, where I have never had a bad meal, and afterwards went to the Harborside for Cognac. The Harborside has the best view in town, looking out, as it does, over Edgartown Harbor. We sat and looked at the lights on the boats and in the windows of the houses down harbor. There were lights on the second floor of the Damon house, and I wondered if Colonel Nagy was still in his room sipping wine and looking at us as we were looking at him. I

›ld Helga everything I'd been told so far, which wasn't ıuch but seemed to be adding up.

"Of course people may be lying," she said when I was ırough. "The Colonel is probably right to suspect that. You ıspect it too, don't you?"

"Maybe that's one of the reasons I got out of the cop busiess. I don't like spending my life not believing people."

"I thought you got out of the business because you got ıot and have a bullet still in you."

"That too. And then my wife left me because she'd been cop's wife for years and she'd been worried all the time bout something like that happening and as soon as she new that I'd not be crippled, she knew she'd had enough. he wanted a marriage where she could expect her husband) come home every night and where she wouldn't be afraid) start a family. After she left I thought she was probably ght, so I left too. Or something like that."

"I read somewhere that for years in New York City no cop ad ever been killed by a handgun at a distance of more than wenty feet. I think that may be true. Most of the cops who et it, get it at close range. You got yours at a distance, I ear."

"Your agency is full of snoops."

"It's one of the things we do for a living. I got your file om the old man himself. I guess he did a checkup on you hen you left the force. Wanted to hire you, I think. How did ou happen to get shot?"

"It was night. An alarm had gone off, and my partner and happened to be right there. My partner took the front, and ran around back. Somebody came out of a door and started unning down the alley. I yelled stop and police and all that, ut naturally the person just kept running, so I ran too. It was ark and both of us kept running into things. Boxes and rash barrels. Then the person I was chasing ran into a sort f dead-end alley. The other end was closed off by a metal ence a construction crew had put up while they were building a building on the other side. I was feeling pretty lucky, ut then the woman turned around and shot me. It was the damnedest thing. I fell over, and she came running back by me, still shooting, trying to get away, I guess. As she went past I shot her till my gun went dry. I didn't know it was a woman until later, not that it would have made any difference."

Helga nodded and then looked out at the lights in the harbor. "My dad is a cop. He's never pulled his gun once in thirty years."

"Most don't. It was just one of those things. I don't think about it much anymore."

"The woman died?"

"Oh yes."

We sat silent for a while, then Helga nodded again. "Thanks for telling me. Now let's think about possible liars in this case."

Good. "Anyone could be lying. Blunt might have been lying to Nagy, Nagy might have been lying to us, Zee might have been lying about the kidnapping, Bonzo might have . . . No, I don't think Bonzo remembers how to lie. Who else is there? The Chief? Spitz? You? Me?"

"Bonzo's the kid up at the bar in Oak Bluffs, right? The one who tipped you off about the people in the guitar."

"Right. I'll tell you who I believe. I believe Bonzo and I believe Zee and I believe the investigators on the case. I don't necessarily believe that Spitz, or you, or the Chief, for that matter, have told me everything you think or know, but I don't think you've lied to me. I don't know about Blunt or Nagy."

"How about you? Have you lied to us?"

"That's for you to decide. I'm no problem to me, I'm only a problem for everybody else."

"I don't know why you'd be lying to me."

"I don't either."

"I want to go with you to the bar in Oak Bluffs. You are going up there later tonight, aren't you?"

"Yes, but it's got nothing to do with your work. It has to do with Zee's kidnapping if it has anything to do with anything at all."

"Nagy was right when he said it was an awful lot of coin-
dence that your friend got snatched just long enough for
e necklace to get stolen and Blunt to get shot. Do you
ink Blunt was lying when he told Nagy that he stole the
ecklace?"

"Do you think Nagy was lying when he told us that story?"

"I don't know."

"I don't know either. I'd like to talk to Spitz again and find
ut what he and Blunt and Nagy talked about that Sunday
ght."

"I want to go with you tonight."

"I don't think so."

"If I don't go with you, I'll go alone. Then there'll be you
atching for the guitar people and me watching you. We can
ave a parade."

"You're a tough customer, Johanson."

"Call me Helga."

I gave up. "Well, we can't go dressed like this. We'd stick
ut like sore thumbs. We need some Fireside clothes." I eyed
er. She and Zee were about the same size. "I've got some
othes you can wear, at my place. We can change there."

"Gosh, this is getting exciting. I get to wear your girl-
iend's clothes! Is this kinky, or what?"

"Kinky, shminky. We just won't tell Zee. Get out your
allet."

She waved for the waitress, paid up, and got a receipt for
er expense account. "Lead the way," she said.

She liked my house. Everybody likes my house. I found a
hirt and jeans belonging to Zee and gave them to Helga.
ee's clamming sneakers were a half-size too small, so
elga would have to wear her own low heels. We changed
separate rooms. I felt a lot better in sandals, shorts, and a
e shirt than in my yachtsman-ashore duds. Helga took her
air down and let it fall straight to her shoulders. She now
oked about twenty-one.

"Make sure you take your ID," I said, "or it may be a dry
ght."

We drove to Oak Bluffs. I parked down by the Reliable

Market, and we went into the Fireside. It was a Thursda
night and the crowd wasn't quite what it would be on
weekend, but the blast of sound from the jukebox and th
smells of drink and smoke were about the same. We found
couple of stools at the bar, and the bartender never batted a
eye when Helga ordered a Cognac. I got a Sam Adams
America's best bottled beer. I looked around for Bonzo, bu
didn't see him.

After a while Bonzo came out of the men's room and sav
me. In the Fireside, the men's room is identified by a stenci
of a little boy trying to button his pants. The ladies' room i
identified by a stencil of a little girl pulling up her panties
The Fireside is nothing if not chic. Bonzo came right over.

"Hi, J.W.! Say, that was some fish I caught. That wa
maybe the best fish I ever did catch." He smiled his foolis
smile at Helga. "A bonito," he said. "A nice one."

I introduced them to each other. Bonzo took her hand
"Any friend of J.W.'s is a friend of mine," he said. Then h
turned conspiratorial and leaned closer to me. "Those guita
people aren't here. They ain't been here all night."

"That's okay," I said. "We'll wait. If they show up, let m
know."

"Good," said Bonzo, relieved that he had not disappointe
us. "If they come, I'll be sure to tell you." A glass went ont
the floor somewhere, and the sound of its breaking alerte
Bonzo to his duty. His dim eyes sought out the accident. "
got to go to work," he said. "These people, they brea
glasses and spill things all the time, you know? My gosh
how they break so much is beyond me."

He went off. Helga smiled after him. I told her the ba
acid story I had heard and how he'd gotten his name from
his fondness for Ronald Reagan's movie *Bedtime for Bonzo*

"He's nice," said Helga.

I was on my second beer when the jukebox began to fil
the beery air of the Fireside with the deafening noise of
particularly awful band. I frowned at Helga. She was smil
ing and tapping her finger on the bar. She leaned toward m
and shouted, "The Gits! Terrific!"

The Gits howled and throbbed at me from loudspeakers all round the bar. There was no escaping them. I looked into the mirror behind the bar and saw a girl standing at the jukebox, punching in more coins. As I watched, she bobbed her head in rhythm with the music and turned away. I watched her walk back and sit down in a booth. Then Bonzo was in the mirror beside my own image. "Hey," he yelled. "There's those guitar people!"

I put a finger to my lips, and he immediately put one to his own. A look of dull cunning appeared on his face. He glanced quickly toward the booth and then, using his other hand to shield the gesture, jabbed a finger toward it. His mouth moved silently. I realized he was mouthing "Guitar. Guitar." I smiled at him and nodded. I put my mouth close to his ear and shouted.

"Got it, Bonzo! Thanks!"

He looked conspiratorially at Helga, again touched his finger to his lips, smiled and nodded, and went off.

The Gits bombarded my ears with screams and electronic howls and booms. No one besides Helga seemed to notice them. Helga was happy. She yelled in my ear. "Great stuff! You don't get to hear the Gits too much! Too new, I guess! The sign of a with-it bar!"

Terrific. The men's room was beyond the booth holding the Gits girl and her companions. I walked back past the booth and glanced at its occupants as I passed. I did the same coming back. Three young people. Two women and a man. Two with olive skins and dark hair, the other woman Caucasian in her coloring, but with those fine, sculptured facial bones I had seen in pictures of people from Iran and Pakistan. The man had a beer, and the women were sipping wine. The Gits woman was bobbing to the beat of the music, and all three were smiling. They apparently felt safe in the bosom of the Fireside. The Gits drowned out any words they might have been speaking.

I went back to the bar and, a bit later, got us a booth where we'd be easier to overlook. I couldn't see the back door, but I could see the front one. About midnight the three young people got up and went out the front door. I put some bills on the table, and Helga and I went out after them.

"You get the car," said Helga. "I'll keep track of them."

They went right toward Giordano's, and I went left up the street to the LandCruiser. I was barely inside when Helga came hurrying up the street and climbed into the passenger's seat.

"They're in a Chevy two-door. They should be coming by any minute."

The parking slots on Circuit Avenue are the diagonal kind. I waited until an average-looking Chevy two-door went by and then I tried to back out. But another two cars were not interested in my problems and passed before I could get out of my slot. The Chevy was now three cars ahead, and I was behind a guy who liked fifteen miles an hour as a maximum speed. I watched the lights of the Chevy disappear ahead of me along Circuit Avenue. Christ! The fifteen-miles-an-hour guy flashed his brake lights. There is a universal principle of some kind that says that the slowest drivers use their brakes most often. Scholars argue whether they are slower because they use their brakes so much or whether they use their brakes so much because they're the slowest drivers. Happily for me, in this case, the fifteen-miles-an-hour guy turned left by the Brass Bass. Now there was only one guy between me and the Chevy.

I goosed the LandCruiser and rattled on after the disappeared taillights of the Chevy. The guy between us was also hurrying along, and on Wing Road I caught up with both him and the Chevy's taillights. Both turned west along County Road and a bit farther along the Chevy's brake lights brightened. The Chevy turned right, and the car between us went on. I slowed, found the dirt road the Chevy had taken, and turned off my lights. I got my flashlight out of the glove compartment and found the name of the street. Ocean View Lane. I put the flashlight back into the glove compartment. On Martha's Vineyard, if you can catch even the slightest distant glimpse of the ocean in the dead of winter when there are no leaves on the trees, developers and home owners call their places names like Sea View, Ocean Vista, and Water View.

The moon was a week or more past full, but I could still see by its light. I drove slowly after the Chevy's taillights until they brightened again and the car took a left. I drove to the turnoff and saw the Chevy stopped at a house set at the end of a driveway. I went past, found another driveway, turned around, drove back past the Chevy's drive, and parked.

I got my flashlight from the glove compartment again, and Helga and I got out.

"What do you have in mind?" she asked.

"I just want to see the number on the house."

"Yeah. Everybody's up and around right now. Better to hit them early in the morning when everybody's half-asleep."

"You got it, kid, but I'm going to do a little scouting right now."

"I'm right behind you, then. I just hope they don't have any dogs."

"Zee never mentioned a dog. If there's one here, we've got the wrong house."

There wasn't a dog. There was a floodlight in front of the house, but I came in from the trees and slipped along close to the house itself, ducking under a couple of windows en route, until I got to the porch. Number thirteen. I could see the license plate on the Chevy from there, so I noted that too. To make things complete, I crept around back and located the rear door. Then I slipped away and found Helga waiting. We went back down the driveway, got into the LandCruiser, and drove away.

"When?" she asked.

"Five-thirty?"

"That's good. Nobody's awake at five-thirty."

"You off-islanders are all alike. You sleep away your lives. Here on the Vineyard we've done a half a day's work by five-thirty."

We got back to my house. It was almost one in the morning. Helga yawned and stretched.

"Find your clothes and I'll take you home," I said.

"The ferry's not running."

"We'll go along the beach."

"That's a long way for you to drive."

"No problem."

She ran her hand through her hair. "You have an extra toothbrush?"

"Yes."

"Any objection to my staying here? I want to be in on it when you hit the house in the morning, and by the time you take me home, it'll be time to leave again."

I thought about it. I needed somebody to watch the back door of the house when I went in the front.

"All right."

There was a tingle of sexual energy in the air. Helga's tongue touched her upper lip. She was a lovely woman. She took one step forward, then stopped.

"What is it?" I asked.

"I'm thinking that my husband probably wouldn't approve of me right now."

Husband. Suddenly I was amused. "You can sleep in the room where you changed clothes," I said. "There's an alarm clock in there. Let's not plan on being at the house until six. That way you can get a whole extra half hour of sleep. I want you wide awake in the morning."

"Well, shucks," she said.

"It's not that you lack womanly charms, it's just that I need to get some rest and I don't think I'd get much with you in my bed."

"You're right about that." She grinned. I thought there was actually a note of relief in her voice. "Well, see you in the morning." She went past me into the spare bedroom. I stood there for a moment then went to my own room and set the alarm for five. It took me a while to get to sleep.

▪ 22 ▪

I was awake before my alarm went off, so I turned it off and got up. There was a good deal of light outside already. I could hear Helga stirring. Had her alarm awakened me? I pulled on some clothes and phoned Zee. Being a nurse, Zee had developed the talent of being instantly awake when her phone rang. Phone calls at odd hours meant trouble for someone in need of her services, and she woke up with her brain already in gear. Besides, she had to go to work at eight and was probably about to get up anyway. I reminded her of that as soon as I heard her voice.

"Thanks a lot, Jefferson. I could have slept another hour!"

"Women of your caliber scoff at the idea of extra sleep. You work from dawn to setting sun with smiles on your faces and songs in your hearts. I think I've found the house you were kept in. I'm going to knock on the door at six. Do you want to be there?"

"You're damned right!"

"Meet me on County Road at the corner of Ocean View Lane. That's one of those dirt roads with a fancy name that they're punching out through the oak brush."

"I'll be there."

"Leave your shotgun at home."

"You leave your shotgun at home! I've got to get dressed. Goodbye."

I made instant coffee, toast, and scrambled eggs seasoned with just a bit of Szechuan sauce. By the time Helga emerged from the bathroom, the food was on the table.

"Eat up. We've got to hit the road."

At twenty to six we were on our way. Zee's little Jeep was parked at the corner of Ocean View Lane. Zee was wearing her white uniform. She and Helga exchanged looks. Zee looked again at the jeans and shirt Helga was wearing. Then she looked at me.

"You're right," I said to Zee. "They're your clothes. Mrs. Madieras, Mrs. Johanson. Mrs. Johanson, Mrs. Madieras. Zee, Helga. Helga, Zee."

They shook hands. They were like night and day, the moon and the sun. Dark-haired Zee, golden-haired Helga. There was a poem there somewhere, probably, but I suspected I should not try to write it.

"I'm going to work in two hours," said Zee, a bit testily. "I don't imagine that it'll take longer than that to decide whether this is the place or not."

"We may not manage it at all, but on the other hand, we might. Shock value may help. A knock on the door at six in the morning, a man with a badge, a woman with a badge at the back door, you standing there behind me. We'll see. Any questions? No? Let's go, then."

Zee followed us in her Jeep. We drove to the house and parked in the driveway. The place was absolutely quiet. No lights, no movement. "I have a pistol," I said to Helga. "Do you want it?"

"No. Sam Spade didn't carry one and neither do I."

"Aha! So that's how you managed to wear that slinky blue gown at the big Damon blast. No gat!"

"Oh dear, my secret is out."

"It's safe with me. Let's go. You know how to look official?"

"Trust me."

I did. We compared watch times, and she went around the side of the house and disappeared. Zee came up. At six o'clock I walked up onto the porch and banged on the door. "Open up!" I yelled. "Police! Open up this door right now! Police! Police!"

I thought I sounded pretty good. I banged and banged on the door and rattled the knob. Lights flicked on inside. I could hear movement.

"Open up!" I shouted. "It's the police!

Nothing happened. There was a confused conference

going on inside. If they had any grass, maybe they were flushing it down the drain. I banged on the door and shouted lustily. I glanced back at Zee. She looked caught between laughter and tears. I banged some more.

The door opened a notch. An eye peeked out. "Police!" I yelled and flashed my brand-new badge. "Open up!"

The eye left me and focused on Zee. Voices chattered in a language I did not know. The eye disappeared. I gave the door a kick and it opened. I went in.

Two young women and a young man stood there half-dressed. Across the room the back door swung open. I went over there and looked out. Helga Johanson had a come-along grip on a second young man and was walking him back into the house. He was groaning but doing what he was told, as I probably would have been doing too if I were in his place. Helga's come-along hold was the one where she causes you great pain and makes you think she's going to break your thumb unless you do what she says. And if you don't do what she says, she *will* break your thumb. She and the young man came inside. I shut the door behind them. Zee shut the front door behind her.

"Well, Mrs. Madieras?" I yelled. "You smell that?"

Her fine nose sniffed. She nodded. "Coriander and cumin. That's the smell, all right."

I glared at the four young people. "You're all in deep shit," I said. "Kidnapping is serious business. Your asses are in slings! Sit down!"

They sat down. "You can't just break in here . . ." said one of the women. "This is America . . . !"

"Shut up!" I said. I pointed at Zee, who was looking around with more curiosity than anger. "You recognize that woman? She's the one you kidnapped last Friday night. You're all headed for a long stretch in jail. Or maybe we'll ship you back to Gwatar and let the Padishah have you!"

The man Helga had collared was brave. "You have no warrant, you have no authority to be here. Get out!" I wondered why he had tried to get away. He didn't seem to be a coward. I ignored his words.

"Look around," I said to Zee. "Walk around. Go to the bathroom, look in the refrigerator, get the telephone number. You, Officer Johanson, search the house. I wouldn't be surprised if you found some SDL literature around somewhere. Subversive organization. Seize it if you find it. Firearms too. Anything suspicious."

"You can't—" said the brave young man.

I pulled out my old .38. They sank deeper in their chairs. "You see this," I said. "It says I can do anything I want." I stuck my face in the face of one of the young women. She shrank back. "And what I want," I said, "is a name. I get it, you all can walk. I don't, you go to jail. It's simple. Even a bunch of fucking foreigners like you can understand. I don't give a damn about you. I want the guy who gave the order. Who told you to snatch the woman? Who?!"

I thought I might have made a B-movie bad guy if I really wanted to. Something out of the thirties, maybe. A crooked cop in a Bogart movie, maybe? I grabbed the woman's robe and yanked her up to me. "Talk!"

She wept instead. "I don't know, I don't know!"

"Hey, look at this," said Helga. She waved some pamphlets and a book. "Sarofimian Democratic League stuff. Bad Padishah, good peasants, bad secret police, good Amnesty International. Standard shit. And this." She handed me a copy of *Free People* by Dr. Hamdi Safwat. "More trash," she said. I admired her. She was getting into the act.

The brave young man stood up, afraid but furious. "That is not trash, you idiots, that is the work of a great man."

I shoved him down. "Sit, and shut up." I looked at Zee. "What have you found, Mrs. Madieras?"

She held up a tape. "The Gits' *Starship Parade*. I must have heard it a hundred times."

"That does it," I said. I jerked the second young man to his feet, spun him, and locked his arm behind him. I twisted it and he groaned. One of the women came at me. I pushed her back. "You're all going up. Make it easy on yourselves."

"No," cried the girl. "He can't go back. The police killed his father . . ."

"Fuck him and his father," I said. "Fuck you too. I want a name and you won't give it to me. Okay, I'll get it someplace else. But you'll be in jail. Good riddance. Let's go, Johanson. County jail for the lot of them."

"No," said the second woman. "No! Not jail! Let Anwar go! It was—"

"Be quiet!" Anwar groaned. "Don't tell them anything!"

"What difference does it make?" she cried. "He's dead, isn't he?" She clutched at my arm. "It was a man named Blunt. Mr. Willard Blunt. He told us to kidnap Mrs. Madieras!"

I let Anwar go and pushed him down onto a chair. He rubbed his shoulder, his dark eyes filled with fear and anger. I looked at Zee. Her eyes were wide.

"Willard Blunt?" I asked the woman.

"Yes. Blunt."

It was time for the good cop to take over. "All right," I said. "A deal's a deal. But I need it all. When did he set it up? What did he tell you?"

"Friday night," said the woman. "He telephoned around six. He told us to follow him to her house and to abduct and hold her, but not to hurt her."

"Be quiet!" said the man who had tried to run. But the woman was through being quiet.

"Hush yourself!" she cried. "Do you want to go to jail? Do you want to be sent back to Gwatar? We need you! Quiet your tongue! Blunt is dead. No one can question him." She turned back to me. "He said he would tell us when to release her. But then we learned he was dead and we didn't know what to do. We had a woman we didn't want. We talked for a long time. No one wanted to kill her. We didn't know what to do. So we took her back to her house." She looked at Zee. "Oh, madam, I assure you that we never meant you harm. We were always sorry for your fear, but we had our orders . . ."

"Do not apologize to an oppressor," said the second woman.

"I'm not an oppressor!" said Zee, with steel in her voice. "I never even heard of you people!"

"You are a naïve woman," said the man who had run. "You are a part of a civilization that has supported the corrupt regime of the Rashad dynasty!"

"And you are a foolish boy!" said Zee. "You mouth political platitudes and call them truth. God help the people of Sarofim if you ever become one of their leaders! You don't know the difference between theories and people. You are a child in a man's body. You are no wiser than that fool of a Padishah! I feel sorry for the people of Sarofim if they are doomed to be led by such as you!"

I don't think he looked any more shocked than I imagined I looked. Zee wasn't through. "This girl here," she said, pointing at the woman who had named Blunt, "has more compassion and common sense than a dozen of your kind! She is living in the real world, not in a land of political dreams where children like you can sit in circles and congratulate yourselves on understanding reality so much better than anyone else has ever understood it! You will do well, young man, to keep your mouth shut until you know a great deal more than you know now! You can start by listening to your women!"

"Damn right!" I said, and suddenly realized that I still had the .38 in my hand. I tucked it away in a pocket, out of sight. "Why did Blunt want Mrs. Madieras kidnapped? She knows nothing of politics."

"I do too know something about politics!" flared Zee.

"I don't know," said the woman. "He thought she knew too much . . ."

"About what?"

She looked at her friends. Her eyes flashed. She was done with concealment. "About the necklace. The emeralds. He was afraid she knew something . . ."

"About the theft?"

"We knew nothing of a theft. There was to be an embarrassment to the Padishah. That was all we knew."

"What?" said Zee. "I knew something about an embarrassment to the Padishah? That doesn't make any sense. I knew nothing about any such thing. I didn't even know anything had happened until three days later!"

"Mr. Willard Blunt thought that you did. He wanted you kept quiet until after the work was done. He telephoned us and told us to take you. He stayed with you until we did that, so that you could tell no one of what you knew."

"But I didn't know anything!"

There were tears in the woman's eyes. "But, madam, he said you did. How could we know otherwise? Can you understand?"

"What did Blunt have to do with the SDL?" asked Helga.

The man who had tried to run gave her a mocking look. "Madam, for forty years Mr. Willard Blunt was a chief American supporter of the political opposition to the Rashad dynasty. No one did more over those years to aid the SDL. Always in secret, of course. On Friday, when he needed us, we repaid him a part of the debt we owed." He looked at me with ill-disguised contempt. "Even you, perhaps, can understand that sort of obligation."

"What did he think Mrs. Madieras knew?"

He shrugged. The women shrugged. The other man shrugged.

"I think you're lying," I said.

"No," said the woman. "I was the one to whom he spoke. He never explained. I assure you he did not."

"How did he know how to contact you?"

"Be quiet," said the other woman, but the first woman gestured her words away.

"We knew about the necklace and the ceremony. We were told to cooperate in an effort to embarrass the Padishah. Two of us, with other friends, landed a boat at the Damon dock and made a great scene. Two others threw firecrackers over the Damon fence and then ran away through the woods. Mr. Willard Blunt coordinated our efforts." She looked at me with bright, suddenly proud eyes. "And our efforts were rewarded beyond our wildest dreams! The necklace has been stolen!"

"And you are accessories before and after the fact."

She stared at me and then put her hands over her face.

"No," said the man who had run. "We knew nothing of the

theft until after it happened. We only knew we were to embarrass the Padishah in a certain way and at a certain time."

"And you were willing to abduct Mrs. Madieras."

He looked at the floor.

"Give me your passports," I said. "You first. Officer Johanson, go with him."

He and Helga went into a bedroom and came back with his purple Sarofimian passport. One by one, the others did the same. I copied names and addresses and then put the passports on a table. I saw a look of hope on their faces.

"One more question," I said, looking at the man who had run. "Who were you going to telephone after you escaped out the back door?"

He glared at me. "No one. I was afraid. I ran."

"You are a poor liar," I said. But I was tired of being a bully. "I have no further interest in any of you," I said. "Mrs. Madieras, you may press charges if you wish."

Zee shook her head. "No," she said.

"If that's the way you want it," I said. I glared at the four young people. "I have your names, should I need them. If I were you, I would leave the island on an early boat."

The expressions on their faces were those of people afraid to feel joy. We went out and shut the door behind us.

"Good grief," said Zee. "Remind me to hire you if I ever want some child abused."

"I was pretty good, wasn't I? I can tell you were impressed."

"I'm going to go to work, where all I have to deal with is damage to the flesh. Nice to meet you, Mrs. Johanson. Maybe I'll see you around."

"Call me Helga," said Helga.

"See you later, Jefferson." Zee got into her Jeep and drove toward Oak Bluffs. Helga and I climbed into the Land-Cruiser.

"She's a beauty," said Helga. "I don't think she liked me wearing her clothes."

"I have a silver tongue," I said. "I'll explain everything.

You're a real actress. I was impressed. Officer Johanson, tougher than nails."

"The kid thought so when I tossed him on his ear and led him back inside."

"What do you think about his run?"

"I think you were right. I think he wanted a phone. I think he wanted somebody to know that the kidnapping jig was up."

"I wonder who."

"Maybe we'll find out. I can arrange for these kids to get some real pressure once they get back to Weststock. They're all Weststock students, you know. Their rooms were full of Weststock stuff. Thornberry Security has worked with the college. We know people there. We can arrange for some squeezing if that's what we need."

Back at my house Helga changed into her nice dress and handed me Zee's clothes. "I'd wash these, if I were you. I may have left some of my smell on them."

"Your smell smells pretty good to me."

"To you, maybe, but not to Mrs. Madieras. You look funny."

"I don't feel funny."

"Take me home."

We drove to the ferry. It was early and there was no line. The ferryman looked at me and at Helga in her party dress.

"No comments," I advised.

We drove to the Damon house. "Your husband has a virtuous wife," I said as she got out. "I'll be glad to tell him in case he doesn't know. Where is he, anyhow?"

"Boston. I'm beginning to miss him." She leaned over and kissed my cheek. "Don't feel so bad. I know you were putting on an act. If you hadn't done it, you never would have learned about Blunt. Tell your girlfriend everything."

"Yes, ma'am."

She got out of the LandCruiser and walked toward the door. "Hey," I said. She turned. "Thanks, Mrs. Johanson."

She smiled and raised a hand and went into the house.

▪ 23 ▪

I drove down to the Wasque reservation parking lot. A cruiser and some other cars were there. There were some young uniformed police officers down below the dropoff on the south side of the parking lot. I stopped and spotted Jake Spitz standing by a car, watching the young police officers walking around getting sand in their shoes. I went over and joined him.

"Looking for Blunt's revolver?"

"Yep. If Nagy is telling the truth, Blunt may have ditched the revolver to confuse things a bit more than they're already confused. If he did, it may be down there somewhere. They found him right about here."

"If he dug a hole and buried the gun, you'll have a hell of a time finding it."

"We're rounding up some metal detectors. If it's there, we'll find it."

"What did you and Nagy and Blunt talk about that Sunday night before Blunt killed himself, if that's what he did?"

He glanced at me. "The case. What we knew. What we didn't know. What we might find out. Looks like Blunt was playing games with us, but we didn't know that then."

"You didn't know much about anything, did you?"

"We knew that the real necklace and the pastes were in the safe before the party and the necklace was not in the safe when Blunt and the Damons went to get it the night of the party. We didn't think anyone had opened the safe in between times. We agreed that Blunt was the logical suspect, but he'd insisted on being searched after the theft and hadn't had the opportunity to pass the necklace off to anybody before the search, so we were pretty stumped."

"Blunt didn't mind being a suspect?"

"Now we know why, don't we? No, he didn't mind. It was only logical that he would be, after all. Why do you want to know what we talked about?"

"So you reviewed what you knew, which wasn't much. Then what?"

"Then we talked about what to do next. Who we should question. SDL people on the island, their sympathizers, you know, college professors and student activists, other enemies the Padishah might have, professional thieves who might have pulled the job, fences who could handle such a hot item, collectors who might have sponsored the theft. We talked about some people like that and made some plans to track them down and ask questions. Why do you want to know?"

"Because I want to know why Willard Blunt suddenly decided to tell all to Colonel Nagy and then shoot himself. I mean, I can understand why a sick old man might decide to kill himself rather than go on experiencing increasing pain until he died, but it all happened so suddenly. If Blunt wanted to kill himself, why didn't he do it last week? If he wanted to confess, why didn't he do it with you at seven o'clock instead of three hours later with Nagy?"

"I don't know. Why?"

"Because he learned something that night that he didn't know before? Maybe at that meeting with you? And he had to figure out what to do with the information?"

"And what he did was confess that he stole the necklace and then shoot himself with Nagy's gun? It makes more sense to think that Nagy stole the necklace and shot Blunt and made up that story he told you."

"Except Nagy is sitting over here on Chappy drinking wine instead of being off in Rio spending the money he'd get from the emeralds."

"I thought of that too," nodded Spitz. "A puzzler, all right."

"So you guys talked about the SDL and agreed that you'd track down any members here on the island. Catch any?"

"Nobody who doesn't have an alibi."

"You talk about anybody else I might know?"

"Kingfish Cassidy. You know Kingfish?"

"No."

"Jewel thief. This smells like his work. But he's in jail in Atlanta, it turns out. Augie Newsome?"

"No."

"Boston fence. Owns a jewelry firm down on Washington Street. Very slick. Handles some big items. We almost had him a couple of times. But Augie's in Florida. New wife. Honeymoon. The store is closed. Dr. Hamdi Safwat?"

"Him I've heard of. Professor at Weststock. Wrote a book."

"Books."

"Books. Big anti-Padishah intellectual."

"Yeah. Friend of Willard Blunt's too. Hamdi would probably love to get his hands on the necklace, but he was at a shindig for summer faculty that night. College president's house. Wally Farmer?"

"Who's Wally Farmer?"

"Wally Farmer is a second-story man who can open a safe like that one in Damon's house in about thirty seconds. But Wally walked in front of a kid riding a bicycle a couple of weeks ago and got his right hand busted. In a cast up to his elbow. Out of comish. Shall I go on?"

"None of them panned out, eh?"

"Not so far. Now what can you tell me?"

I told him about the four young Sarofimians.

"Well, Jesus Christ," he said. "You let 'em go?"

"Zee didn't press charges. What would you have done, run them in for throwing some firecrackers over Damon's fence?"

"You're some cop, you are."

I gave him the list of their names and their passport numbers. "You can find them if you need to. I don't think they know any more than they told me."

"Maybe not, but I'll check them out anyway. Some of these young revolutionary types are pretty clever and not noted for telling cops true tales. Well, at least we don't have to wonder about who did the kidnapping anymore. And we were right about one thing, anyway: the kidnapping was hooked to the theft. What do you think Mrs. Madieras was supposed to know?"

"Beats me."

"And where did Blunt go after he left Nagy and me that Sunday night? He went off to see somebody. Maybe that's where he learned whatever it was that made him decide to confess and kill himself. If that's what he did."

"He went to see Amelia Muleto. They were old friends." I told him what Amelia had said of the visit.

"He didn't confess and he didn't tell her he intended suicide?"

"No. She said he looked frail and kissed her when he left. She thinks now that he was saying goodbye for the last time. If she's right, it means that he'd already decided to die that night."

"Maybe she's lying."

"Maybe everybody's lying. I've known her for thirty years. I'd trust her with my life."

"Yeah. I wish they'd get here with those metal detectors. What's next on your detecting agenda?"

"Actually, I thought I'd do my laundry and then pickle some zucchini."

He looked at me. "That makes as much sense as anything," he said with a grin.

And that's what I did, being careful to toss Zee's clothes in with my other coloreds. While the solar drier beamed upon them, I pickled and bottled all of the zooks I could find, then froze most of my ripe tomatoes for winter use. I freeze them whole in plastic bags. By the time I had the toms in the freezer, the clothes on the line were dry and I took them in. I stuck my nose into Zee's shirt. If Helga's scent was there, I couldn't smell it. I folded everything foldable and put it back in its place, found a Sam Adams in the fridge, and sat down at the phone.

I got Dr. Hamdi Safwat's phone number without any trouble, but nobody answered my call. Dr. Safwat was one of the few remaining human beings on earth without an answering machine. I interpreted this as an indication that he was a modest fellow who didn't think he needed a record of all the people who telephoned him. I made another call, this one to Jasper Cabot. Jasper's secretary answered, discovered who I claimed to be, and hooked me to her boss.

"Yes, Mr. Jackson?"

"I have a question. Do you want a report first?"

"The question first."

"Do you know the name 'Periezade'? I think it may be Sarofimian."

There was a silence at the end of the line. Then Jasper Cabot spoke in an expressionless voice. "I've not heard that name for many years. Periezade Safwat was a young woman I knew in Sarofim. She was taken by the Padishah's secret police, and I never saw her again."

Of course. That was it. "Yes. Now I remember. Her father protested and someone mutilated and killed him. Willard Blunt might have been in love with her. That fits. The elder sister of Hamdi Safwat . . ."

"It is a Persian name of considerable antiquity. There are no doubt other Periezades in the world."

"I think this is the one." I told him what Nagy had said of Blunt's last conversation with him. Jasper Cabot listened without interruption.

"Yes," he said, when I was done. "I believe you're right. Wergeld, as you no doubt know, is the price paid by the family of a killer to the family of the victim. Old German and Anglo-Saxon law. Blunt was of Anglo-Saxon ancestry. Very old family. Wergeld for Periezade. The necklace as payment for her life. Yes."

"He must have loved her more than you knew."

"To take revenge after forty-five years? So it would seem. He never married, you know."

"Maybe he was homosexual."

"Willard? Oh no. He was never interested in men. Not in that way. He liked women. Over the years he had many women friends. Some became mistresses. No, it's as though the two women he could have married were denied him and after losing them he simply abandoned the idea of taking a wife. I assure you that many of our wives attempted to marry him off to some very wonderful women, but though Willard took some of them to his bed, he never proposed marriage to any of them."

"The other woman whom he might have married being Amelia Muleto?"

"Amelia Stonehouse in those days. Yes. When she married young Raymond Muleto, her family was shocked, but I think Willard's heart must have been broken, if I can use so old-fashioned a phrase. He never criticized her, however, but served her loyally throughout his life. She was always of special concern to him, and he personally took care of her inheritance."

"He continued to love her?"

"There are such men. It would account for his bachelor life."

"Yes. The detail about Periezade makes Nagy's story more convincing, doesn't it? It's not a name he would have made up. The girl disappeared almost fifty years ago."

"I agree. I'm therefore inclined to believe his tale. It would seem, then, that Willard did kill himself with Nagy's gun."

"Why not with his own? And why the confession to Nagy?"

"You are the detective, Mr. Jackson, not I. Have you other news that might clarify the issue?"

I brought him up to date. The kidnapping interested him.

"Willard a kidnapper too? My old friend was apparently not entirely the man I thought I knew. Kidnapping? Theft? Suicide? Perplexing . . ."

"It ties together somehow. I'm just not sure how."

"And Willard Blunt is at the center of it all. I am concerned about the content of the telephone call you received. Do you think that your life and that of Mrs. Madieras are actually in danger? Perhaps you should drop the case."

"If we're in danger, I don't think it's because of the work I'm doing for you. I think it's something personal."

"And you spoke to Colonel Nagy about it."

"Yes. If the Padishah is the bad guy, maybe he'll just forget about Zee and me and go home, now that we've been warned. He won't want to mess up relations between the U.S. and Sarofim."

"Not if he's rational; but Colonel Nagy has apparently suggested that he is not, that he is a petulant child."

"But he can be controlled by his advisors. I hope."

"Yes. I hope so too, Mr. Jackson. Keep me advised of your progress. Have you received my check?"

"I haven't been to get the mail for a couple of days."

"Then I suggest that you go today."

I took that advice, and there was the check. I went right home and phoned Jeremy Fisher. "I want to come and have another look at your catboat," I said.

"You know where it is," said Jeremy.

"I do," I said. "I'll be right up."

▪ 24 ▪

The catboat was in the barn behind Jeremy Fisher's house. I parked in the yard, waved to Jeremy, who was sitting on his porch having a pipe and watching the traffic go by at the end of his driveway, and went in to see if the boat was still as desirable as it had been the last time I'd looked at it. It was. Perfect for cruising or fishing or just goofing around. Catboats are perhaps the best possible boats for day sailing around the shoaly waters south of Cape Cod. They can sail in very thin water, of which we have a lot around Martha's Vineyard, can turn on a dime, and are so beamy that they heel very little in anything less than a gale. This one had a cuddy cabin with two bunks as well as the normal huge cockpit. It was gaff rigged and had an ancient eighteen-horse Evinrude hanging on an outboard-motor mount on the port transom. I had no difficulty imagining myself sailing down across the flats in Katama Bay or even fetching Nantucket on a fair day. Like many Vineyarders, I had never been to Nantucket. This boat would give me an excuse to go there.

I went up to the house and sat beside Jeremy and did some initial dickering. He wanted more than I was willing or able to pay, so I offered him less than that. I inhaled his pipe smoke and agreed that the Vineyard was getting so dang many cars on it these days that you took your life in your hands just trying to get to the hardware store.

He came down a little and I went up a little and things looked promising when I left.

On the way home I thought of what Jasper Cabot had said and wondered if Nagy had really had his pistol taken away from him or whether, after Blunt told him that he had stolen the necklace, Nagy had shot him right there, then put the gun in his hand to make it look like suicide. I wondered if it made any difference who had killed Blunt, who was dying anyway. I also thought about how Blunt had managed the theft, if, indeed, he really had done it. I had a semi-idea about how it might have happened, but didn't quite have it straight yet. One thing was certain: if Blunt had stolen the necklace, he'd either had help or the necklace was still on the island somewhere. Where? With the pistol under the sand somewhere where the Padishah of Sarofim would never find it? Why not? That would be a serious blow to the Rashads, and Blunt might well have wanted to give such a blow before he died.

Too many options. William of Occam would have recommended the simplest one that accounted for everything. But which one was that? Where was old William when you really needed him?

I had a surprise waiting for me at home. A cruiser in my yard. I parked beyond it and got out. The Chief and Jake Spitz and another man got out of the cruiser. None of their faces had much in the way of expression.

"This is Mr. Wapple," said the Chief. "He wants to talk to you."

Mr. Wapple put out his hand. He had an average sort of grip.

"To get right to the point, sir," he said, "I represent the White House. There are sensitive discussions going on in Washington regarding a certain foreign policy matter of which you may be generally aware. I've been asked to come up to the island here and request various parties involved in investigating last weekend's theft and suicide to, as it were, not pause in their inquiries but pursue them with discretion until the negotiations in the Capitol can be completed. I've spoken to your Chief here, to Mr. Spitz's superiors, and to Mr. Jason Thornberry and have gained their cooperation. I hope I can count on yours as well, Mr. Jackson." He smiled.

"I'm working for Jasper Cabot," I said. I glanced at the Chief. His face was blank.

Mr. Wapple's smile stayed on his face. "Yes, yes. I'm afraid that Mr. Cabot has been out of his office when I've tried to contact him, but I'm sure he will agree to my request when I do get in touch with him."

"Well, as soon as you do and he gives me the word, I'll walk away from the whole thing."

"Maybe you shouldn't wait," said Spitz. "I mean, hey, they don't want us to drop the case, they just want us to stay off of the Padishah's toes for a day or two. That right, Mr. Wapple?"

Mr. Wapple's smile faded a bit. "That's right, Mr. Spitz."

"I'm the soul of discretion," I said. "I never step on people's toes. What's happening here, Chief?"

The Chief got a little red in the face. It looked more like anger than embarrassment. He stuck his pipe in his mouth. "We're always glad to cooperate with the White House," he muttered.

"I'm not completely convinced that you don't step on toes," said Mr. Wapple, his smile now only a faint line across his face. "I'm told that you're not averse to causing trouble."

"For instance?"

"You made threats to the Padishah. That issue has come up in the Washington discussions. We don't need any more of that sort of thing."

"I didn't know about that," said the Chief, taking his pipe from his mouth.

"I didn't either," I said. "I did mention that if he didn't take his hands off of Helga Johanson she might kick his balls up into his brain cavity, but I don't think that I threatened him. I'd guess that the Padishah's advisors are spreading this story around as part of a negotiation for a better deal from Uncle Sam. Not that that'll be difficult. Government guys like Mr. Wapple's boss have a long tradition of supporting fascist governments as long as they're nice to our military."

Wapple's smile was now a memory. "And there's the matter of your invasion of the house of the young Sarofimians this morning. You used your badge to gain illegal entry and then threatened your victims with a pistol. You're liable to arrest on several counts. The President, as you know, ran on a strong law-and-order plank, but he also deeply resents the unlawful use of police authority." He leaned slightly forward. "We cannot afford any additional actions of this sort, sir." He turned to the Chief. "Tell him."

The Chief looked me in the eye. "You used your badge illegally. You didn't have a warrant. You waved a gun. You're in trouble."

"Who told you all that?"

He nodded at Spitz. "He told me what you told him. And Helga Johanson backed him up."

I looked at Spitz. He shrugged.

"There's no reason that this issue needs to be pursued," said Wapple, suddenly suave. "I'm sure that all parties will benefit from, say, three days of circumspect activities regarding the whole matter of the Padishah and last weekend's unfortunate occurrences. I suspect, Mr. Jackson, that at the end of that time your Chief may be more understanding of this morning's incident."

It was clear that he didn't know the Chief, who did not like his officers screwing up their work or his department's reputation.

"The Padishah and his party are scheduled to return to Sarofim in three days," explained Spitz unnecessarily.

I got out my wallet, took out my brand-new badge, and put it in the Chief's hand. He took it without hesitation. "Sorry it didn't work out," I said. I looked at Mr. Wapple. "If you think you can hang an arrest on me, hop to it. By the time you manage it, if you manage it, the Padishah will be long since home in the family harem. And while you're trying to scare me with your law-and-order presidential plank, you might give some thought to who's going to testify against me about this morning's adventure. Zee Madieras? Ha! Those Sarofimian college students? They know that Zee can hang a kidnapping charge on them if she decides to. I don't think they'll testify to anything. Helga Johanson? Hell, if I did something illegal, she was in on the whole thing." I walked over to Wapple and put my nose close to his. "I already had one threat hanging over my head before you decided to wave yours at me. I don't like threats or threateners. They tend to make me edgy. I get uncooperative. If you'd gotten Jasper Cabot to ask me to back off, I'd probably have done it. But now I think I'll stay with it. You fly back and tell the President to send somebody else to see me the next time he wants me to do him a favor. Now get off of my land."

I turned away and winked at Spitz, then spun back at Wapple. "Off! Go bully some little kid or kick a dog or something."

Wapple's face was white. The Chief turned away and coughed.

"Come on," said Spitz, taking Wapple's arm. "You've done your best, sir. I'm sure Mr. Jackson will cooperate. Let's give him a chance to cool down. Come along."

"These negotiations in Washington are important," cried Mr. Wapple as they led him to the cruiser. "National security could be involved! Don't you forget that, you . . . sir!"

"A pox on your negotiations!" I shouted. "And another one on national security!" I thought that had a fine theatrical ring to it.

They drove away. I went inside and found a Yuengling and washed Mr. Wapple out of my mouth. As someone once observed, life is just one damned thing after another. I felt pretty good and realized that the badge had been a weight I was glad to be rid of. It was too tempting to use it exactly the way I'd used it, and I'd not been pleased with the way I'd felt afterwards. Good riddance.

I looked at my watch. Zee would be off work in a couple of hours. If I was right about Colonel Ahmed Nagy being the foreign threat to her and me, I only had three more days to worry about her. I went out into the yard and stepped over the chicken-wire fence into the garden. The Bad Bunny Bunch hadn't found a way through yet, but they were an ever-present danger. Maybe I could sic Mr. Wapple on them.

I did some weeding and checked on my latest planting of green beans. In not too long I'd have another mighty bean-fest to share with Zee. I could make a whole meal out of nothing but fresh-picked green beans boiled and served with just a bit of butter and salt. Fresh vegetables almost never need much help to be delicious.

By the time my bottle of Yuengling was empty I had come to my cauliflower row. I have an annual fight with cauliflower and rarely produce much that's impressive. This year was no different, but I did have a couple that were doing very nicely. I admired the bigger of them and suddenly had an irresistible yen for fried cauliflower. I went inside and got another beer and phoned the hospital. The lady who answered the phone in the emergency room took my name, said just a moment, and a bit later said that Zee was busy.

Sure. Zee had been a little irked this morning. Maybe she still was. I went out to the garden again and harvested the head of cauliflower that had caused my tastebuds to leap into action. Inside, I washed it and cut it up into handy nibbling-size pieces and put it in the fridge. Then I got into the LandCruiser and drove to the hospital. On the way I passed Ocean View Lane. Were Anwar and his friends still there, or had I scared them across the Sound to America? I parked in the emergency room parking lot and went inside through the glass doors. Zee, looking terrific in her white uniform, was standing at the reception desk writing in a folder.

"Hi," I said. "I've come to invite you to share a deep-fried cauliflower with me."

She looked up, then looked down again and wrote some more. "Just the three of us, I presume."

"Just the two of us. I can explain everything."

"I'll bet you can. You've had all day to think up your story."

"I come in peace," I said. "I know you're mad, but you shouldn't be. There's a perfectly sensible explanation. I want to give it to you."

"All right, give. I'm listening."

The receptionist on the other side of the desk gave me a

matronly smile and listened without apology. I wondered if she was the one who had answered the phone.

"I'd prefer to give it over a chilled glass of Absolut and a hot plate of fried cauliflower," I said.

Zee said nothing.

"Sounds good to me," said the receptionist. "If she doesn't want to listen to you, I will!"

"Okay," I said. "And tomorrow you can pass the message on to Mrs. Madieras, here, if she wants to know it. What time do you get off?"

"I'm out of here at six."

"All right, all right," said Zee, "I'll come for cauliflower."

"Shucks," said the receptionist. "Now I have to go home to Homer and the kids. Maybe next time you'll ask me first?"

"Sure. You might try getting Homer to fix your cauliflower for you."

"Homer's idea of a sophisticated meal is a peanut butter and marshmallow sandwich. I don't think he knows how to boil water."

"See you in a bit," I said to Zee. I gave her a big smile. She lifted her chin and walked away. She had wonderful legs. I watched them go around a corner and out of sight, then raised my eyebrows at the receptionist. She gave me a friendly look. I went out to the LandCruiser. So far, so good.

▪ 25 ▪

I put two glasses in the freezer beside the bottle of Absolut and got ready to fry up the cauliflower. Oil in the wok, some milk in one bowl, some flour in another. Not too much later, Zee's Jeep came down my long driveway, stopped, and produced its driver.

The first thing she said was, "Did she have to wear my clothes?"

"Yes." I puckered hopefully, and she reluctantly allowed her cheek to be kissed.

I handed her an icy glass of vodka. "Sit. Admire the view." I escorted her to my best white lawn chair, salvaged from the Big D, repainted, and as good as new. Archie Bunker's chair was next on the repair list. "I shall return," I said.

The only people who don't like fried cauliflower are the kind you really shouldn't hang around with anyway since sooner or later they'll corrupt whatever good taste you have in other areas of your life as well. Like a lot of excellent recipes, the one for fried cauliflower is simple: get your oil hot, dip your cauliflower in the milk, then the flour, shake off the excess flour, and drop the cauliflower into the oil. As soon as it's golden brown, take the cauliflower out, drain it, lightly salt it, and *eat* it! None of it ever goes to waste at my house. I made up a plateful and took it out to Zee.

She sniffed the aroma. She looked at the plate.

"If madam is not pleased, the chef will be charmed to commit suicide in a manner of madam's choosing."

"Madam is not pleased yet."

"Then it will be my pleasure to begin the suicide immediately after I have had a final meal of this most excellent vegetable." I went back inside and cooked a plate for myself, then returned, plate in one hand, vodka glass in the other. Zee's plate was half empty. I wasn't surprised. A small nurse can eat a large horse at the end of a working day.

"You can delay the suicide for the time being," she said, munching.

"Madam is too kind."

"Well," she said as I sat down. "Let's have it."

I told her the truth about my adventures with Helga. By the time I was done, her cauliflower was gone and she was eating mine. I got up and went inside and cooked up what was left. I brought it out with the Absolut bottle.

I poured. We sat and looked out over the pond to the Sound. Sailboats, white against the darkening water, were trying to catch a whiff of evening wind to take them into harbor. Along the spit of sand separating the Sound from the pond, the parked cars were thinning out as the August people reluctantly abandoned the beach.

"All right," said Zee. "You were right. There was an explanation. But it felt funny seeing another woman in my pants."

"No one can fill your pants but you, dear," I said.

"Thanks a lot."

"I think you should stay with your Aunt Amelia for a couple of days. You have the weekend off, and I'd like to do some fishing. Maybe we could go up to Lobsterville and try for weakfish."

"My gear's at home. Are you protecting me again?"

"You'd both have a good time visiting. You can tell her all there is to know about being kidnapped."

"I've talked to her on the phone and told her everything about that. I don't want to talk about it anymore. I didn't like it. I hated being tied up. I think it's made me claustrophobic." She suddenly shivered in the warm evening air.

I felt a shaft of pain in my soul. I wanted to hold her so tightly that she would lose all of her fear. But before I could move she seemed to reach inside of herself and find some of that secret, unsuspected strength that women discover when they must have it, the strength that takes them through the deaths of parents, sisters, lovers, children, through the sicknesses and betrayals and cruelties of life, and allows them to endure and even find joy when many men, equally afflicted, would either go mad or turn to stone or die.

She sat up straight. "But I think it's also made me a better nurse," she said. "Now I understand better what it's like to be totally helpless, like some of my patients. I thought I understood before, but now, having had no arms or legs or eyes for all that time and never knowing if I'd ever have them again, I understand better. Having someone take me to the bathroom, having someone feed me, never hearing a voice, all that . . . was for the good. I should probably be grateful. I hated it, but I should probably be grateful."

I didn't think I would be, in her place. I thought that the hate and fear would be all I could get out of it.

"I don't want you alone for the next three days," I said. "On Monday the Padishah and his gang are headed for home. After that I don't think we'll have to worry about what the guy on the phone said."

"You really think somebody will try to hurt us?"

"I don't know. The Padishah has a bad reputation at home. People he doesn't like end up dead. I just don't want you to be alone this weekend."

"Don't worry so much about me."

"Tell the sun not to shine."

"I'll be very careful."

"We've been through this before. You don't know who's coming after you, so you might not know he's there until . . ."

"Until it's too late? After surviving being tied up for three days, I don't feel very afraid of the Padishah."

"Nagy's the one to be afraid of, not the Padishah."

"Well, let's ask the Chief to keep an eye on Nagy, then. He can have a man keep an eye on him over the weekend. No Nagy, no trouble. Simple. I can go home, and you can stop worrying."

"Except for one thing." I told her about Wapple and his request from the White House. "Everyone's cooperating," I said. "Everyone's being very discreet. Everyone's agreed not to ruffle the Padishah's feathers. Orders from headquarters. I doubt if the Chief will see fit to put a man on the Padishah's personal bodyguard."

Zee looked out into the evening. On the Sound a bit of wind from the southwest had answered the sailors' whistles, and the white boats were leaning toward Edgartown. "Maybe you're right," she said. "I know you. If I go home, you'll probably camp in my driveway with one of your dad's old shotguns." She looked at me. "Won't you?"

"It would be best if you went to Amelia's. You'd be safe there."

"I think I'd rather stay here."

Surprise and a rush of desire stopped my speech. I took a sip of icy vodka and willed my brain to control my hormones. "It would be better if you'd stay with Amelia."

"You're a real flatterer. I make you an offer you can't refuse and you say no. I must be losing my touch." She looked at my face, saw something there, and nodded. "Ah, I get it. If he comes here after you, you don't want me under your feet."

"He's not coming here," I said as convincingly as I could.

"Then I'll stay. You can be manly, and I'll be right here for you to protect. Or vice versa, as the case may be." She got to her feet. "Home first for fishing gear, then back in a flash." She came over to me. She was like a dark sun shining. "If we get to sleep soon enough, we can be at Lobsterville at daylight. What do you think of that plan?"

I got up from my chair. The top of her head came just to my chin. She put her arms around my neck, tipped her face up, and pulled my lips down to hers. Our kiss was long, and when it ended we were breathless. She laid her head against my chest. "Maybe I don't have to go home," she said. "We can stop by my place in the morning and pick up my gear on our way."

My brain was no longer in the fight. I couldn't think of a single argument against her revised plan. My eyes discovered the vodka bottle on the table. "You're Absolut-ly right," I said. I picked her up in my arms and walked into the house.

There was no best time to make love with Zee. Every time was the best time there ever was. In the fading evening light I carried her to my bedroom and stood her on her feet. She put her hands to her head, and the dark hair that had been pinned up for her day of nursing came tumbling down, thick and blue-black over the white collar of her uniform. A flock of goats moving down the slopes of Gilead. I put out my own big hands and unbuttoned her blouse. Her skin was tanned and smooth. Her lips were like a scarlet thread and her mouth was lovely. She dropped the uniform on the floor. I touched her throat. Her breasts were firm and sleek. Like two fawns that feed among the lilies.

My own clothes were off, and she came smiling and naked and pressed herself against me, arms around my waist. Such sweetness. She was all fair, my love; there was no flaw in her. We lay on the bed, and that long hair flowed over me like liquid night. She ravished my heart with a glance of her eyes. Love sweeter than wine, lips like nectar, love like a well of living water from which we drank until we could drink no more.

Afterwards Zee poked a finger into the little depression that contains my belly button and smiled a lazy smile. She put the finger into my mouth. "Taste that."

"Salty."

"Sweat. You have a little puddle of it in the middle of your belly. Maybe you haven't been getting enough exercise lately."

"I have no one to blame but you. Besides, you're a little slithery yourself."

"You're quite right. Time for a shower. Come on."

We got off the tumbled, sweaty sheets, found beach towels, and went out into the night and showered together under the stars.

Then we went back inside and went to bed. Zee curled herself against me and was asleep in minutes, her arm around my waist, her knees tucked up against the back of mine, her skin smooth and warm against my own. I lay awake and thought about Colonel Nagy, Jake Spitz, and the stolen necklace. I listened to the night wind in the trees and to the rustle of nocturnal creatures moving through the leaves under the oak brush. Everything sounded normal, and finally I too went to sleep.

At five we were at her house in West Tisbury. While she collected her fishing gear and put her rod on the roof rack, I wandered through and around the house and found no sign of anyone having tried to enter. An hour later, on the Lobsterville beach near the only parking spot that Gay Head's xenophobic citizens allowed along the road, I landed a nice weakfish just after Zee lost one she almost had in.

"I'm refraining from saying that fishing is really a man's game," I said. "I hope you appreciate that."

"Oh, of course. It's a real pleasure to fish with one of the few males who's totally free of sexist inclinations." She made her cast. I watched the lure arc out and splash into the water. It was a lovely cast.

"We're a rare and vulnerable minority," I said, "but there are some of us around. Say, do you want me to show you how to do that right?"

We fished until an hour after the sun came up over the Chilmark Hills and the water began to dance with light. Before we decided it was time for breakfast, we had nailed four fish, two each.

"Tell you what," said Zee. "We'll go to my place and you can cook one of these guys up for breakfast along with some eggs and toast and coffee. I'll pour the orange juice. And afterwards you can wash up while I read the paper. What do you say?"

"Suits me. You can fillet the other fish while I'm cooking."

"That's man's work," she said.

"I don't think you've got this role stuff down, yet. I'm Nimrod, the mighty hunter, and you're Vesta, goddess of the hearth. I bring home the bacon and you cook it up in a pan and never let me forget I'm a man. God, I love that song!"

"I think you've got your myths mixed up about as bad as they could be. Okay, I'll fillet the fish. I do it better than you do, anyway."

"You can't rouse my masculine vanity with that tricl Fine, you fillet the fish."

"Okay, okay."

The road from Gay Head leads around the south end c Nashaquitsa Pond and into Chilmark. In the early mornin light that loveliest of island landscapes was ethereal as dream. A layer of mist that lay over the pond had not ye burned off, and the anchored boats seemed painted on a mi ror. Zee found the Cape classical station on the radio, an Vivaldi accompanied us all the way to her house. It was th Vineyard as it was supposed to be.

"Did you know that Bach belonged to the Vivaldi Societ but Vivaldi did not belong to the Bach Society?" I asked.

"No," said Zee.

"It's a little-known fact," I said.

"So what?" asked Zee.

I raised a professorial finger. "Knowledge is to be value for its own sake," I said.

"Gotcha."

No one was waiting for us at Zee's house. Together, w set the kitchen table. Then, while Zee filleted three fish, I fi leted the fourth, peeled and sliced some potatoes, and gc the coffee started. A bit of butter in the frying pan to cook u the potatoes, then in with a bit more butter and the fish fi lets, then, while everything else was cooking, poached egg in a second pan. Nothing to it. I dropped bread into th toaster. The fine smells of coffee and food filled the kitcher

Zee walked in, wiping her hands, eyed the stove and gc out the orange juice.

"Perfect timing." She turned on the morning news and sa down while I poured coffee and loaded up our plates. We at slowly and steadily while the announcer informed us hov the world beyond the Vineyard had not significantl changed since yesterday. We ignored the weather repo since it was a mainland station and the Vineyard has its ow private weather systems that no one really seems to be abl to predict. The sports report was of the Red Sox in anothe August slump. What else was new? The Red Sox are heart breakers because they're always just good enough to give you hope and never good enough to justify it.

"No bull pen," said Zee. "No left-handed power. Great outfield, but shaky up the middle. Same old Red Sox."

"We ought to go up for a game sometime. If you're sitting in Fenway Park, even watching them lose can be fun."

"Yeah, we really should do that. This is good stuff, Jefferson. Did anybody ever tell you that with just a little bit of advice, you could probably cook as well as I do?"

"I think you've mentioned it from time to time."

"Well, I really mean it. This is good!"

"Why don't you get your bathing suit and we'll go to my place and get mine and some food and beer and newspapers and books and we'll hit the beach just like the summer ginks."

"You're on. Listen."

I listened. The announcer was telling us that the Padishah of Sarofim had completed a state visit to Washington and had returned to the island of Martha's Vineyard for a last weekend at the summer house of his host, the well-known financier Mr. Edward C. Damon, before returning to his homeland on Monday.

"So he's here," said Zee.

I had been wondering when he'd show up. "We knew he was coming. Not to worry. If it ever got out that he or his henchmen tried to do a number on a couple of American citizens, he'd be in what some folks call deep international doodoo. He'll be gone on Monday. Nothing's going to happen."

And nothing did. Then.

▪ 26 ▪

When we got out of the LandCruiser at my house, somebody at the Rod and Gun Club was already popping away on the target range.

"They must shoot up all of their money," said Zee, looking down that way through the trees behind my place.

"The serious ones all reload just because of that."

Whoever was shooting was doing it systematically. There would be a silence, then two shots coming so fast they sounded almost like one, followed by a split-second silence, two more quick shots, another split-second silence, and then two more of the incredibly fast shots. After a while the sequence would be repeated.

"What's that all about?" asked Zee.

"It sounds like Manny Fonseca or one of his pistoleering buddies. You know Manny?"

"Manny Fonseca, the woodworker? I know him."

"Well, Manny puts three targets up, then practices his draw and shoot. Two shots in each target. You know, like John Wayne in *Stagecoach*. Ringo against the Plummer brothers? I think Ringo only had one bullet per Plummer, but Manny likes to put two in each target. Sounds like he's shooting his .45 today."

"Boys will be boys."

"Manny and the guys like to shoot just like we like to fish. Maybe they do less damage. We killed four fish this morning, but all they kill are targets."

"They're still playing cowboys and Indians."

"A gun is just a tool."

"I still don't like them."

"Remember that this coming winter when I'm out there

freezing my fanny in my blind and you start thinking about my famous duck with honey and marmalade."

"Get your bathing suit. I want to get wet before I take my late morning nap on the beach."

I collected food, drink, and gear. When I came outside, Zee was sitting in a lawn chair watching two of the Bad Bunny Bunch watching her.

"Why don't you plant a bunny garden?" she asked. "You know, a garden without a fence. One just for the bunnies."

"What an un-American thought. We don't go around building bunny gardens. I never heard of such a thing. Get out of here!" I yelled at the bunnies. They didn't move.

"Where do they live when they're not trying to find a way through your garden fence?"

I gestured toward the woods. "In there somewhere. They probably have a bunny condo or something."

"I think they live in holes in the ground."

"Could be."

"They're cute. Let's shoo them away and then follow them and see where they go."

"You go right ahead. I'm going to the beach."

"Tomorrow we'll do it," said Zee.

"Tomorrow you can follow bunnies if you want to, but I don't think I will. I plan to devote myself entirely to meditation and spiritual exercise."

It was turning into a beautiful day. We drove down to Katama, then turned east over the beach. There were the to-be-expected late-August clammers trying their hand on the Katama flats, and out on the bay, the pro quahoggers were leaning back on their rakes. There weren't too many 4x4s on the beach today, but tomorrow there would be more than you could count. The weekends are the only time working islanders have for beaching, and on a fair day the beach between Katama and Wasque sometimes looks like a parking lot for 4x4s. There are more every year.

We drove on to Chappy and took the narrow road through the dunes, over the splintering wooden roadways that the Trustees of Reservations built at great expense to save those very dunes, and on to Wasque where we paused and watched a good many people fail to catch any fish. It was family day at Wasque. Umbrellas had been put up, and children were running around with balls and toys while their mothers watched them and their fathers made their casts into the empty waters of the rip. It was amateur hour. The casts were going every which way. We checked out the 4x4s and didn't see any that belonged to serious fishermen.

"Forward, ho!" said Zee.

We took the road to Pocha Pond and were pleased to find no one there before us. I parked in the lee of the tall reeds that grow there, and we spread my double bedspread on the sand. An old double bedspread is far better for beaching than even the largest towel. You can spread out and relax and not end up with half of you in the sand. We nailed down the bedspread with a cooler on one corner and a beach chair on another, then stripped to our bathing suits. Mine was almost as small as Zee's. I would be in style at Cannes, but I was quite daring by Vineyard standards.

The water is shallow at that corner of Pocha Pond, and we had to wade out quite a way before we could swim. The pond was warm and clear, and we had it all to ourselves. Zee, who could swim like an otter, dived and did flips and turns, then swam along parallel to the rocky west shore of the pond. I swam with her. After a couple of hundred yards of this, we went ashore and walked back to the bedspread. By the time we got there we were dry.

It was a lazy day. After we finished the *Globe,* it was nap time. I have no difficulty at all going to sleep on the beach under a warm sun and proved it. We woke up for lunch, and afterwards, while Zee read her book, I went out with my quahog rake and my small basket and got myself some chowder clams. For reasons that totally elude me, Pocha Pond is home to many large hard-shell clams and practically no small ones. How the clams manage to get big without going through smaller stages is one of the mysteries of Chappaquiddick.

Quahogging is a pastime that allows the quahogger much

opportunity for thought. You rake the bottom of the pond and then bring up the rake and have a look at what you've got. You keep the quahogs and dump the seaweed, rocks, and empty shells back. This process does not require much intellectual focus. While I raked, I thought about the theft, the kidnapping, Blunt's suicide, and the anonymous telephone call. The first three were only puzzles, but the last was more than that. I would be glad when the Padishah and his crowd were gone. I wondered if the Padishah was actually foolish enough to risk the mutual security treaty with the United States for the sake of achieving a petty revenge for largely imagined insults.

Would Colonel Nagy obey his master if the Padishah ordered him to extract revenge on Zee and me in some way? The Padishah might be unstable, but Nagy was not. And would Dr. Mahmoud Zakkut, the Padishah's political advisor, not strongly advise against any rash action being taken on American soil?

I thought of the tale Jasper Cabot had told me of the disappearance of Hamdi Safwat's sister and the mutilation and death of his father, of the current reputation the Rashad dynasty had for the suppression and torture of its domestic critics and the tendency of those critics to die of "natural causes." I remembered the anger and fear of the four young Sarofimians I had bullied only yesterday, and I wondered if, indeed, Nagy or some other agent might actually act on the orders of an angry, childish dictator such as Ali Mohammed Rashad, Padishah of Sarofim. I looked ashore. Zee sat in her beach chair, reading. A Jeep came out of the dunes behind her and went north toward the Dyke Bridge. Several had passed by since we'd arrived. Above the dunes, sea gulls soared. The wind moved the reeds behind the LandCruiser and wrinkled the surface of the water where I stood waist deep. The sun stood in the western sky, bright and warm. The sky was a pale blue dome. A few clouds floated over the spot where I knew Nantucket lay behind the haze on the horizon.

Everything I saw spoke of peace and beauty.

But Vietnam had been beautiful too. A rifleman with a decent scope could pick both of us off from the north side of Pocha and never show himself to either of us. I felt his eye between my shoulder blades and turned and looked, but of course saw nothing because there was no rifleman.

I filled my basket and waded ashore. Zee smiled.

"Nice batch. Chowder tonight?"

"You bet."

"You have some white wine at home?"

"Is the Pope Polish?"

"I found your pistol in the glove compartment."

"Yeah, well . . ."

"It was here and you were way out there."

"I didn't really think I'd need it."

"And you didn't. You really thought you might?"

"I don't know." I found a Beck's Dark in the cooler. "Did you ever notice that Beck's Dark and Dos Equis taste like they came out of the same barrel?"

"No. Maybe they have German brewmeisters in Mexico."

"I think it would be a good idea if you spent the next couple of nights with Amelia. I'll drive you over after supper."

She put her book on her knees. "We went through this yesterday, remember? The way I see it, you and I are in this together, but if you don't want me at your house, I'll stay in my own. I have no intention of hiding out at Amelia's."

"You are a very stubborn person."

"I'm stubborn? You're the stubborn one!"

I lay down and put my hands behind my neck and looked at the sky. Those little lines and squiggles that you can see when you do that floated in their watery way on the edges of my vision.

"That Friday night when I dropped you off at Amelia's, the night you were kidnapped. What were Amelia and Willard Blunt talking about when you sneaked up to the door and listened. You thought it might be romance, I remember. What was it really?"

"What a question. It wasn't the romance I thought it might be, I remember that. Let's see. Something to do with

Willard Blunt's nephew or grandnephew. Oh, I remember. They were making a present for him. A surprise. I thought it was a cute idea."

"What was it?"

"A book with a hollow place in it. The little boy would get a pretty dull-looking book, but when he opened it he'd find something really nice. One of those superhero wristwatches. It would be the boy's first watch. He and Amelia were pretty excited about it."

"That was it?"

"Yes. Why?"

"Nothing more?"

"No."

"For Blunt's nephew or grandnephew? You're sure?"

"Yes, I'm sure. Why do you ask?

"What happened next?"

"I put on the dress, and Aunt Amelia and I worked on fitting it. Willard went into the den and worked on the book. I think he watched the Sox on the tube."

"Did he make a phone call?"

"He could have. There's a phone in the den. I guess he must have, if he called those young people who grabbed me."

"We can check that out. We know the number of the telephone at the house the Sarofimian kids lived in. The phone company will have a record of calls from Amelia's house. Did Blunt say anything about anything that might have had to do with the theft?"

"Nothing I can remember. He worked on the book while Aunt Amelia and I worked on the dress. Then we all went out to dinner. And, no, Mr. Blunt didn't say anything then, either. He was just charming and sweet and sophisticated. Unlike some people I know who like to ask questions but don't answer them."

"I'm pretty charming myself," I said. "I'll prove it. You can stay with me. See how charming I am? But I want you to know that it's only because of your primary and secondary zones."

She put down her book and came over and sat on my belly, her knees on either side of my chest. "You don't have zones," she said. "You have zone. You're all one big zone. It will be the death of you." She leaned down. There wasn't much cloth between her and me. I put up my arms and pulled her close against me. Her skin was hot. She had a great laugh.

27

When we got back to my house in mid afternoon, the Rod and Gun Club shootists were still at it.

"Must be a competition coming up," I said, when Zee raised a brow.

"Dibs on the shower!" She grabbed her beach towel and was gone in a flash. I took the cooler inside and unpacked it and hung the bedspread on the line. Then I leaned my Remington twelve gauge against the wall by the front door and went outside.

"You're next," said Zee, coming inside while she dried her hair. "I even left you some hot water."

"You're a sweetheart."

"You don't know the half. When you get out, you'll find an Absolut martini waiting for you up on the balcony."

I did. She'd also brought up some cheese, crackers, and smoked bluefish pâté. Paradise enou. Zee was in jeans and sweatshirt and was brushing out that wonderful long blue-black hair so the wind could help dry it. She was watching two of the Bad Bunny Bunch trying to find a way into my garden.

"Wretched Robert Rabbit and Horrible Harry Hare," I said. "Wretched Robert is the one with the floppy ear, and the one with the dark spot on his shoulder is Harry. They're the two easiest ones to identify. The others all look a lot alike, so it's hard to make a case against them. These guys are the gang leaders, I think. Bold as bears. Look at them. Hey, get out of there! See? No respect for my property."

"I'm surprised you don't sit up here with your shotgun and blast them. You're a sportsman."

"Maybe I will. Maybe I'll do just that. I'll use my twelve gauge. Be nothing left but a bunny tail and maybe an ear. You want to join the shoot? I mean, it's your idea."

"No thanks. What were you thinking about on the way home? What was on your mind?"

"Just you, my love."

'No. I was on your mind when we left the beach, but by the time we got here you were thinking of something else. What?"

"The case."

"I thought you gave your badge back to the Chief. Look there. I think Harry's thinking of digging a hole under the fence!"

"Get out of there, Harry!" I threw an ice cube, which Harry ignored. "Damned rabbit! Maybe I will get my shotgun." I started to get up. It was a feint that worked.

"No you don't," said Zee. "I'll run them off. Get out of there, you two!"

She went down the stairs and out to the garden, martini glass in hand. The bad bunnies watched her approaching, then slowly hopped away.

"They're fleeing in terror," I called. "Would you consider taking a job as a scarebunny? All you have to do is stand in the garden."

Zee looked up at me. "This is my golden chance. I'm going to follow these guys and see where they live. Want to come?"

"I'll watch from here. My interest in rabbit burrows is not as highly developed as my interest in martinis and hors d'oeuvres. But do carry on, by all means."

"When I become a famous writer about rabbits, you'll remember this opportunity and weep." Harry and Wretched Robert hopped reluctantly into the woods, and Zee went after them. For a while I could see her moving erratically through the oak brush, ducking under branches and around thorns. Then she was gone.

Beyond her, the Rod and Gun Club shooters continued their target practice, shooting up God only knows how much money. The bunched shots, two two two then silence, then two two two and silence again, suggested that the shooter was still triple targeting.

I ate crackers and cheese and bluefish pâté and thought about Amelia Muleto and Willard Blunt. I was still on my first martini when I heard a car coming down my driveway. I was down the stairs and standing in the front door when the car came into view. One of the Damon fleet, I thought. The car stopped, and a small, brown, elderly man got out. He peered at me through thick glasses.

"Mr. Jackson? Mr. J.W. Jackson?"

"Yes."

"How do you do? I am Dr. Mahmoud Zakkut. May I speak with you?" His English was a bit guttural, and I remembered that he had studied medicine in Germany. I looked into the car. He was alone. He put out a thin hand. I came outside and took it.

"I recognize you, Doctor. I saw you last Saturday night at the Damon party."

He peered around and nodded. "Yes. Much has happened since that night, as you no doubt know. This is a very pleasant place, Mr. Jackson. May we sit outside?"

"Sure."

We walked out onto the lawn. He seemed none too steady on his feet, so I took his arm. He thanked me. I sat him in my best repainted Big D chair, and I sat in Archie Bunker's chair. He looked out across Anthier's Pond toward the far road where the beach people were collecting their umbrellas and children and going home for the night.

"Very lovely. Sailboats. Like butterflies, don't you think?"

"I like the view."

"It is a most attractive place, this Martha's Vineyard. I can now well understand its fame as a resort."

"You'll be leaving soon, I'm told."

"Yes. On Monday. It will be good to be home again, for though Sarofim is nothing like your island, it has beauties of its own which endear it to its citizens. You understand."

"Yes."

We looked out across the water. The pistols popped at the Rod and Gun Club.

"Well, to business," he said at last. "I am here as a representative of His Highness Ali Mohammed Rashad, the Padishah of Sarofim. His Highness feels he has suffered a grievous injury from you which he cannot allow to go unpunished. You are an American, so I will not expect you to understand the sensibilities of a monarch such as His Highness. As His Highness's political advisor, I have counseled him to forget the indignation he feels, but I have been unable to influence him. Thus, here I am as his agent." He peered at me through his glasses. "Do I make myself clear?"

"To tell you the truth, I was expecting Colonel Nagy."

"Of course. And your expectations were correct. Look behind you, sir."

I did, feeling a sudden chill. Nagy stood in the doorway of my house, punching shotgun shells out of my twelve gauge. He nodded.

"Good afternoon, Mr. Jackson. You will appreciate the fact that we needed to distract you so as to gain this advantage over you. It is your territory, after all, and you could be expected to defend yourself." He put the shells in his pocket and leaned the shotgun against the wall. Then he dipped his hand under his shirt and produced the pistol I'd seen in his room. "Please stay right where you are, sir. Dr. Zakkut."

The doctor elevated himself with difficulty from his chair and walked slowly to his car. The Colonel came forward. "As you can now guess, I came through the trees while Dr. Zakkut drove down your road. A simple, but effective tactic. Although a frail, old man such as Dr. Zakkut seems no threat at all to a strong young man such as yourself, he can, however, be distracting. While you talked here and looked out at this lovely view, I took the opportunity to enter your house by its back door and search it. Mrs. Madieras is not there. Too bad. I'd hoped she would be. She was not at her own home earlier today, either. Do you have any idea where she is?"

"At work." I willed her deeper into the woods.

"No, not at work. A nurse's uniform is in your dirty clothes hamper. I imagine it is hers."

"Yes. She left it here earlier in the week." I had an almost irrepressible fear that Zee would come walking out of the woods at any moment. I could not bear the thought.

"Of course. No matter. We'll find her later."

Zakkut was walking slowly back, carrying a small black bag. I had time to wonder if every doctor in the world had a small black bag. Zakkut put the bag on the table and opened it. He brought out a roll of duct tape and put a pair of scissors in the pocket of his jacket. Nagy cocked his pistol and pointed it at my head.

"Don't move, sir. Dr. Zakkut is going to tape you to your chair. Please don't struggle. I assure you that we are taking this measure only to prevent you from attempting some violence which you might regret later. We have no intention of harming you or anything that belongs to you. But I have my orders and I will shoot you if I must. Please. Sit still."

"If you have no intention of harming me, why do I need to be tied up?" I spoke loudly, so Zee could hear me and know not to come into view. Nagy frowned and let his eyes roam around the yard before they returned to me.

"It will become clear to you, sir. For now, please allow the doctor to do his work."

I judged the distance between us. Too far. Zakkut came around so that I was between him and Nagy. He wrapped the heavy gray tape around and around my arm and the arm of the chair. When he had wrapped enough to satisfy himself, he cut the tape with the scissors. He then knelt and taped my leg to the leg of the chair. He and Nagy then circled and changed places, and Zakkut taped my other arm and leg. That done, he went to the table and put the tape and scissors into the bag, and Nagy put his pistol away under his belt.

"Thank you very much," he said. "I appreciate your cooperation."

Zakkut was fumbling in his black bag. I didn't dare look toward the woods where Zee had disappeared. The pistols popped at the Rod and Gun Club. I tested the duct tape on one arm. The chair groaned, but the tape did not give. I gave that some thought. The Colonel stepped forward, touched the tape with his long brown fingers, and stepped away again.

"Wonderful stuff. I'm taking some back with me. We really don't have anything like it in Gwatar. It leaves no sign of a struggle, you see. Not like rope or metal cuffs. Both of those leave unmistakable marks. My men will be very interested in this tape."

"Now that you have me here, what next?"

"Nothing to fret yourself about, sir. The doctor is going to give you a shot of potassium chloride. In some spot where it won't be noticed. An old scar, perhaps. You have your share of them, I note. Shrapnel, yes?"

"Yes. Potassium chloride is a salt substitute. What else does it do?"

"Please, Mr. Jackson, don't trouble yourself unnecessarily about the inevitable. Let us say, simply, that it will put you to sleep."

"I don't want to be put to sleep," I said in my loud voice. "You said that you had no intention of harming me!" I looked at Zakkut. He was filling a hypodermic syringe from a small vial.

"Yes. Well, of course that was not entirely true. I do intend to harm you. However, experience has shown that if a subject can be persuaded not to resist, it's much easier to perform actions upon him that otherwise would be much more difficult. You will recall the lengths to which the Nazis went to persuade the Jews to voluntarily enter the gas chambers. They were told they were going to be fumigated or given showers. The Germans' work was much simpler than it would have been had the Jews known what was actually going to happen to them. I was pleased when the same principle worked with respect to you."

I tugged at the tape. The chair creaked. "What does that stuff do?" asked my big voice.

"Well, if you insist on knowing, I will tell you." The Colonel stood several feet away. He was a very careful man. "Potassium chloride in an IV solution is a common and very effective injection for people suffering from certain illnesses resulting in dehydration. Anorexia nervosa, for example. It is well known to the physicians of Sarofim, since ours is a warm desert country where dehydration is common. Dr. Zakkut gives those injections. It's all quite legal and conventional, I assure you."

I was suddenly aware that the shooting had stopped. I heard the sounds of birds and the wind in the trees, but nothing more. Did the Colonel or the doctor notice the change? I needed to delay things and to distract their ears. I nearly shouted.

"Tell me, Colonel, was that story you told about Blunt taking your pistol true? Did he commit suicide? Or did you kill him?"

"Must you speak so loudly, Mr. Jackson? I assure you, sir, I told you the truth. Blunt shot himself with my pistol. Rather embarrassing for me, but not, as it turns out, to my Padishah's diplomatic hopes. Your government, like ours, is sufficiently anxious to conclude an agreement between our countries that the fact that my pistol was the death weapon has been seen as unimportant. However, if the necklace Blunt claims to have stolen actually has been delivered into the hands of our political opponents, that will be a serious problem for my master and, alas, one that is beyond my abilities to rectify. You and Mrs. Madieras, on the other hand, are problems which I can solve. Did I tell you that potassium chloride has other interesting medical characteristics? Given in a large enough undiluted dose, it will cause the subject to have a heart attack."

I looked at him. He smiled. My voice got bigger. "You may not be blamed for Blunt's death, but you can't expect to get away with murdering me!"

"Of course I can. Because you will not be murdered, you

will die of natural causes. Heart attack. Most unexpected in a man of your apparent health, but hardly an unknown sort of event. When you're dead, I'll remove this tape and there will be no sign of violence at all. You will be found in this chair. I assure you that no one will suspect what your mystery writers call foul play, because potassium is normally found in your system and there will be no discoverable chemical imbalance in your body."

The Colonel was too far away.

"Help!" I yelled as loud as I could. "Help! Help! I'm being murdered by Dr. Mahmoud Zakkut and Colonel Ahmed Nagy! Help! Help! Murder!"

"A wonderful medicine," said the Colonel, frowning at my outburst. "Dr. Zakkut learned of it while studying in Germany. We have had great success with it in Sarofim. I think I should gag him, Doctor. He has a very loud voice. It's just possible that someone could hear him."

Do it, Colonel, I thought. Don't just talk about doing it. "Help, help!" I bellowed. "Murder! Murder! I'm being murdered!"

The Colonel shook his head. "I should tell you that I have long since stopped being surprised at the screams of apparently strong men. Still, it is disappointing, sir. I thought perhaps you would be different."

He did as I willed. He stepped to the table and got the tape out of Zakkut's bag. Beside him, Dr. Zakkut held his hypodermic needle up and examined it. He nodded, satisfied. I listened and heard only wind and birds. Come closer, Colonel. I took a deep breath.

"Help! Murder! Help!"

The Colonel approached and bent over me, a wide piece of tape in his hands, a look of annoyance on his face. "Yes, you disappoint me, sir. Ah, well, no matter." He brought the tape down toward my mouth.

My muscles leaped, and I heaved with all of my strength against my bonds. Adrenaline surged through me, and a roar came from my throat. The tape on my arms held, but, as I'd hoped, Archie Bunker's chair did not. I tore the right arm away and smashed it into the Colonel's face. He spun and staggered away. Dr. Zakkut's eyes widened. He hesitated, then came toward me. I tore away the left arm of the chair and kicked with first one leg, then the other. The old chair legs groaned but held. Zakkut danced in and thrust the needle at my legs. I swung an arm at him and he leaned away. I kicked again. A leg tore from the chair and I was on my feet, most of the chair still taped to one leg and other parts of it taped to the rest of me.

Colonel Nagy's face was bloody, but he had recovered some of his wits, at least. I went for him, but he leaped back. The wreckage of the damned chair was an anchor. I kicked at it but it clung to me. I spun back and saw Zakkut coming at me with his needle. I swung at him with the piece of chair taped to my left arm but he was just beyond my reach. He was frail but intent. I was furious. I spun and leaped for Nagy, but the chair tangled my legs and I went down in a heap. Nagy danced to one side and put his hand beneath his shirt.

Then, behind him, I saw Manny Fonseca and Zee coming out of the woods. Manny was wearing his favorite camouflage shirt and shooting cap. Around his waist was the heavy belt holding his pistol holster, his extra clips, and God knew what else. He and Zee were panting from their run. There were scratches on their faces from the brush they'd come through.

I pointed at the Colonel and shouted. "This one's got a gun and knows how to use it!"

Seeing my eyes, the Colonel whirled to face them.

It was Manny Fonseca's worst and finest moment. All that practice finally came into play. The Colonel's hand came out of his shirt, and his pistol swung up as Manny made his draw. Manny's right arm locked, his left hand cupped his right hand, and he shot the Colonel twice through the chest.

As Manny fired, Dr. Zakkut leaned over me and thrust the hypodermic needle into my leg. Zee screamed. Manny never missed a beat. He swung his pistol and shot Zakkut twice. The bullets lifted the fragile Zakkut away from the hypodermic's plunger and slammed him into the table, spilling him and the contents of his black bag onto my lawn.

The hypodermic swayed back and forth in my leg, its deadly dose of potassium chloride undelivered.

I reached down and pulled the needle out. A moment later, Zee reached me and took me and the remains of Archie Bunker's chair in her arms.

•

▪ 28 ▪

The last of the police cruisers had gone out of the yard, and Jake Spitz was the only lawman left. His rented car was parked beside the LandCruiser. It was evening, and he was having a Molson. Zee and I were sticking to Absolut martinis. The three of us had finished off the smoked bluefish hors d'oeuvres long since and were reduced to cheese and crackers, which were also going fast.

"I was afraid that Manny Fonseca was going to shake himself to pieces after it was over," said Zee. "I never saw a man so weak in the knees. I made him sit down before he fell down."

"He never shot anybody before," said Spitz. "Guy did okay, if you ask me."

"He sure did," said Zee. I looked at her. "Scary," she said. She squeezed my hand.

I squeezed back and looked at Spitz. "What'll all this do to the big treaty plans? Will our guys in Washington still go through with it, knowing that they're making a deal with a psychopath?"

"Hey," said Spitz. "Why not? It wouldn't be the first time."

"You mean they'll go through with it even though the Padishah tried to kill Jeff and me?" asked Zee.

"They don't tell me their plans," said Spitz. "But it wouldn't surprise me. Balance of power; national interest transcending individual issues. Stuff like that."

"By the way," I said. "I appreciated the tip about Nagy and the Padishah, even if it didn't help much in the end, thanks to my dumbness."

Spitz took a nip of beer. "How'd you know it was me?"

"Who else would plant a bug in the Padishah's suite? Not the local cops; not Thornberry Security—their only job was to guard the necklace. Who else could it be but you? Especially since your outfit isn't always hand in hand with the State Department and since you're a maverick guy who doesn't always even agree with your own bosses' policies. Two days ago, when I told Nagy that I'd been tipped off about a threat, I watched him scan his room and I figured he was wondering where the bugs were."

"Ah," said Spitz. "That's why we didn't hear anything more after that. He found the bugs and put them out of commission. Too bad you tipped him. Otherwise we might have heard about today's plan in time to stop it before all this happened. Not that I think the world's much worse off without Zakkut and Nagy. Good riddance, I say.

"Sorry I didn't pick up on Zakkut being involved. I should have guessed that he might be. He was studying medicine in Germany during World War II, you know. Afterwards, when he went to work for the Padishah, the secret police got a lot more sophisticated about how they handled political prisoners. Not so much baseball-bat surgery. More death by natural causes. Now we know why."

"No problem," I said. "All it cost me was a chair."

"How do you think the government will handle this?" asked Zee.

"I'm just a poor old FBI agent," said Spitz, "so don't ask me. If I was to guess, I'd say the scenario would be something like two crazed zealots acting completely on their own did this, and the Padishah is horrified. You can ask Standish Caplan if you see him. He's got a future in the State Department, I think, and he can probably put as good a spin on this mess as anyone. I gotta go. I still haven't found that stolen necklace."

"Do you think you will?"

"No. I think it's out of the country by now."

"I think you're right," I said.

He looked at me. "You think so?"

"Yeah."

"You know something I don't?"

"Naw."

"Naw. Did I tell you that we found a Webley revolver out on Chappy this morning? Right next to the road under about a foot of sand. Sending it to the lab for prints, then up to Boston so your boss, Jasper Cabot, can identify it. Funny thing, a Quaker like Blunt bringing home a pistol for a souvenir. You never know about people, do you? Well, I gotta go. Glad it all worked out. See ya."

He went.

"I'm starving," said Zee. She got up and pulled me up. "Let's eat some real food and go to bed."

"It's only about seven-thirty. You can't be sleepy yet."

"That's right," she said.

In the morning Zee and I slept in. I got up finally and made some blueberry waffles and brought them and the fixings and coffee back to the bedroom. Zee's smile lit up the room, and she dug right in. Never stand between a hungry nurse and food.

At nine o'clock, I held a finger to my lips. Zee stopped chewing and listened.

"Hear that?"

"What?"

"Silence."

"So?"

"Manny Fonseca is always on the range early Saturday morning. Today he's not there. I guess he did enough shooting yesterday to last him for a while."

"Poor Manny," said Zee. "Good old Manny. When I saw Nagy sneaking out of the woods, I just took off through the brush toward the shooting range. Manny was there with a guy I don't know, and the two of them were terrific. The guy went for a phone to get the cops, and Manny came running back with me. I'll never forget him."

"The old Wampanoag-hating, pistol shooter isn't all bad, eh?"

"No. Maybe nobody is." She chewed and swallowed a bite of waffle. "Except maybe the Padishah. I haven't found much that's good about him yet. I really have to wash my hair, Jeff."

"Women will never seize control of the world if they keep taking time out to wash their hair," I said.

"Women don't want to seize control of the world," she said. "How many times do I have to tell you that? Men are the ones who want the world. That's why they keep their hair so short. It's a sure sign. You have to take me home. You don't have any good shampoo here."

"I do too."

"No you don't."

I took her home and kissed her and drove back to Edgartown to Amelia Muleto's house. She was in her gardening clothes.

"Come in, J.W. I'll put some water on for tea. I hear that you had some excitement up your way yesterday. I want to hear all the details. You are all right, aren't you?"

"I'm fine."

I sat while she went into the kitchen. After a bit she brought the teapot into the living room.

"Now tell me everything," she said.

I told her.

"The Padishah is a bastard," she said. "I always knew it. I think it's genetic. All of the Rashads are rotten. At least the last generations have been. Willard Blunt always said they were madmen, all of them! I'm so happy you didn't get hurt."

"Zee saw the present for Willard Blunt's nephew."

"I beg your pardon?"

"You remember. The Friday before the big Damon shindig. Zee came here and found you and Willard Blunt making a surprise present for his nephew. The hollow book. The book you showed to me earlier."

"Oh. Oh yes. His grandnephew, it was, I think. Yes. We put a superhero watch inside. I'm sure the boy loved it."

"I think Willard Blunt ordered Zee's kidnapping because of that present. What do you think?"

She held her cup in both hands, then set it down in its saucer. "What do you mean?

"I think you know."

She shook her head. "No, I don't. Perhaps you'll tell me."

"Yes. The first thing is that Willard Blunt was an only hild. He didn't have a nephew or a grandnephew. You know ıat. More tea, please?"

She poured. Her hands were very steady. She picked up er cup.

"I want you to understand that what I'm saying is just beveen you and me," I said. "If you tell anyone else, I'll deny ver saying any of it."

The cup shook a bit in her hands. Then it steadied. "Go n."

"Here's what I think happened. It's the only explanation I an come up with. Let's call it a story. Feel free to edit it if ou want to. You know, add, subtract, change things . . ."

"All right."

"I think that you and Willard stole the necklace as a eam. I imagine the two of you go back a long way in your islike for the Padishahs of Sarofim. Both of you were oung and idealistic when Blunt went off to Sarofim in the var and saw a girl and her father destroyed by the Rashads. don't think Blunt ever got over what happened and I nagine he told you about it and that you gave him a lot of ympathy. I think that when he learned that the necklace vas going to pass out of your estate and be returned to the 'adishah, the two of you decided not to let him have it, but o get it into the hands of the political opposition. A sort of ast chance to damage the Rashads, as it were. I'm not too ure of the details, but I think that's the motive. Am I okay, o far?"

"Please go on."

"I think you did it this way: Blunt brought the necklaces, ne real one and the pastes, to the Damon house, and Dr. 'oussef, the curator of the National Museum of Sarofim, erified that the pastes were pastes and the real emeralds vere the real emeralds. Youssef testified that he looked at he pastes first and then, while Blunt put the pastes and their ox into the safe, he checked out the real emeralds, then put that necklace into its matching box and that box in the safe and locked the door."

"Yes, I believe that is the report I heard."

"I think that while Youssef was looking at the real necklace, Willard dropped the pastes into his pocket and put an empty box into the safe. It would have been pretty easy. They were alone, and Youssef didn't care about the pastes anyway. All he cared about was the real emerald necklace. What made everything work, I think, is that everybody trusted Willard and was interested in the real necklace, and nobody was really interested in the pastes. Is this what they call a dénouement?"

"More tea, J.W.?"

"Thanks. Then I think that Willard brought the pastes to you. I'm not sure where you carried them, but on Saturday night you took them to the party with you. You're a pretty nervy lady, I think."

"Thank you."

"When trusty Willard and your sister went upstairs to get the pastes, he opened the safe, opened a box, and put the real emeralds around her neck. She thought she was getting the pastes, and since they were good pastes and she probably didn't look at them too closely and wasn't really interested in them anyway, she didn't notice the difference.

"The same was true for everyone else. We all thought we were seeing the pastes, so that's what we saw. Your sister put the necklace around your neck, and you wore it as you left the room, and soon all eyes turned to watch your sister come downstairs with the real thing. I think it was a lovely plan. I was right beside you, and I never doubted that the necklace you were wearing was the one with the pastes. No one else did, either. A hundred people would have testified under oath that you were wearing the pastes. Blunt was a smart old guy.

"I think that when you acted pale and wan and stopped at the ladies' room it was all part of the plan. I think that there was a small glitch in that plan when Helga Johanson went into the ladies' room with you, but you managed to switch ıe real necklace for the pastes anyway. And then you put ıe pastes, which were what everybody thought you'd been vearing anyhow, into the safe in the library in front of two vitnesses, Helga and me.

"There's not much else to it. Upstairs, both boxes in the afe were empty. The emeralds had been stolen. There was rush to the library safe and there, sure enough, were the astes. All you had to do was wait around until they let you o home, and off you went, emeralds and all. Slick. And utsy."

"I do not have a gut, J.W. And I was not faking being ill ıat evening. It was tension, I think. I was worried about Zee nd I had never been a jewel thief before. I found the whole ıing quite nerve wracking. I knew that there was a stall in ıe ladies' room where I could be alone and switch the neck-ıces, so I didn't mind Ms. Johanson going in with me. She ras very kind, in fact. I carried the necklaces in my sash, by ıe way. I sewed a little pocket there, just big enough to hold ne of them. I felt very strange, I can assure you, walking round my sister's house for hours while all those policemen rere searching high and low for the necklace. I don't think am really cut out for a life of crime."

"That's probably a good thing. The police have enough roubles already. I think that when you got home, you put the ecklace into that hollow book, wrapped it up, and waited or the post office to open on Monday. That was a dangerous eriod, that waiting time. If anyone had caught on to the ıeft, you'd have been nabbed with the goods. But no one id catch on, and the next day, guess who you got to mail the ook for you."

"I hope you aren't angry."

"No. I'm glad to have helped damage the Padishah, if you rant to know the truth. Thanks for the opportunity. I rouldn't have any objection to any of this if it hadn't cost ee three days of being treated like an animal. I couldn't tand being taped to that damned chair for twenty minutes. ee had three days of it. That was rotten."

She nodded her head. "I know it was. But I ask you to believe me when I tell you I didn't know anything about that. I never would have allowed it, had I known."

"I believe you. And I believe that Willard Blunt knew that you wouldn't put up with it and that's why he never told you. I figure that Zee came in that Friday and caught the two of you with the book. You both stayed with the story that it was a gift for his grandnephew. But Blunt was afraid that Zee had seen enough to put two and two together and would tie the stolen necklace to the hollow book. He knew he was going to be everyone's logical first suspect, after all, and you and he were old buddies, and Zee was a smart woman. He needed to get her out of the way until he could get the necklace off of the island on Monday. After that he didn't care if she guessed anything or not. The emeralds and the book would be gone, and there'd be no evidence to support her suspicions.

"He had arranged for some SDL kids from Weststock to come down and throw some red herrings across his trail that night. The firecrackers over the wall, the party crashers at the dock. The plan worked pretty well, by the way. Afterwards a lot of cops wasted a lot of time trying to track those people down. Blunt phoned his SDL people from your house and arranged for them to kidnap Zee after he took her home and to hold her until they heard from him on Monday."

"But he died on Sunday night."

"That's right. He died on Sunday night. Suicide, according to Nagy, and I think he's right."

"Suicide? I thought . . ."

"Willard Blunt subscribed to the Hemlock Society idea that a terminally ill person is justified in taking his own life. I agree with him, by the way. On the other hand, he was a Quaker who didn't approve of taking another person's life. Finally, he genuinely hated the Padishah and his agents and probably wanted to kill them even though he ethically disapproved of violence imposed on others. An interesting moral dilemma. He resolved it by taking Nagy's pistol and killing himself with it. Two birds with one stone: he was free from suffering, and Nagy, the Padishah's agent, looked like murder suspect, which could also be bad for the Padishah."

"That's pretty farfetched, J.W."

"There's more. Early Sunday evening, he and Nagy and ke Spitz, the FBI man, had a talk, and Nagy had suggested oking into what Blunt's old pal Professor Hamdi Safwat as up to."

"Ah. I see."

"Right. The book I mailed was sent to Safwat. I think that lunt wanted to deflect a serious inquiry into Safwat's part this operation until the necklace was out of the country. he not only stole Nagy's pistol, but told him that he himlf had stolen the necklace. He told the truth, in fact, and by ooting himself, which sooner or later he was going to do yway, he distracted investigators from Safwat. A third bird ith the same stone. He came to you that night, remember?"

"Yes. He came to say goodbye for the last time. He didn't y that, but I knew."

"He couldn't tell the SDL kidnappers anything because he dn't know how the night would actually turn out. He didn't ow if he could find Nagy or someone else to whom he uld confess. But Nagy was true to his word and walked me that night, and Blunt met him.

"When the SDL people learned of his death, they didn't ow what to do with Zee. They decided to take her home ain, but they could just as easily have decided to kill her d bury her someplace. Revolutionaries have a tendency to ll people who are inconvenient to them. I wish I could talk ith Blunt and have him tell me whether I'm right or off in ft field about this, but it feels right to me."

"And where do you think the necklace is now, J.W.?"

"I mailed it to Hamdi Safwat last Monday. By now I agine it's in Europe or even Sarofim itself. I think I'd have t it and some junk jewelry on the neck of some woman L member and had her wear it when she flew to London wherever. Then I'd have had her take a flight to Amsterm and give it to somebody to hold until it was politically right time for the necklace to reappear. Something like at."

"You're a nice boy, J.W. I've often said that. Shall I mal us some more tea?"

"I've changed my mind about not telling this tale to an one. There are two people I want to tell. But I won't unle I have your permission. Jasper Cabot is one."

"Jasper?" She thought for a moment. "Well, I don't s why not. I trust Jasper. He is an old friend." She smiled me. "I assume Zeolinda is the other person."

"Yes. I don't like to deceive her about anything."

"I understand. Yes, do tell Zee. Like you, I don't want try to hide this from her. The three of us are too close f such deceptions. You love her, don't you?"

"Yes, but I don't take that to mean that I have any clain on her."

"Does she know?"

"I'm sure she does. How did I do solving the crime?"

"You did very well. I'm proud of you. You know whe the bathroom is. I notice that you've been getting squirm Tea will do that to you."

I got up without a further invitation.

▪ 29 ▪

The day after Labor Day begins a new season for Martha's Vineyard. Most of the tourists are gone, the water is still warm, the air is clear and clean, and the bluefish are beginning to come back. What could be better? I had my new Martha's Vineyard Striped Bass and Bluefish Derby pin on my hat and was with Zee off Makoniky Head on the north shore. We were anchored just off the rocks and were casting northeast with the wind. We had three nice blues in the fish box and we were both on again.

The fish were jumpers and were out of the water as much as they were in it. About forty feet off the boat, mine went high into the air, gyrated, and tossed the plug even higher.

"Wow! Way to go, fish!"

Zee hauled hers in close, and I scooped it up in the net. A nice eight-pounder.

"Way to go, Zee!"

We added her fish to the box, and I glanced at the sun. The tide was running west against the wind, but the wind was dying. Time to get going if we wanted to fetch Menemsha by dark. I put up the big gaff-rigged main, hauled in the anchor, and began the beat westward along the shore.

"So this is what they mean by boat fishing," said Zee.

"Yes indeed. It's a different game."

"You can get to all those places you used to get locked out of."

"Yep. I figure we can fish the whole damned island in the *Shirley J.* No more worrying about whether the Gay Head town fathers and mothers block off their roads to down-island fisherman. We'll sail right up to the beach and nail the fish whenever we want to. Same goes for every place else too. The world is ours."

"It's great having a boat. No doubt about it. I love it."

"We'll be in Menemsha Pond just in time for cocktails."

And we were. I dropped the hook and furled the sail, and we lay at ease in the lee of the Gay Head hills. I filleted the fish and threw the carcasses overboard. Food for smaller fishes. I put the fillets back in the ice chest, then mixed up a sauce of mustard, dill, and mayo and set it in with the fillets. By the time I'd done that, Zee had the martinis ready. We sat in deck chairs and watched the evening come in on us.

"Good old Jasper Cabot," I said. "Here's to you and your checks, Jasper."

We sipped our drinks.

"What was the *Shirley J*'s name before she was the *Shirley J*?"

"Jeremy called her *Wanderer.* He said he didn't care if I changed her name, because he was done with her. Here's to you, Jeremy."

We sipped. To the north, the little village of Menemsha, Walt Disney's idea of what a fishing village should look like, lay in the last of the evening sunlight.

"So Jasper paid pretty well, eh? Down payment on the *Shirley J,* anyway. Not bad, J.W."

"He seemed satisfied."

"Did you see the *Globe* this morning?"

"No."

"The necklace has showed up in Paris. The Sarofim Democratic League had a news conference. Showed the emeralds. Hung them around some beautiful woman revolutionary's neck. She gave a speech. The police arrested several people. Up in Weststock, Hamdi Safwat gave another speech. Exciting times."

"The latest revolution is gaining momentum, eh?"

"Seems that way. You know, this isn't a bad way to live. Let's circumnavigate the island. We can anchor tomorrow in the lee of Nomans and do a little fishing, then sail down along South Beach and fish some more at Wasque, about three casts offshore. We can sneer at the poor slobs on the beach who can't reach the fish we'll be pulling in and then go up to the Jetties and maybe pick up Iowa and take him out for a ride. Then we can duck in and spend the night in Cape Pogue Pond."

"You can't anchor overnight in Cape Pogue Pond anymore. New rules. Not smart rules, but new ones."

"Edgartown is getting as bad as Gay Head, what with all its damned regulations! What we'll have to do is put up our black sail and sneak in at night, like pirates."

"Good idea. Where'll we get a black sail?"

"Your girlfriend, Helga Johanson, can make it as a thank-you gift for your hospitality to her."

"Helga Johanson is home with her husband over in America. Besides, Helga is not the seamstress type. She's in the detecting business."

"Well, you're not."

"Not anymore. I'm a sailor, a mariner. I go down to the sea in ships. My detecting days are over. I'm a captain. Forget Helga Johanson."

Later, we lay in our bunks looking out of the hatch at the stars in the September sky. I was thinking of how many sides there are to people, how complex even the simplest seeming of them are, and how contradictory they can be in both their thoughts and acts. Zakkut, both doctor and murderer; Nagy, both protector and killer; the Padishah, both despot and hopeless movie fan; Amelia Muleto, gardener and jewel thief; Willard Blunt, at once vengeful, gentle, suicidal, and pacifistic; none of them only what they seemed. Probably even Bonzo was more than I might guess.

A northeast wind slowly swung the stern of the boat around until we could see the dark mass of the Gay Head hills blocking out the lower western stars. The sight reminded me of the latest tale about Manny Fonseca, and I laughed.

"What is it?" asked Zee's voice from the other bunk.

"Did you hear about Manny Fonseca?"

"No. What?"

"I saw his wife, Helen, downtown a couple of days ago. She had a hard time keeping a straight face. Seems that Manny got hold of some old family records and found out that one of his grandmas was a Vanderhoop from Gay Head. Manny's an official Wampanoag Indian! All these years he's been insulting himself! His wife thinks it's really funny, but Manny is fit to be tied. Who's he going to light into now?"

Zee laughed. "Poor Manny. He's had a tough end-of-the-summer. Amazing."

Amazing, indeed. Manny Fonseca was another of those people who were more complex than they perhaps wanted to be. I was still alive thanks to his fanaticism about pistols, which I had seen as a comic minor vice. And now he was a Wampanoag, the last thing in the world he wanted to be. Could Amy Lowell find a pattern in all this?

"Speaking of amazing," said Zee. "We are not being amazingly bright. Here we are, lying inside on these bunks that are so narrow only one person can get in one, and outside the stars are shining. We should be out there sleeping together on the deck and save these bunks for a time when it's cold or raining or something."

The wind came around more to the north, and the stars swung across the open hatch. The water lapped the *Shirley J.*

"When you're right, you're right," I said, and threw back my blanket.

Zee was ahead of me. We put our foam mattresses on the deck and arranged our blankets and crawled in. Zee snuggled up against me.

"This is better."

It certainly was.

"And another thing," said Zee. "Now I really do think you should plant a little garden without a fence, just for the bunnies. Because if it hadn't been for them, I wouldn't have been off in the woods, and . . ."

"Another good idea," I said.

"I have lots of good ideas," she said sleepily. "Aren't the stars beautiful?"

"Yes."

We held one another there between the dark waters and the glittering sky, afloat on Middle Earth, halfway between heaven and hell, until, at last, we slept.

Enter the Wonderful World of Philip R. Craig's Martha's Vineyard Series

Martha's Vineyard is home to ex-Boston cop J.W. Jackson and his much-adored family. Yet this idyllic vacation spot offers no escape from danger—and from the peaceful beaches to the quiet towns, murder sometimes rears its ugly head.

Turn the page and get a glimpse into the world of J.W. Jackson, and see why "Spending time with Craig on Martha's Vineyard is the next best thing to vacationing on the island itself."

—*Minneapolis Star-Tribune*

During his career as a cop on the back streets of Boston, J.W. Jackson saw enough evil to last a lifetime. So he retired to the serenity of Martha's Vineyard to spend his days fishing for blues and wooing a sexy nurse named Zee. But in **A Beautiful Place to Die,** *when a local's boat mysteriously explodes off the coast, killing an amiable young drifter, Jackson is drawn reluctantly back into the investigative trade.*

■ ■

Now the *Nellie Grey* was in sight, moving smoothly out with mild following waves, the wind at her back. She came past the lighthouse and we could see Jim and Billy. They waved and we waved back, and they went on out beyond the shallows that reach east from Cape Pogue. Beyond the *Nellie Grey* the long black boat altered her course to hold outside the *Nellie*'s turn as she swung south beyond the shallows to follow the beach toward Wasque.

"Come on," said George, lowering his binoculars, "let's go back to Wasque so we can watch them fish the rip. The east tide will be running and there may be something there."

Susie, looking sad, nodded and turned to the Wagoneer.

"We'll follow you down," I said, "but then we're going on into town. We want to sell these fish."

"And I've got to get some sleep," said Zee. "I've got duty again tonight, and right now I'm frazzled out."

Just at that moment the *Nellie Grey* exploded. A great red and yellow flower opened from the sea and expanded into the air. Petals of flame and stalks of debris shot up and arched away as a ball of smoke billowed from the spot where the *Nellie* had been. A moment later the boom of the explosion hit us, and the sea around the *Nellie* was one of flame. I thought I saw a body arc into the burning water.

A university professor visiting Martha's Vineyard has fallen in love with the island's gently lapping waves and whispering island breezes. But on a warm June day, she's swallowed up by a dark and merciless sea, never to be seen again. And in an attempt to preserve his beloved home's peace, intrepid sleuth J. W. Jackson dives into the investigation of this mysterious and "accidental" **Death in Vineyard Waters.**

■ ■

She gave a small smile. "Of course not. I believe a salesman would say it comes with the territory. Besides, there may be something to the idea. Why should flesh and spirit be separate, after all? D. H. Lawrence thought that the separation of the two was the major malaise of western civilization, you know." Her fingers played on my arm and then suddenly withdrew, as if she had just become aware of them being there. "Dr. Summerharp is just an old . . . woman without a good word for anyone. She needs love and understanding, not hatred."

"Dr. Hooperman was not so generous in his feelings."

"Ah, well, he must be forgiven, too. Momentarily done in by gin, I believe. I recall that my husband invited you to visit us at Sanctuary. I echo that invitation. Please do come up." Her eyes looked up at me from beneath hooded lids.

"Thank you." I was suddenly sure that her husband would never leave her no matter how involved she might sometimes be with some other man or woman. I looked at my watch. "I'm afraid I must go and save my car," I said.

She offered her hand. "A pleasure seeing you again. Do come and visit us."

I went down the library walk. Glancing back, I saw that she was watching me. We exchanged waves. Three cars behind mine a meter maid was scribbling out a ticket. I just beat her to the Landscruiser, thus thrice escaping the clutches of the law in a single day. Not willing to press my luck, I left town and went home, where I worked at things that I'd been meaning to tend to but hadn't because I'd been occupied with Zee. Now I had the time. Too much of it, really.

That evening, I looked up "moldwarp." I learned that it was a name for the common European mole. I had now pulled even with Hotspur on one word, at least.

Precisely one week later I read that Marjorie Summerharp was dead.

J.W. Jackson loves the crisp Vineyard autumn days and the beginning of **Off Season.** *But this fall, the natives are getting seriously restless. Animal rights activists are squaring off against the deer slayers, and environmentalists are at odds with land developers. And when the verbal arrows become real ones, it is J.W. who must lead the hunt for a killer.*

■ ■

When you live on the Vineyard all year round, it's easy to understand why the tourists like it so much, but it's also nice to know that they mostly come only in the summer. The rest of the time the island belongs to you.

And the year-rounders make both the worst and best of the off season. For some, it's a time for malevolence. Old antagonisms, put on a back burner during the busy money-making season, reappear. Meannesses, both petty and grand, manifest themselves in and out of court. Tire slashers make their presence known. Anonymous telephone callers and letter writers harass their victims. Drink and drugs continue to mix with driving and the abuse of relatives and associates. Arguments break out over fences or in committee meetings, threats are exchanged, angry letters appear in the papers.

For other islanders, the winter season is a time of special blessing when, no longer obliged to structure their lives around the activities of a hundred thousand visitors, they can pursue their private intellectual and aesthetic interests. Their enthusiasms for culture and the arts flourish, with concerns, benefits, dances and lectures being attended on a nightly basis. People go to theater, listen to speakers, plan charitable events, gossip and otherwise use the off season to good advantage.

In **A Case of Vineyard Poison,** *wedding bells are about to chime for ex-Boston cop turned island fisherman J.W. Jackson and his lady Zee. And Zee's automatic teller machine tells them a rather substantial "present" has been deposited in the bride-to-be's account: one hundred thousand unexplained dollars. But when authorities discover that the college student lying dead in J.W.'s driveway recently withdrew a hundred grand from her own account, J.W. must match wits with a murderer who may be gearing up to kill again.*

"You're looking at a wealthy woman." She smiled and waved her two receipts.

Nurses don't normally get wealthy so fast. "I want you to know," I said, "that it's your dear, sweet heart that has drawn me to you, and that your millions mean nothing to me."

"In that case," said Zee, "I'll just keep the hundred thousand to myself."

"A hundred thousand? Dollars?"

"Look," said Zee, handing me the receipts. "I have about fifteen hundred in my checking account, but look at these."

I looked. Each receipt said that Zee had a hundred thousand more than that in her account.

"I got two receipts, just to make sure," said Zee. "Both times it said the same thing. Maybe I should go right to the tackle shop and get myself a hundred thousand dollars' worth of leaders and lures. What do you think?"

"I think Rio might be a better plan, because I have a feeling that banks, being banks, probably have laws that protect them when this happens and put people like you in jail if you run off with the hundred thousand."

"Rio it is, then. They'll never catch us."

When J.W. Jackson foils an attempt to terminate former mob boss Luciano Marcus on the steps of Boston's Symphony Hall, it puts a definite damper on his newlywedded bliss. But **Death on a Vineyard Beach** *promises more than just off-island danger, for the mayhem follows J.W. and Zee back home to Martha's Vineyard, and keeping the circling sharks from the kill may just be more than J.W. can handle.*

■ ■

Later, in bed, I listened to the sounds of the night: the odd calls of nocturnal creatures, the swish of leaves, the groans of tree limbs rubbing together. Once or twice I thought I might be hearing unusual noises in the yard, but when I slipped out of bed for a look, there was no one there.

The next morning, when Zee was home from her graveyard shift and asleep in the bedroom, another car came down our driveway. I didn't recognize this one, or the two guys who got out of it. They were young, bronze-skinned guys with dark eyes and muscular bodies.

"You Jeff Jackson?" the first asked.

I had the garden hose, and was watering the flowers in the boxes on the front fence.

"That's me."

"I have a message for you," he said, coming up to me. "Stay out of Linda Vanderbeck's hair!"

And so saying, he hit me in the jaw with his right hand and followed with his left.

At first, the girl J.W. Jackson encounters strolling alone along South Beach seems like your typical teenager. But there's nothing typical about young Cricket Callahan, the spirited only daughter of the vacationing President of the United States. What Jackson can't figure out is why the feisty First Kid is so intent on eluding the Secret Service, or why the Chief Executive himself wants J.W. and Zee to watch over the errant sixteen-year-old. In **A Deadly Vineyard Holiday,** *the answer unfortunately comes in the form of a dead body . . .*

■ ■

put another basket and rake into the Land Cruiser, and we drove out to the pavement and turned toward Edgartown. 'here was a car parked beside the bike path a hundred feet r so up the road in the direction of Vineyard Haven. I ıought there was someone in the driver's seat.

The car was still there when we came back with our quaogs an hour and a half later.

I pulled into the driveway and stopped and looked at the ar.

"What is it?' asked Zee.

"I'm not sure," I said.

As I got out of the Land Cruiser and crossed the highway, thought I saw the driver taking my picture. Then, as I alked along the bike path toward the car, its driver started ıe motor, made a U-turn, and drove away.

I thought the car had a Massachusetts plate, but I couldn't ıake out the number.

I walked back to the truck.

"What was that all about?" asked Zee.

"I don't know," I said. "Probably nothing."

But I didn't think it was nothing.

In **A Shoot on Martha's Vineyard,** *J.W.'s idyllic summer hits a snag when a movie scout from a land called "Hollywood" invades the beaches—and takes a liking not only to the island locale, but to Jackson's lovely lady Zee as well. And when a longtime nemesis turns up dead—and J.W. is the prime suspect—the ex-Boston cop will have to cast his line to find the real killer.*

■ ■

I liked having Zee's hand in mine. I liked being married t her, and having Joshua making us three. I didn't want t do anything to unbalance us.

One of the things I liked about our marriage was that was stuck together without any coercion of any kind. Ther was no "We have to stay together because we said w would" or "You owe me" or "You promised me you'd lov me" stuff nor any "Think of the children" stuff, either, eve though we had said we'd stick together, and we did ow each other more than we could say, and we did love eac other and, now, we did have Joshua to think about.

Basically Zee and I were married because we wanted t be married, and for no other reason.

I wondered why I was thinking such thoughts, and sus pected that it was because of two things: the first was a so of restlessness that had come over Zee since Joshua ha made his appearance. Her usual confidence and independ ence were occasionally less pronounced, occasionally mor her normal fearlessness was sometimes replaced by an u easiness that I'd not seen in her before, and at other tim she became almost fierce.

A postpartum transformation of some kind? I didn know. Maybe she saw the same things in me, and all that e ther of us was seeing was the fretting of new parents wh didn't really know how to do their job and were worried that they were doing it wrong.

The second thing bothering me was more easily identified. It was Drew Mondry.

Him, Tarzan; Zee, Jane.

They even looked like Tarzan and Jane. Both were suntanned and spectacularly made, with his blond hair and brilliant blue eyes contrasting well indeed with her dark eyes and long, blue-black hair. Golden Tarz; bronze Jane.

And there was that little charged current that had run between them this morning.

May I call you Zee? I'll phone you later.

In **A Fatal Vineyard Season,** *the arrival of Julia Crandel and Ivy Holiday, two actresses staying on the Vineyard for the summer, has incurred the wrath of local gangsters. Worse still, a deadly stalker from one of the ladies' pasts has found out where they are hiding, and it looks like it's up to J.W. Jackson to follow his conscience and protect two frightened, helpless off-islanders . . . and put himself in danger as well.*

■ ■

The two young women exchanged looks, then put smiles on their faces. "Yes," said Julia. "You're right. We'll just be vacationers like everybody else."

"We'd love to have you up for drinks before we go," said Julia later as they got into their car.

"Tomorrow I'm off with the kids to see my mama over in America," said Zee. "I'm afraid I won't be around for a while."

"Too bad," said Ivy. She looked at me. "Maybe you'll come by, J.W."

"I've been known to have a cocktail," I said.

The car drove away.

"She has great come-hither eyes, doesn't she?" said Zee.

"Who?"

"You know who."

"Oh, her."

Martha's Vineyard is a magic place that can isolate you from the real world for a while and cleanse your soul, and I hoped that it would do that for Ivy Holiday and Julia Crandel. But as the old Indian medicine singer said when his spell failed, sometimes the best magic doesn't work. Two nights later, someone kicked in the front door of the Crandel house, took a knife from the kitchen, and went upstairs after Ivy and Julia.

A surprise visit from a dear old friend only adds to the joy of good weather, great fishing, and loving family for J.W. Jackson this idyllic island summer. But his elation turns to dread when a rundown summer shack burns to the ground, and an unidentified corpse is discovered in the ashes. Fearing it may be that of his friend, J.W. dives into an ugly mass of arson, extortion, and secrets—and in **Vineyard Blues,** *the ex-Boston cop may just be headed down a road toward murder.*

■ ■

That night, sometime after Zee came home, climbed into bed beside me, and we both snuggled to sleep, I was awakened by the fire whistle in Edgartown calling to the volunteers. Then I heard sirens and more sirens, and I was disturbed by the direction they seemed to be headed. I listened, then eased out of bed and went into the living room and turned on the scanner. Voices and static crackled from the speaker. I heard the name of the street where Corrie had been staying, and had an almost irresistible urge to go there. But I knew that the last thing the firemen needed was another citizen getting in their way, so I remained where I was.

In time I heard someone say that the place seemed to be empty, and I felt a surge of relief. Apparently, everybody had gone to a party at another house, said the voice.

That would be the party the twin had mentioned, where the college kids would combine fun with charity as they tried to help those who'd gotten burned out earlier, and where Corrie had been asked to do some singing for the good cause.

Another bad fire, but at least no one had gotten hurt, in spite of the arsonist who I now believed was pretty clearly at work. The fire marshal could handle it. I turned off the scanner and went back to bed.

It wasn't until the next morning, as I made breakfast and listened to the radio news, that I learned I was wrong about no one being hurt. A body, as yet unidentified, had been found in the ruined remains of the house.

J.W. Jackson abandoned Boston, hoping to leave the violence of the big city behind. But in **Vineyard Shadows,** *when the past comes looking for him in the guise of two brutal thugs, the former cop knows it's time to put down his fishing pole and start opening doors he'd hoped were closed forever.*

■ ■

I got the details by talking with the survivors, since I wasn't at the house when it happened. Instead, I was on the clamflats in Katama with my son Joshua. When we came home, there was a cop at the head of our driveway, and an ambulance was pulling out and heading toward the hospital in Oak Bluffs. I turned into something made of ice.

The cop recognized my old Land Cruiser and waved us in. I drove fast down our long, sandy driveway. The yard was full of police cars and uniforms. Sergeant Tony D'Agostine met me as I stepped out of the truck.

I was full of fear. "Stay here," I said to Joshua, and shut the truck's door behind me.

"There's been some trouble," said Tony.

"Where's Zee? Where's Diana?!"

"Take it easy," said Tony, "it's all over."

"Where are they?!" I pushed him aside, and went toward the house. He followed me, saying something I wasn't hearing. I saw what looked like blood on the grass. Jesus! Cops stood aside as I came through them.

That was the beginning of it for me.

With the arrival of warm weather and good fishing, everything should be just fine for J.W. Jackson and Zee. But something's wrong. A mysterious man named Mahsimba, who is on the Vineyard searching for two priceless soapstone eagles missing from his African homeland, has embroiled him in problems both personal and professional. And in **Vineyard Enigma,** *J.W. couldn't have known that helping Mahsimba would pit him against powerful figures in the Vineyard's art world, including some who would stop at nothing—even murder—to add forbidden objects to their collection.*

■ ■

"In any case," continued Mahsimba, "with the discovery of the ruins came European treasure hunters and so-called experts on ancient cultures. One of the treasure hunters was a man named Willi Posselt. In 1889 he discovered four eagles carved from soapstone and traded for what he considered the best of them. Over the years, a total of ten eagles were found in Great Zimbabwe and shipped elsewhere, to museums and private collections. The whereabouts of eight of them are known, and my country is working very hard to have them returned to their homeland. I'm here on your island in search of the two missing ones. think they may be here, and Stanley Crandel thinks that you may be able to help me find them."

On a chilly, pre-tourist March day in Vineyard Haven, J.W. and Zee are out dining when shots ring out. A man lies bleeding in the street, but luckily he's wearing a bulletproof vest. But this is a strange choice of clothing unless you're expecting to be shot. And soon, in a case involving a ruthless real estate developer, a jilted lover, and a mysterious vagrant, J.W. investigates what may be his most baffling case yet.

Rich in ambience and with a touch of murder most foul, ***A Vineyard Killing*** *is now on sale in hardcover from Scribner.*

■ ■

"Wait!" cried Zee.

But I didn't wait. When I got to the street I lanced in the direction of the firecracker sounds, saw noth-ng, and ran out to the fallen man. I got my arms under him nd dragged him back to shelter in front of the deli. He was hite-faced and moaning between gritted teeth.

"Help is coming," I said. "Do you know where you're it?"

He put a hand on the center of his chest. "Right here. It urts. God damn!" He was gasping for breath.

I tore open his coat and saw two slugs half buried in a bul-tproof vest.

"You're wearing armor."

"Yes."

"A fortunate choice of clothing. Lie still."

On the far side of the street the man with the cane had oth arms around Donald Fox, holding him back.

"Stay right where you are till the cops get here," I called them. "He's going to be okay." Then I looked at the deli oor, where John Skye and Mattie were hanging on to Zee, nd said, "You stay right there, too!" Mattie and John hung n harder."

I heard the first of the sirens. “You’ll be fine,” I said t
Paul Fox, “but stay where you are until the medics ge
here.”

His eyes were wide and full of fear.